Salt

The Evermore Trilogy Book 1

Cleo Sweetland

For all the sisters;
Whether you are born a sister, made a sister,
or have sisterhood thrust upon you.

Contents

Preface

The series of events which take place throughout The Evermore Trilogy happen over the course of one unforgettable summer through the eyes of our main characters with each book focusing on a different girl's point of view.

Prologue

My head pounds, and everything feels hazy, like I'm stuck in a fog. I open my eyes but my vision blurs; all I can see are vague shapes and colours. Dust hangs in the air, floating lazily in the dim light, and I can't quite remember where I am or how I got here. There's a strange almost metallic taste in my mouth and my ears are ringing.

I try to move but my limbs are heavy, like they're weighed down by something unseen. As my eyes start to focus I realise I'm lying on the floor of the living room at Evermore, and it looks like it's been torn apart by a storm.

Books are scattered everywhere, pages ripped and fluttering about like they're trying to escape. The walls are cracked, chunks of plaster and wood splintered all around me. My hand brushes against something soft and I turn my head slowly to see the vague shape of a body lying nearby, motionless. My breath catches in my throat. There are more people here, people I think I recognise but I can't be sure. It's as if a bomb went off, tearing through everything, leaving nothing but destruction in its wake.

I shift my body and suddenly a sharp, searing pain shoots up my arm, I cry out, the sound echoing around the broken room. My vision narrows and dark spots dance before my eyes. It feels like I have been staring at the sun for too long, everything is too bright and too dark all at once. My hand moves instinctively to the source of the pain and I feel something warm and sticky. Blood. My blood. It's wet beneath me, soaking into my clothes, warm and yet somehow chilling. Panic begins to rise in my chest, my heart hammering in my ears as I struggle to push myself up to see more clearly.

As my eyes adjust to the light I look around again, the fog slowly lifting from my mind. I remember fragments of moments from this house, laughter, arguments, secrets whispered in the dark, all of it flashing through my mind like a broken film reel. I remember arriving here, every detail, all the things we have been through.

And yet, even with everything that's happened this summer, I would have never expected that one of us would end up dead.

1

The morning that started the chain of events which would change my life forever was as normal as any other.

The sun rose in its usual quiet splendor, spilling gold across the rooftops, the birds sang their songs in blissful ignorance, and the house exhaled the comfortable stillness of an early hour.

No one would have sensed the invisible shift, least of all me, as I padded downstairs, my socked feet barely making a sound on the wooden steps.

But one thing which probably would have been agreed upon if anyone had known what was coming was that you never truly understand the sacrifices you're willing to make when death is staring you in the face.

Until, it's too late.

∞∞∞

Mum and Dad were already gone by the time I stepped into the kitchen, the silence of their absence as loud as a held breath. Sunlight streamed through the front windows, slicing across the countertop in warm beams. A note lay on the breakfast bar, neatly written, as always, perched beside an envelope full of cash.

I picked the letter up, twirling one of my dark brown curls around my finger.

Sasha,

We left early and didn't want to wake you, hope you didn't get to bed too late! Hope you and Sloane have a good drive, let us know when you arrive safely! Miss you already, all our love,

Mum & Dad

I smiled, the cash was their little way of making sure I wouldn't want for anything while they were away.

I glanced at the old grandfather clock against the wall, 8:06am, I'd managed about six hours of sleep, which explained the dull weight pressing behind my eyes. Yawning, I drifted toward the black Tassimo machine, slipping in a caramel macchiato pod with the easy, automatic movements of my everyday routine. The scent of coffee curled into the air as the machine hummed to life.

With a quick glance behind me to make sure the coast was clear I flicked my fingers and the cupboard door swung open. Two mugs glided elegantly towards me, one a bright pink and the other a deep, stormy black with the words 'Death Before Decaf' emblazoned across the front. My lips quirked, Sloane's favorite. Funny how my magic always knew what I wanted without me really having to tell it.

The coffee dripped steadily into my mug, but my mind wasn't in the kitchen anymore. It was still tangled in the echoes of last night.

Sloane had shown up at my door just after midnight, her dark eyes wide, her entire body thrumming with a nervous energy that was almost tangible. She'd barely made it inside before launching into a furious tirade about how she couldn't take another second in that house.

It wasn't unusual for Sloane to rant about her foster parents. Mallory and Rory Harding were the kind of people who took in children for the money, not that I had any idea what they spent it on, except for their love of alcohol, of course. Her clothes were always second hand, her room barely furnished, and I couldn't remember a time Sloane had ever mentioned a gift or a kind gesture from either of them.

Fostering for Mallory and Rory was definitely not an act of kindness, they had never once treated Sloane like she mattered. All those years stuck in that suffocating house, knowing that the people who were supposed to care for her couldn't care less.

But last night's argument seemed to have been different.

Something had set her off in a way I'd never seen before.

It had taken half an hour, and several shots of vodka, to slow the frantic edge of her words. Even now, my memories of the conversation felt fragmented, like trying to piece together a dream after waking.

I remembered the sharp bite of alcohol on my tongue as I tried to keep up with the shots she was knocking back, starting with vodka in solidarity before quickly deciding that water would be a better choice for me. I remembered the tension in her shoulders and the way her foster brother, Marcus' name kept slipping through her lips.

I knew, without needing to ask, that something had happened.

The coffee machine beeped, jolting me from my thoughts. I picked up my mug, letting the warmth bleed into my fingers as I took a slow sip and placed Sloanes mug under the spout.

My chest ached a little, but not from exhaustion. From something deeper.

I had spent years watching Sloane exist in that house, counting down the days until she turned eighteen, until she could leave and never look back. She had endured so much for so long, but now, now she was finally free.

I shifted my thoughts, letting the dark clouds of worry dissipate as I thought about what was waiting for us.

Evermore.

My parents' summer home had been my sanctuary since childhood. Hidden deep in the countryside, surrounded by endless stretches of wild green and dense whispering woods, it was the place where magic truly felt alive.

I was going to miss my parents this summer.

For as long as I could remember, every year when school finished, we'd packed up and escaped to the old house by the coast, where the days stretched long and full of promise, filled with the scent of pine trees and the crackle of bonfires.

But this year, for the first time, I'd be there without them.

Gabrielle and William Ward, world-renowned authors, literary legends, and most importantly, the best parents I could ever ask for, were finally doing something for themselves. A six-week book tour, spanning continents and oceans, meeting the fans who had devoured their words for years. It was their dream, and I was so proud of them.

Still, I couldn't pretend I wasn't jealous. Travelling the world had always been a dream of mine too, airports and foreign cities, ink-stamped passports and stories waiting to be lived. I could already picture them wandering through bustling streets in Paris, strolling along the canals of Venice, signing books beneath neon signs in Tokyo.

They had promised to keep in touch. I'd made them swear, on pain of death (or at least, eternal guilt), that they'd send me a postcard from every city they visited. I couldn't wait to read their stories, not the ones they wrote for the world, but the ones meant just for me.

As I watched the dark liquid pour into the black mug, my mind drifted to all the things to come over the next few weeks. Number one on the list was finally being able to introduce Sloane to Fi.

Fi, my other best friend.

The girl in the woods.

The witch who had been my first real glimpse into the world of magic.

A small smile played at my lips as I remembered that first summer, the breathless excitement of discovery, the way my entire world had tilted on its axis the moment I realised I could do magic too.

I had told Sloane everything, of course. She was the keeper of my secrets, the one person I trusted beyond all doubt. She had even sworn a pinky promise to never tell a soul.

Grabbing both mugs, I made my way upstairs, nudging my bedroom door open with my hip.

Sloane was sprawled across my bed, a tangled web of limbs and lilac sheets, snoring softly. Her bags, haphazardly packed in a frenzy, were strewn across the floor, a final testament to her departure from the life she had left behind.

I set her coffee down on the bedside table and crouched beside the bed, a mischievous grin tugging at my lips.

Then, without warning, I yanked on her leg.

Sloane lurched awake with a gasp, fists raised in some half-formed attempt at self-defence. Her black hair, usually sleek and perfect, was a chaotic mess, sticking up at odd angles.

"Fuck sake, Sasha!" she groaned, voice thick with sleep.

I burst into laughter, barely able to catch my breath.

"Sorry," I wheezed, wiping at my tear-streaked cheeks. "Brought you coffee. Happy birthday."

Still grumbling, Sloane flopped back against the pillows and grabbed her mug.

"Soooo…" I began, glancing at the bags on the floor. "All packed and ready to go?"

She let out a slow breath, fingers tightening around the ceramic like it was the only thing grounding her.

"Yeah," she said. "I grabbed everything that mattered before I left. I'm not going back, Sash. Ever."

Excitement sparked in my chest at her words.

I had known this moment was coming, we had been waiting for it for years, but hearing it aloud, knowing she had finally broken free… it was different.

She was different.

However I couldn't help but notice Sloane seemed slightly conflicted about it, her words sounded like she was happy but she was screwing the duvet cover up into little bunches with her free hand and her bare feet were tapping against the mattress. She was a bundle of nervous energy.

"You okay?" I quirked a brow in her direction.

Sloane let out a long breath and a flicker of something bright crossed her expression, burning away the remnants of exhaustion. Whatever she was just thinking about had apparently passed.

"Yeah, I just can't believe I'm finally rid of them... *and* I can't believe I finally get to go to Evermore!"

The shift in her mood was obvious and I couldn't help but grin.

"Come on," I said, nudging her with my foot. "Let's get ready. The sooner we hit the road, the better."

I walked over to the huge window that overlooked my back garden and threw my cream, organza curtains open.

"Alexa, play Taylor Swift."

Behind me, Sloane groaned dramatically and burrowed deeper into the duvet just as Death By a Thousand Cuts exploded from the tiny speaker.

Laughing, I turned to my vanity, the cool glass of my dressing table pressing against my fingertips as I reached for the small bottle of hair oil. As soon as I unscrewed the cap, the rich scent of warm vanilla and coconut filled the air. I tilted the bottle, letting a few drops pool into my palm before rubbing them between my fingers. The oil felt smooth and silky as I ran it through my thick curls, taming the wild strands that had been disheveled overnight.

In the mirror's reflection, I caught sight of my bed just as a hand emerged from the depths of the quilt, groping blindly for the black mug on my bedside table. Fingers curled around the handle, and then, just as quickly, the mug disappeared back into the blanket cocoon before reemerging to be placed carefully back down.

I snorted to myself and rushed over to the bed, yanking the covers back in one swift motion.

Sloane erupted from beneath them like a horror movie jump scare, eyes still half-closed but already scream-singing the bridge of the song at full volume. She bounced on the mattress, her hair a static mess, her voice completely off-key, and yet somehow, she made it work.

I doubled over, laughing so hard my stomach hurt.

Sloane was the kind of person who carried the weight of the world on her shoulders and still found a way to crack jokes, to throw herself into joy like she could outrun all the things that haunted her. I admired that about her, but I also saw the exhaustion behind her sharp humour, the weight in her eyes when she thought no one was looking.

Sloane suddenly grabbed my wrist and yanked me onto the bed with her. I shrieked, but soon we were both jumping, belting out the bridge of the song as if we were performing to a sold-out crowd. When the last notes had faded into silence, we collapsed onto the mattress, breathless and giggling.

After a moment, I sat up, catching my breath, and reached down to the side of the bed, feeling around until my fingers closed around the tiny package I had hidden there the night before. With a grin, I held it out to her.

"Sasha, what the hell, man? We don't do presents!"

"Yeah, well, it's only tiny, and it's your 18th! Just open it!"

She eyed me warily but took the gift, the black wrapping paper glinting under the twinkle of the fairy lights strung across my headboard. She ran her thumb over the smooth surface before pulling at the white ribbon, unraveling it with deliberate care. The tape peeled away with a soft crinkle, and then she turned the small object over in her palm.

A matte black bat keyring.

She frowned, studying it with quiet

curiosity before glancing up at me, a silent question in her dark eyes.

"It's for your key to Evermore," I explained, watching her closely. "I mean, I haven't got you one yet, but I will. Then, even after this summer, you can come and go as you want. You'll always have a home with me, Sloane."

Her jaw tensed, and for a second, she didn't say anything. Then, just as quickly, she scowled to mask the emotion welling up behind her eyes.

"Thanks, Sash," she muttered.

It was all she said, but I knew how much it meant.

I smiled.

She was always the one who acted like she didn't need anyone, but I knew the truth. She was my best friend. I would do anything for her, just like she would do anything for me. We had been through so much together, and I knew, this summer would be different. This summer would be the start of something new.

"Anyway!" I announced, springing off the bed. "Let's get ready, we have a whole summer of fun ahead of us!"

I crossed the room to my floor-length mirror, running my fingers through my curls one last time before sighing and twisting them into two space buns that perched like little ears on top of my head.

I studied my reflection.

I'd always been tall, a fact I had hated as a kid but learned to appreciate as I grew into my curves. My dark caramel skin glowed, thanks to my mothers Jamaican heritage and the shimmering body lotion I applied religiously. My legs were toned from all the running I did and despite having to fight my mane of thick hair every morning it did mean that my eyelashes were long and my brows full. I let out a deep breath, smoothing a hand down my arms, feeling the warmth of my skin beneath my fingertips.

It was going to be a good summer. I could feel it.

I threw my wardrobe doors open, grabbing my favorite pair of wide-leg jeans and a little white crop top. The denim was soft and worn in, fitting just right, and the top left my shoulders bare, catching the morning sunlight. A quick swipe of black mascara and a lick of clear gloss on my full lips completed the look.

Spinning around, I spotted Sloane across the room, dressed in black, as always.

Her leggings hugged her small frame, her platform Converse (also black) adding little to her height. An oversized, black-and-white striped t-shirt draped over her, giving her a slightly chaotic, Beetlejuice-esque vibe. A thick wing of jet-black eyeliner sat atop her dark eyes, and her fingers, the onyx paint on her nails chipped at the edges, drummed absentmindedly against her thigh.

She caught me staring and flashed a goofy thumbs-up. "Ready when you are."

Just after 10 a.m the sun shone high in the sky, already radiating heat as we loaded the last of our bags into my white Volkswagen Golf.

I slid into the driver's seat, the leather warm beneath my thighs. As soon as my phone connected to the car, I tossed it to Sloane.

"DJ duty?" I asked.

She grinned, scrolling through my playlist. A moment later, Lana Del Rey's smoky voice crooned Season of the Witch through the speakers.

I rolled my eyes as Sloane threw on her oversized sunglasses, lowering them slightly to smirk at me.

"What?" she teased. "It's the summer vibe."

I couldn't help but laugh, shaking my head as I backed out of the driveway.

As the car sped down the road away from home, the windows were cracked just enough to let the wind rush in, whipping loose strands of my hair into my face.

I glanced over at Sloane, a grin tugging at the corners of my lips. "I still can't believe it. You're actually coming to Evermore this year."

Sloane leaned her head back against the seat, exhaling slowly. "Honestly, I can't either." Her voice was light, but something in her expression wavered. "After all that time begging to go with you, it still feels surreal."

For years, we had asked, pleaded, with her foster parents to let her come to Evermore. Every time, the answer had been a flat-out no. Instead, she was stuck behind the reception desk of their run-down car garage, dealing with grease-streaked paperwork and leering customers while I spent my summers swimming in the lake, lounging in the sun, and dancing around bonfires on the beach.

It had always seemed so unfair.

But now, at eighteen, she was finally free. No more garage. No more being told what she could or couldn't do.

"I still don't get it," I said, shaking my head. "You had to sit behind that reception desk all summer while Marcus actually got to work on cars. Why didn't they train you to do something useful?"

Sloane scoffed, rolling her eyes. "Because

Marcus was the golden child. His parents acted like he had the Midas touch. He was always going to inherit the garage. Didn't matter if I could handle the tools too, they were never going to let me near the cars. I was just there to answer the phones and smile at creeps."

Her voice was light, but the bitterness underneath it was sharp enough to cut.

I wrinkled my nose in disgust, gripping the wheel a little tighter. "I went there once, remember? That place was gross."

It was more than gross. It smelled of burnt rubber and stale cigarettes, with oil-slicked floors and cracked leather chairs in the waiting area. The radio had blared old classic rock, the kind of songs men in their fifties played too loud while knocking back cheap beer. But the worst part was the customers, the way they looked at Sloane like she was just another part of the shop, something to be leaned on or ignored.

Sloane snorted. "Yeah, well. That was my life."

"Marcus doesn't deserve to be handed that garage," I muttered, shaking my head. "Even if it is a total dump."

"Exactly," she sighed. "He barely even works. Always acts like he's some sort of car genius, but I swear he spends more time looking busy than actually doing anything.

But, whatever. It's not my problem anymore."

She said it casually, but I caught the way her fingers curled slightly against her thigh, like she was holding back something deeper.

I smiled anyway. She was right. No more being trapped at the garage. No more Marcus. No more begging for permission to live her own life.

I glanced over at her again, a surge of excitement bubbling up. "Do you remember how many times we used to plan this? Lying on my bedroom floor, coming up with every possible way to convince them to let you come? I swear, we tried everything."

Sloane laughed, her face lighting up for the first time since we'd gotten in the car. "Oh, God, yeah. I think the most desperate was when we tried to convince them that working at that fish market on the beach would be more 'educational' than sitting in a garage answering phones."

I giggled. "That one was good. I thought it might work, too. I didn't stop to think about how little they cared for your education in reality."

"Yeah, until Marcus started whining about how he couldn't handle the garage alone. Like he does anything." Sloane rolled her eyes again, but her tone was lighter this time. "But you know what? Screw it. Let him have it. I'm done with all of that."

I smiled, my best reassuring smile.

Sloane cracked open a can of Coke, the sharp hiss of carbonation slicing the air. She raised it in an exaggerated toast. "Here's to freedom."

I grinned, lifting an imaginary glass. "Here's to Evermore."

It wasn't until just over halfway into the drive, that the first missing child poster came into view.

The flash of red caught my eye first, capital letters spelling out MISSING in a desperate, almost accusatory font. On this one, a girl's face. She couldn't have been older than eight, her smile bright and gap-toothed, frozen in time.

I swallowed hard, gripping the wheel tighter as the poster blurred past us.

I'd gotten used to them over the years. They were stapled onto telephone poles, taped to petrol station doors, hanging from noticeboards at supermarkets. But that never made it easier.

I focused on the road, but the image clung to the edges of my mind, pressing down like a weight on my chest.

A memory stirred, the feel of fingers grabbing my arm, nails digging into my skin. The burn of his hateful glare.

My stomach twisted.

I blinked hard and rubbed my eyes with one hand, forcing the thoughts back into the locked box where they belonged.

Beside me, Sloane shifted, watching me carefully.

"All right?" she asked, suspicion creeping into her voice.

"Yeah, yeah. Fine." My voice was too quick, too forced. I reached for the volume dial and turned up the music, drowning out the lingering ghosts in my head.

None of that mattered anymore, it was years ago and I had worked hard to move on from those thoughts. This *was* going to be the best summer of my life and a brief memory from the past wasn't going to spoil that.

2

*F*ive years old

There are so many things I remember from that first visit to Evermore. The way the raindrops ran down the car window like tiny silver rivers. The first breath I took when we entered the front door, fresh but warm, like sea air and old books, the kind of scent that settled into my lungs and made it feel like home. The grand staircase which looked so big on that first visit but seemed to reduce in size with each subsequent trip. Each summer, as I grew taller, it seemed to shrink just a little, until one day, I was looking down from the top and wondering how it had ever made me feel so small.

But of all the things Evermore has given me, memories, lessons, moments that shaped me into who I am, the gift I cherish most is Seraphina Fox.

But, I'm getting ahead of myself.

My parents, Gabrielle and William Ward, had just published their third book that summer. Ever since I could remember, they had been writing, scribbling on napkins, muttering into dictaphones at odd hours, disappearing into their study with cups of coffee that always went cold before they remembered to drink them. Even as a child, I understood that their work was important. I didn't know the specifics, but I knew the feeling of it, the weight of their dreams pressing down on our home.

I have vague memories of their early struggles. My mother crying in the living room when they thought I was asleep, my father holding her, whispering reassurances I didn't understand. I remember sitting at the top of the stairs at two years old, gripping the wooden bannister, watching as he promised her that next time would be the time.

It wasn't.

Until, one day, it was.

And just like that, everything changed. Someone, somewhere, had finally seen their talent for what it was, extraordinary. A writing duo like no other. My mother brought the energy, the drama, the sweeping emotion; my father, the intricate prose, the clever turn of phrase. Together, they were unstoppable.

They were, and still are, amazing parents. But when the publishing house signed them on for a whole series of books, they disappeared deeper into their writing. Hours turned into days, weeks, months of them living in their fictional worlds while I was passed between nannies and babysitters, always cared for but never quite with them.

It wasn't until I was four, when I refused to go to my mother for a goodnight kiss, preferring the comfort of my latest nanny, that something shifted. That was the moment she decided enough was enough.

That's where Evermore came in.

The sprawling estate was meant to be a solution, a way for us to be together while they worked. Each summer, we would pack up and move there for six weeks, the length of my school break.

There was a housekeeper, Eva, who lived on the property in a small cottage with her son, Jasper. She looked after Evermore when we weren't there, and when we were, she looked after me too. It worked, in its own way. For forty-six weeks of the year, we were an ordinary family. But for six weeks in the summer, my parents disappeared into their stories, writing at least two books to be released throughout the next year.

I saw them often, a quick cuddle in the morning, a kiss goodnight before they retreated back into their world of words. And then of course there was our Wednesday morning breakfasts, when they would sit with me at the big oak table and ask about everything they had missed.

I know they missed me. And I missed them. But it worked. It was what they needed to do to be fully present for the rest of the year.

And despite that, despite the way the summer months felt like a separate life, I loved Evermore. I loved Eva and Jasper.

The first time I met Eva, she swept me up into a hug so big it nearly swallowed me whole. She was unlike anyone I had ever met, small and bustling, always in motion, her cropped hair forever dyed some vibrant shade. Her clothes were a wild mix of colours and patterns that should have clashed but never quite did.

Jasper, on the other hand, took time to warm up to. He was three years older than me and never let me forget it. Every summer, we had to start over, circling each other cautiously until we inevitably fell back into our usual rhythm of bickering and companionship. He pretended he played with me out of obligation, but I knew better. He enjoyed it, he just didn't want to admit it.

And he was there, that first summer, the day I met Seraphina.

Not directly. But he was there.

That first day was spent settling in, unpacking, exploring, letting my parents proudly lead me through the grand rooms and out into the sprawling gardens. I remember the excitement that buzzed in my chest at all the space, all the possibilities. The high ceilings, the hidden nooks and crannies, the way the lawn sloped gently toward a rose garden that bled into the edge of the woods.

That evening, I stood by the pool, peering down toward the trees, already longing to disappear into them.

The next morning, my mother took my hand and led me down to Eva's cottage. I clung shyly to her legs as she knocked on the door, but that didn't last long. Within minutes, I was in Eva's arms, she smelled like cinnamon and fabric softener and I giggled as she tucked a lollipop into my pocket and whispered conspiratorial plans in my ear.

While they talked, I crouched on the path outside, digging in the dirt with a stick. I could feel Jasper watching me from the porch, he was sitting with some kind of superhero toy, nothing that would have interested me at that age but I kept him in my peripherals, mostly ignoring him, until a butterfly, autumnal wings fluttering, landed on the tip of my stick.

I barely breathed.

And then, just like that, it took off, drifting down the path toward the rose garden.

So, of course, I followed.

The bushes were tall, carefully tended, their scarlet petals bursting against the green. I chased the butterfly through the first row, then the second, giggling as it danced just out of reach.

And then I saw her.

At first, I thought she was a fairy.

A pretty blonde girl sat in front of me, her hair long and cascading in tousled waves down her back. She wore a dress, layered fabric in colours of muted pastels draped her as she knelt in front of the roses with her eyes closed. A faint smile lingered on her pink lips and her small hand was raised, finger outstretched. She sighed lightly and gently reached out towards a closed rosebud in front of her.

She paused for a moment, I could hear my heartbeat in my ears, then she tapped the bud.

I watched as the petals unfurled, slowly, deliberately, stretching open like the first yawn on a Sunday morning.

I was mesmerized.

I must have made a sound because suddenly, her deep green eyes flicked open, meeting mine. They were framed by dark lashes, striking against her golden hair.

The butterfly fluttered around her head, and she lifted her hand, letting it land on her outstretched finger.

She smiled.

A warm, knowing smile. The kind that made me feel safe. The kind that made me feel like I just made a friend.

I took a step forward—

"Sasha!"

The moment shattered. How long had I been gone? It felt like minutes but it could have been longer.

I spun, searching the lawn.

"Sasha!" My mother's voice was sharper now, laced with panic.

I turned back to the girl, to ask her name, to ask if we could be friends—

But she was gone.

I rushed to where she had just been kneeling, my heart pounding, eyes scanning the garden for any trace of her. Nothing.

My chest tightened. Had I imagined it?

Then, slowly, the butterfly drifted back down, landing on the blooming rose she had touched. The one that had just a moment before, been only a bud.

I stared.

She was real.

"Sasha, there you are!"

My mother's arms scooped me up, pressing me against her chest. "Sweetheart, you can't just disappear like that."

Eva and Jasper came skidding around the corner, both flushed, both relieved.

"She's here," my mother assured them, smoothing my curls down as she carried me away.

And that was the first time I ever laid eyes on

Seraphina Fox.

3

We pulled up onto Evermore's cobblestone driveway just as the clock edged toward noon. The sun sat high in the sky, a shimmering gold coin against an uninterrupted stretch of blue. There wasn't a single cloud, one of those rare British summer days where you could almost be tricked into thinking you were somewhere much more exotic.

Sloane let out a slow, disbelieving breath, pushing her sunglasses onto her head as her gaze swept over the estate.

"Jesus fucking Christ..." she murmured. "I mean, you told me all about this place, but it's literally insane, Sash."

Before I could even respond, she was already out of the car, practically throwing herself onto the driveway, the door slamming shut behind her.

I didn't move right away. Instead, I sat

there with my hands resting on the wheel, staring out at the house that I had spent thirteen summers in. Even after all these years, Evermore still had the power to take my breath away.

It wasn't just the beauty of it, the intricate brickwork, the towering bay windows that stood proud at the front of the house or the ivy creeping up the right-hand side like something out of a fairytale. No, it was something deeper. Mostly, I thought, the thing that makes this house so beautiful are all of the memories that I had made here.

This was home. It had always been home.

I exhaled slowly, finally opening the door. The warm breeze carried the scent of salt from the distant sea, mingling with the sweet, earthy perfume of roses blooming.

I knew eventually Evermore was where I wanted to live, where I wanted to raise a family and spend my days, once I'd finished seeing the world of course.

Sloane was already at the front steps, tilting her head back to take in the grand columns framing the entryway. She turned suddenly, throwing her arms wide with an incredulous grin.

"As if this is where I'm living for the next couple of months!" she yelled.

I laughed at her excitement, stepping onto the driveway and stretching out the stiffness from the long drive. I had no doubt this place would change her.

Sloane had grown up in a house where love was scarce, where walls were cracked and ceilings leaked, where voices were raised in anger rather than affection. Her foster parents had been more like specters than guardians, their presence felt only in the damage they left behind. Coldness had followed her like a shadow her whole life. But here, standing in the sunlight outside Evermore, she looked different. Lighter. Like maybe, just maybe, she was starting to believe she could have something more.

"Sasha! Sloane! How are you, my darling girls?"

A blur of colour rounded the corner of the house, and before I could even react, Eva was barreling toward us, arms outstretched.

She reached Sloane first, pulling her into a crushing embrace. I bit back a laugh.

This summer, Eva's hair was a candy floss pink, the short crop a little longer on top than usual. Last year, it had been half blue, half green, one of my favorite looks yet. She wore a flowing yellow kaftan embroidered with delicate daisies, and her neck was adorned with layers of beaded necklaces, each one seemingly telling a story of its own. I half-expected to see the heavy amethyst pendant she used to wear, the one that left an indentation on my temple every time she hugged me too tight.

"Hi, Eva! I've missed you!" I ran over, joining in the hug.

Eva pulled back, holding both of us at arm's length, her face glowing with warmth.

"Oh, I've missed you too, sweet! Your mum gave me a ring last week and told me to be expecting you both. Sasha, your room is all ready, and I've set up the one across the hall for Sloane. Oh, Sloane, darling, I bet you think I'm a complete lunatic, running up to you like that! But I've known all about you for years, every summer, all I heard was 'Sloane this, Sloane that.' I feel like I know you as well as my own son!"

I let out a laugh, shaking my head. Eva was impossible not to love. She was light incarnate, an endless summer day in human form.

The smiley and colourful woman was the complete opposite to Sloane's jet black blunt hair cut and permanent scowly demeanour, yet even Sloane was clearly taken in by the bubbly lady who stood in front of us.

"Thank you so much, Eva. We're so grateful," I said, meaning it.

"Don't mention it, my love. I've stocked the fridge for you, that should last you a week or so, but let me know if you need anything. I've got to run into town for a few bits, but you know where I am! Love you, darling, see you soon!"

She bustled back down the steps, climbing into her little blue Beetle, and with a final wave, she was gone, the car disappearing down the long drive.

Still laughing, we stepped inside.

The foyer was just as I remembered, soft blue walls that seemed to drink in the sunlight, making the whole space feel like the inside of a seashell. A White Linen Yankee Candle flickered on the console table, its scent crisp and clean. The high shelves, dustless as ever, held trinkets of summers past: decorative shells, a glass bottle filled with sea glass, and the wooden lighthouse lamp we had bought at the beachside gift shop in town, cast a soft glow across the room.

And then, of course, there was the staircase.

Sweeping and grand, it never failed to steal my breath. It was the kind of staircase made for midnight confessions and slow descents in ballgowns.

"She's wicked, we literally must protect her at all costs," Sloane sniggered, dropping her bags at the base of the stairs.

She turned, glancing up at the staircase,

and I heard her breath catch.

"Will I ever stop saying wow?"

"I haven't," I admitted, grinning.

Sloane shook her head. "Right, onto business, where's the coffee machine?"

I rolled my eyes, about to follow her into the kitchen when a sudden knock at the door was immediately followed by it swinging open.

Fi stood there, barefoot as always, her dirty blonde hair tumbling in waves down her back, tiny wildflowers braided into the strands. A floaty sage-green dress billowed around her ankles, and she had that look about her, like she had just stepped out of some otherworldly place.

"Sasha!" she shrieked, launching herself at me.

"What the hell was that?" Sloane peered around the corner, looking alarmed.

"Oh my god! Sloane! Happy Birthday!" Fi cried, pulling her into the hug as well.

I grinned, giddy with the sheer joy of it all. Sloane, however, looked utterly baffled, clearly wondering how she had ended up in two three-way embraces in under fifteen minutes.

Fi extended her arm, revealing three identical bracelets on her wrist.

"Girls, I made you both a bracelet. They match mine, it's made from malachite, for protection."

"Protection from...?" Sloane asked skeptically.

"Who knows?" Fi responded with a grin. "Hopefully nothing."

I bit my lip to keep from laughing at the utterly perplexed look on Sloane's face as Fi tied the bracelet around her wrist.

A thought I had been mulling over for weeks finally spilled from my lips.

"Fi, I think you should move into Evermore for the summer, you already told your parents you would be here basically everyday, and it's the first year without Mum and Dad around. We can make midnight margaritas literally every night!"

I had been thinking about asking Fi to stay since Sloane and I had first started making plans and of course, throwing a reference from our favourite film in there was guaranteed to seal the deal.

Not that I really even had to try and convince her, I could tell by the smile on Fi's face that she had agreed before I'd even finished my sentence.

"I would literally love to!"

And just like that, it was set.

My best friends. My favorite place. A summer of magic.

∞ ∞ ∞

By ten to seven, after multiple gin and lemonades (or tonics, in Sloane's case) and a slice of homemade birthday cake that Fi had brought over after her trip back home to grab her stuff for the summer, we were making our way over the grassy dunes toward Wistow Bay, on the hunt for a party she had heard about. I held up my long burgundy dress with one hand as I walked, trying to minimize the risk of tripping and making a complete fool of myself at the first party of the summer. My beige Birkenstocks pressed lightly into the sandy path between the dunes, the cool grains shifting beneath my feet.

The beach sprawled out before us, a huge bonfire already blazing in the centre, its bright glow licking at the darkening sky. Off to the side, a group of guys had set up a makeshift bar out of pallets, while to the right, a large sound system blared Billie Bossa Nova by Billie Eilish. The bass reverberated in my chest, the sultry melody twining with the distant hum of laughter and the rhythmic crash of the waves.

Fi didn't hesitate, she grabbed both of

us by the wrist and dragged us straight toward the bar, where she swiftly handed us each a beer before pressing a quick kiss to my forehead. Then, just as quickly, she was gone, disappearing into the throng of dancing bodies.

She moved with effortless grace, twirling her arms above her head without spilling a drop of her drink. The pale blue skirt she wore shimmered in the firelight, catching and reflecting the glow with each sway of her hips. Her golden hair fanned out around her like a halo as she spun, completely lost in the rhythm, her movements so fluid it was as if she belonged to the music itself.

Beside me, Sloane stared after her, utterly baffled.

"Is she always like this?"

I laughed, taking a sip of my drink. "You get used to her. If you ever lose her at a party, just head to the dance floor, she'll be there all night."

We made our way over to a large, sea-worn log that had long since settled halfway up the beach, wedged deep into the sand. It made the perfect spot to sit and watch the party unfold, the fire flickering by Fi as she danced, the sea stretching endlessly beyond the glow. The evening air was thick and balmy, wrapping around my skin like silk, the heat of the bonfire warring with the occasional cool breeze rolling off the waves.

"Do you remember that party on the beach when we were fifteen?" I asked, smiling at the memory.

Sloane chuckled, shaking her head. "How could I forget? We told your parents we were going to mine, then hopped on a bus out of the city. I remember feeling so rebellious. God knows why they believed us, we never went to mine."

I laughed. "Right? Now that I think about it, I wonder if they knew and just decided to let us have our moment. That was our first real taste of adventure. The bonfire was huge, and the music was so loud we could hear it from the bus stop."

"It was perfect," Sloane said dreamily. "Until it got cold. And then, of course, my shoes got stolen."

"Oh my god, yeah!" My eyes widened as the memory rushed back. "I couldn't believe someone actually took them. You had to walk all the way back to the bus stop barefoot."

Sloane nodded, laughing. "I was freezing. And that bus ride back into the city? It felt like the longest ride of my life. My feet were numb by the time we got to yours."

"We were so terrified sneaking back in," I grinned. "I still remember how we tiptoed past my parents' bedroom, holding our breath."

"And you gave me those shoes," Sloane said, her voice softer now, a small smile playing on her lips. "Your trainers. You insisted I keep them."

"Of course I did." I shrugged. "I couldn't let you go home barefoot. Plus, they looked better on you anyway."

She laughed, shaking her head. "I still have them, you know. They're completely worn out, but I couldn't bring myself to throw them away."

"Really?" I blinked, touched. "I can't believe you kept them all this time."

"Of course I did." Sloane met my gaze. "They remind me of that night. Our first little rebel adventure. They always make me smile."

I reached over and gave her hand a squeeze, my fingers brushing against the dark velvet of her mini skirt. "That was one of the best nights," I said softly. "And we've had so many more since."

"Yeah," she agreed, squeezing back. "And plenty more to come."

The night stretched on, warm and hazy. Whilst we sat, I pointed out the odd local that I knew the name of and shared bits of gossip that Fi had filled me in on over the years.

Eventually, Fi made her way over to us,

collapsing onto the sand with a happy sigh. Sweat glistened on her collarbones, her face flushed with the warmth of both the fire and the dancing.

"Hello, my beauties!" she grinned, presenting us both with a fresh beer. "Are you having fun?"

"This place is mint," Sloane said, still gazing dreamily at the crowd. "Are there a lot of parties down here?"

"Oh yeah," Fi nodded. "All summer long. It's nice and secluded, so it's always been pretty safe to let loose on this side of the bay."

"Awesome."

I yawned, stretching, exhaustion washing over me in waves. "On that note, girls, I am absolutely beat. Take my key and enjoy yourselves, I'll get you both your own tomorrow, but there's a spare hidden out back I can use tonight."

Sloane barely acknowledged me, I could see her eye-fucking some light-haired stranger across the fire. I flicked a glance at Fi, and we shared a knowing look.

"Make sure she gets home in one piece," I laughed, tossing my key to Fi.

"See you in the morning, love," she called after me.

Swaying slightly, I stepped onto

Evermore's patio, the dusky sky ablaze with deep ambers and reds, clouds streaking across the horizon like a forest fire.

Reaching for the faux rock that housed the spare key, I turned it over in my hand, only to find it empty.

"Dammit," I muttered, realising I'd have to go grab one from Eva's. I made a mental note to ask her about the missing key.

The lawn was glistening from the light emanating out of the cottage windows as I crossed past the rose bushes towards the house. I was more tipsy than I realised, and I had to steady myself against the stone wall as I walked up the path.

I was just leaning up against the bright red door, trying to decide how mad Eva would be for waking her up at this time of night when it flung open from the inside and I went flying face forwards, straight into someone's arms.

Someone's very strong arms.

Warm hands caught my waist, steadying me with an ease that sent a sharp awareness through my body. The scent of cedar and peppermint wrapped around me, heady and clean. My breath hitched.

"Woah," a deep voice startled me.

I knew that voice.

I tilted my head back, my gaze locking onto a familiar pair of chestnut brown eyes, their depths flickering with firelight.

Jasper.

Shit.

"I—uh—sorry." My words tangled in my throat. "I leant the girls my key and the hidden one isn't in its spot. I was just coming to ask Eva if I could borrow hers. I didn't mean to touch.. I mean trip into you."

Jasper's gaze flicked over me, his brow arching slightly.

"Have you been drinking, Sasha?"

"Only a couple," I snapped, trying to regain some dignity.

His lips twitched, amusement glinting in his eyes as he turned to grab the spare key.

I exhaled, willing my heart to stop hammering. But as he moved, my gaze betrayed me, flicking down to where his joggers sat low on his hips.

I clenched my jaw, dragging my focus back up.

Jasper turned, key in hand. "You gonna be alright getting back?"

"Fine." I turned on my heel, only to nearly trip over a flower pot.

"Looks like it," he murmured, laughter in his voice.

I didn't look back. But I could feel his gaze on me the entire way up the lawn.

∞ ∞ ∞

Lying in bed half an hour later, I kicked off the grey patterned sheets, heat simmering beneath my skin. Restless, I sat up and shoved open my bedroom window, hoping the cool night air would bring some relief. It was frustrating, only an hour ago, I could barely keep my eyes open in front of the flickering fire, yet now sleep felt impossibly out of reach.

My thoughts drifted back to the night's events, circling around a single, unexpected focal point, Jasper.

I frowned. Where was this coming from? A fleeting, thirty-second interaction, and suddenly, my mind was unraveling over a guy I'd known since I was five.

I replayed the brief moment his body was pressed against mine, his firm stomach beneath his white t-shirt, the subtle shift of muscle beneath my hands.

A familiar ache stirred low in my stomach, and I scowled at myself. *Honestly.* It had just been too long since I'd had any, that was all. *Nothing more, nothing deeper.* It had been nearly a year since I broke up with Jared, my boyfriend from school. To his credit, he was lovely but that was where it ended. We'd slept together plenty of times, but satisfaction had always eluded me. More often than not, I'd find myself staring at the ceiling afterwards, much like I was now.

Sighing, I squeezed my thighs together and rolled onto my side. *Enough of this.* Grabbing my phone, I shoved in one headphone and clicked on my latest true crime podcast, letting the familiar narration fill the silence.

Maybe, if I was lucky, it would drown out the filthy thoughts that were invading my mind.

4

Five years old

It wasn't until a week later that I saw Seraphina again. The week had been filled with my parents slowly retreating into their respective study's to begin writing. At first, they hovered, making sure I was settling in, but soon enough, they seemed content that I was comfortable with Eva and the sprawling estate to explore. And I was.

Looking back, I cringe at how much time I spent trailing after Jasper. He was older, and while he tolerated my presence with surprising patience, I think he was relieved when the second week of the holidays arrived and he could escape to his dad's house. I, however, was less thrilled. With him gone, the house suddenly felt bigger, emptier. I spent that morning wandering through the halls, the floorboards creaking beneath my small steps, while Eva bustled about in the kitchen.

I must have been getting under her feet because she eventually turned from her baking, wiped her hands on her apron, and said,

"Why don't you go outside for a while, love? But don't go past the end of the garden."

Her voice was kind, but firm, and I knew better than to argue. So out I went, the summer air warm against my skin, the scent of roses heavy and sweet as I drifted toward the garden. I don't remember consciously deciding to go to the edge of the property, but soon enough, I found myself there, standing at the border of the roses, staring into the woods beyond.

I hesitated, glancing back at the house. Through the kitchen window, I saw Eva watching me. She lifted a hand in a little wave, and I waved back before sinking onto the grass, absentmindedly picking up a fallen rose. The petals were so soft against my skin, like silk, and for a moment, I was lost in the texture of it, the way the colour deepened at the edges.

Then—

"Hi!"

I startled, my head snapping up.

"Hello?" I called hesitantly, scanning the bushes.

A rustling. And then, there she was.

Seraphina.

Her hair was different today, neatly braided

into two Dutch plaits, and threaded with ribbons. She wore frayed denim shorts and a crochet vest in lilac and yellow, the fabric loose and airy. Her feet were bare, adorned with an array of brightly coloured anklets that jangled as she plopped down beside me, as if she belonged there, as if we were old friends and this was the most natural thing in the world.

"What are you doing?" she asked, tilting her head.

"Nothing," I said quickly, suddenly self-conscious.

She studied me with those sharp green eyes, and I had the strangest feeling, like she could see right through me. Not in a mean way, but in a way that made me squirm, like she was looking at something inside me I hadn't noticed yet.

I shifted, smoothing my hands over my curls in a futile attempt to tame them. My hair never listened, always springing right back up the moment I let go.

"What's your name?" she asked.

"Sasha," I replied. "What's yours?"

"Seraphina," she said. "But call me Fi."

She stood abruptly, moving with an energy that was almost too much for her small frame. "Everybody does, except my dad. He always calls me Seraphina because he says that's what they named me, so that's what he'll use. But it's a bit long, isn't it? I like Fi. I do like Seraphina too, but Fi is easier to say."

I blinked up at her, barely able to keep up.

She giggled. "My dad also says I talk too much and too fast. I do agree with him on that."

And then, she smiled. That same warm, inviting smile from the week before, and suddenly, I didn't feel so awkward anymore.

I watched as she reached out and ran her fingers over the rose petals. My breath caught, anticipation curling in my chest. I kept my eyes on her hand, waiting.

"How did you do that thing the other day?" I asked quietly.

Fi smiled, trailing her fingertips over the flowers, then she stilled, found a rosebud and tapped it softly.

And just like before, it bloomed.

I watched, transfixed, as the petals unfurled, slow and deliberate.

Fi turned to me. "You mean that?"

I nodded, my heart thumping.

"You could do it too."

I gaped at her. "I can't."

"You can," she said simply.

I shook my head, but Fi just grinned. Before I could protest, she grabbed my hand.

Her skin was warm, soft against my own. She took the fallen rose from my other hand, turned my palm upward, and placed the flower in the centre. Then, she closed her eyes, *bringing her free hand above the rose.*

A twitch.

A shift in the air.

And then the rose lifted.

Just a little. Floating there, weightless, above my palm. Fi's hand guided it up, but when she opened her eyes, she wasn't looking at the rose. She was looking at me.

The rose dropped back into my hand. "Your turn."

I let out a breathy laugh. "I can't do that. I don't even know how you did that."

Fi's eyes sparkled. "Close your eyes."

I hesitated, then did as she said.

"Think of something happy."

Happy? I screwed my eyes tighter, searching my mind, until—

Sloane.

I saw her clear as day, my best friend from home. We were huddled under a blanket fort, the one Dad built for us. We had snacks and stuffed animals, and Sloane, giggling, carefree, stuck carrot sticks in her mouth like buck teeth, sending us both into peals of laughter.

I smiled.

"Look," Fi whispered.

I opened my eyes.

The rose was floating.

I barely breathed, afraid even the smallest movement would break the spell.

Fi grinned. She wiggled her fingers, then

tucked her hands beneath her legs, showing me she wasn't doing it anymore. This was me.

"Witchy!" She whispered.

I lifted my fingers slightly, and the rose gave the smallest of wobbles in the air.

My chest ached with something vast and impossible.

Magic.

Real magic.

Looking back now, I'm amazed at how easily I believed. But that's the wonderful thing about being a child, isn't it? Magic isn't something to be questioned, it just is.

And in that moment, I understood something.

I was a witch.

I used to picture witches as green-skinned, warty old women with pointy hats, but now I knew better. Magic didn't come wrapped in dark cloaks or cackling voices, it hid in plain sight. In the woman at the market selling lavender bundles with a knowing smile, in the street musician whose fingers moved a little too fast over the violin strings, in the way the wind carried whispers through the trees. If I was a witch, then surely others were too, tucked away in the ordinary world, unnoticed by those who didn't know where to look.

I had tried to hint at it to my parents the following Wednesday morning, nervous but hopeful, slipping magic into the conversation like a secret I was testing to see if they could hear. But they had only chuckled, their responses wrapped in affectionate dismissal.

"Childhood imagination," my mother had mused. My father, ever the storyteller, had handed me an old copy of Grimm's Fairy Tales from his vast study.

"For your research," he had said with a wink, as if that was the closest I would ever get to real magic.

But real magic had already found me.

Then came the day I met Fi's parents, Briar and Linus.

It was a warm morning and Eva had taken Jasper and I into the local town.

Wychbold Cove felt like something from another time, nestled between rolling green hills and the sparkling coastline. Its winding cobbled streets, worn smooth from years of footsteps, twisted and turned in unpredictable directions, leading visitors on a gentle maze through the heart of the town. The black and white Tudor houses, some leaning slightly as if whispering to one another lined the streets with their exposed wooden beams and ornate windows. Clematis and climbing ivy wrapped around door frames, adding splashes of greenery to the scene, like nature's own embellishments, while the smell of salt from the nearby beach lingered in the air. Narrow

*alleyways branched off from the main street,
leading to hidden courtyards and steep stone
steps that beckoned to those curious enough
to explore. At the highest point of the town, a
little church stood quietly, its weathered stone
walls watching over everything below. Its bell
would chime softly, marking time as the day
drifted along, and from the steps in front of it,
you could see the glistening sands of the beach
beyond the rooftops.*

*The sandy streets leading down to the
beach were lined with small, brightly coloured
shops, each with hand painted signs which
proudly displayed their names. Locally owned
businesses thrived here, the bakery with its
window full of fresh pastries, the bookshop
spilling out into the street with old wooden
crates filled with novels and the cosy cafes
where everyone knew your name. Shop owners
waved to each other across the street, offering
friendly smiles and small town gossip to
anyone passing by. Flower boxes hung from
window sills, filled with bursts of colour, and
the sense of community was palpable in every
corner.*

*It was a town where time seemed to move a
little slower, where everyone knew each other
and took the time to stop and chat. The beach
below with its golden sands stretching out to
meet the gentle waves, was always just a short
walk away, a peaceful retreat at the end of a*

quiet, winding road.

Fi and I had played together every day since our second meeting, she had shown me how to perfect making the flowers float and we were working on me opening the rose buds myself. I was upset at the thought of leaving Evermore for the day, and not being able to rush down to the rose garden right after breakfast to find her. I remember dragging my feet and lagging behind as Eva walked along in front holding Jasper's hand. She kept glancing back at me and wiggling the fingers on her spare hand to get me to take it, but I was being predictably stroppy and just sighed at her. A bemused look had crossed her face before she'd turned and carried on the way she was going.

And then I saw her.

A flash of blonde hair. A flower crown tilted slightly to one side. Big green eyes peeking out from between the shelves of a shop window, crinkling as their owner grinned.

"Eva!" I yelped, sudden excitement replacing my sulking. "Can we go in here?"

She turned, glancing up at the shop's sign as she followed my gaze.

The Alchemy.

As soon as we stepped inside, I was hit with a scent I couldn't name, earthy, sweet, and mysterious all at once. Incense, I would later learn.

Shelves overflowed with bottles and jars,

each filled with curious things, dried herbs, crystals that reflected the dim light, stones and powders labeled in looping, elegant handwriting. Candles, both lit and unlit, lined the floor, their flames flickering even though there was no breeze. Tapestries and dreamcatchers swayed gently, as if the very walls were breathing.

Somewhere in the background, I Put a Spell on You by Nina Simone played, the music curling through the air like a whispered incantation.

A man stood behind the counter, smiling warmly.

"Hello, folks! Come on in!"

He had reddish-brown hair with curls which mirrored my own, a wild mass that refused to be tamed. His spectacles perched low on his nose, half-moon lenses that caught the light. His clothes were smart but quirky, a button down shirt and trousers but in the most beautiful greens and blues, the threads holding the clothes together seemed to be made of silver, glinting like stardust and the buttons were sparkling gems.

Eva tilted her head. "What a lovely shop," she mused. "I've passed here plenty of times, but I've never really noticed it before."

"Ah," the man said knowingly. "That's the thing about our little shop, you don't really notice it until you need it. Or until it needs

you."

He winked at me.

A small hand slipped into mine, and I turned to find Fi beside me, her fingers warm, her grin wide with excitement.

"This is my friend, Papa," she said, tugging me forward.

The man let out a chuckle, his eyes crinkling in a way that reminded me so much of Fi. "Oh, Sasha," he said, his voice full of warmth. "We've heard lots about you, little lady."

Heat crept up my neck. I could feel myself blushing, but before I could say anything, Fi's father turned toward the back of the shop, cupping his hands around his mouth.

"Briar! Sasha is here!"

There was a rustling sound, then the soft jingle of beads clinking together. A woman emerged through a beaded curtain, and for a second, I swore I was looking at Fi, just thirty years into the future.

Briar had the same long, tousled, dirty-blonde hair, though hers was pinned in a way that seemed impossible, like it should have unraveled at any moment, but somehow held. Loose tendrils framed her face, falling in delicate curls around a pair of large wire glasses perched at the tip of her nose. Her arms were covered in the finest, most intricate tattoos I had ever seen, delicate ornamental designs that wrapped around her wrists and climbed her forearms like vines.

And then she smiled at me. A slow, radiant smile that made the whole shop feel even warmer.

"Oh, how beautiful you are, little Sasha," she murmured, kneeling in front of me. She smelled like flowers, real ones, fresh and wild, the kind my dad sometimes brought home for my mum.

I didn't know what to say.

Then, Briar stood and turned to Eva, taking her hands between her own. "And you must be Sasha's mother?"

Eva laughed, shaking her head. "Oh no, I just look after the house, and Sasha, when her parents are working." She shot me a teasing glance. "Though apparently not very well, since she's managed to make a whole new friend without me noticing."

Briar's lips twitched as she turned her gaze back to me, her eyes twinkling behind her glasses. "Ah," she said knowingly.

"Our Seraphina will have been sneaking into that beautiful garden again," The man added, stepping around the counter. "My name is Linus and this is my wife Briar. We live in a cottage in the woodland just beyond the Evermore gardens. Seraphina loves to play and explore in the area. We hope she hasn't caused any trouble."

"Absolutely none at all," Eva assured them.

"She's always welcome, the little dot. I'm sure Gabrielle and William will be thrilled to hear Sasha has a friend other than my Jasper."

At the mention of his name, Jasper, who had been lingering awkwardly by the door, shuffled uncomfortably. He eyed Linus and Briar with a mixture of wariness and curiosity, like he wasn't sure what to make of them.

Eva knelt in front of my new friend who was still holding my hand.

"I was going to take the children to the beach," she said. "Would you like to come too?" She glanced up at Briar and Linus. "If it's alright with your parents, of course."

Fi's entire face lit up as she turned toward them, hopeful.

"Of course it's alright," Linus said cheerfully. "We'll be here all day Eva, feel free to drop her in on your way back through."

And just like that, Fi and I were beaming at each other, practically bouncing on our heels.

We left The Alchemy heading down through the town toward the beach. Jasper spotted some school friends as soon as we arrived and ran off to join their football game, while Eva settled onto a blanket with her book. That left Fi and me free to roam the shore, dipping our toes into the foamy waves, gathering tiny shells from the rock pools, and most importantly building sandcastles.

Fi was the one who suggested we make fairy

castles.

"But we don't have buckets," I pointed out, frowning at the piles of damp sand slipping through my fingers.

Fi only smiled. "We don't need buckets."

She glanced over at Eva, making sure she wasn't watching, then wiggled her fingers over the sand.

I held my breath.

Slowly, grain by grain, the sand began to move on its own. It shifted and stacked, rising like a tiny city, sculpting itself into walls and towers and winding staircases. The windows were little holes, carved out by unseen hands. The front of the structure opened into a doorway that looked just big enough for something small to step through.

I gasped. Every time I saw magic, even the smallest bit, it filled me with a deep, buzzing excitement, like there was something inside me waiting to be unlocked.

Fi nudged me. "You try."

I swallowed, plunging my hands into the warm sand. I squeezed my eyes shut and focused, just like she'd taught me. I filled my mind with happy thoughts, Sloane and me giggling at the back of the classroom, Mum reading bedtime stories, Fi and me sitting amongst the roses at Evermore. I imagined the sand rising, shifting, building itself into something beautiful.

When I opened my eyes, there it was.

My castle wasn't as grand as Fi's, but it stood, solid and real. A little lopsided, a little uneven, but mine.

I grinned.

Fi clapped. "Let's decorate them!"

For the next couple of hours, we adorned our castles with shells and pebbles, ate ice cream that melted faster than we could finish it, and even attempted to join Jasper's football game, though that earned us plenty of amused snorts and sideways glances from Jasper and his friends. Before long, the sun was dipping lower in the sky, and we were walking back through town, dropping Fi off at The Alchemy before heading home.

∞ ∞ ∞

The rest of the summer blurred by in sunshiny days and starlit nights, in whispered secrets and stolen moments of magic. Every day brought something new, another spell, another adventure, another step closer to a world I never wanted to leave.

And then, too soon, it was over.

I stood beside the car, my suitcase packed, my heart impossibly heavy. Tears slipped down my cheeks, silent but unstoppable. Six weeks hadn't been enough. A whole summer hadn't been enough.

Fi clung to me, sniffling against my shoulder. "You'll write?" she whispered.

I nodded, my throat too tight to speak.

Briar and Linus stood a few steps behind her, smiling gently. Eva wrapped me in a bear hug, and even Jasper, reluctant as ever, patted my shoulder with a gruff sort of fondness. I was sure I could see the telltale shine of tears glistening in his eyes.

I climbed into the car, pressing my forehead against the window as we pulled away.

As my father turned our car out of the drive, Evermore disappeared from view, and with it, the people I had come to love.

I took a deep breath, forcing a small smile.

I was going home to Sloane, and that at least, made leaving a little easier.

5

Despite feeling slightly hungover the day after the party at Wistow Bay, I had dragged myself into town and got Sloane and Fi keys cut for the house. My head still carried the remnants of last night, a dull throb behind my eyes, the vague sense that if I moved too fast, the world might tip sideways, but it wasn't unbearable. The real motivation had been avoiding another awkward encounter with Jasper in the middle of the night. So, I'd also gotten a spare key for the faux rock and with the original spare replaced, there were now two in there, safely tucked away for emergencies. Sloane had attached her key to her bat keyring with an air of satisfaction, spinning it between her fingers like it was some kind of prize. Fi, on the other hand, had reached deep into the seemingly endless pockets of her patterned skirt and pulled out a mishmash of braided cords in a riot of colours, bits of fabric, feathers, and something that might have once been part of a festival wristband, all knotted together in a way that looked both deliberate and accidental. She held it up, examining it critically before weaving the key somewhere among its chaotic form. Fi never explained things like this. She just did them.

∞ ∞ ∞

Later on that day, sprawled outside, the afternoon stretching lazily around us, the warmth of the sun seeped into my skin, countered by the occasional whisper of a breeze that carried the scent of salt and sun-warmed stone. I lay back on the lounger, eyes half-lidded, listening to the rhythmic hush of the ocean mixing with the gentle ripple of the pool. The light danced on the water, the surface shifting between blue and gold. My body felt heavy, relaxed, except for the persistent gnaw of hunger making itself known in the pit of my stomach.

"I'm starving," I muttered, pressing a hand against my stomach as if that might quiet the rumbling.

Fi, stretched out beside me with sunglasses perched on her nose, smirked. "What do you feel like eating?"

I tilted my head slightly, considering.

"Something hearty. But not too heavy, you know? Maybe pasta? Or a big salad with grilled chicken?"

Sloane, who had been lying on my other side, suddenly sat up, a sheepish look on her face which immediately caught my attention. Fi and I exchanged a glance, suspicion blooming between us.

"What?" I asked, narrowing my eyes. "What's that look for?"

Sloane hesitated, biting her lip, which only made me more curious. Sloane was many things, but hesitant wasn't usually one of them.

"Okay, so... there's something I need to tell you."

I raised an eyebrow.

Sloane took a deep breath. "Every Tuesday, while you were in your English class, I... well, I've been going to your house."

I blinked. "Right..?"

"I've been going to your house," she repeated, her voice quieter now. "To learn how to cook from your mum."

For a second, I just stared at her, trying to process that sentence. My brain lagged, like I was attempting to illegally download music on a nineties desktop computer. A laugh bubbled up before I could stop it.

"What?!"

"I know, I know! It sounds crazy, but I

didn't want anyone to know until I was ready," Sloane said quickly. "Your mum's been teaching me to cook. Proper meals, you know? Because I didn't know how. I mean, I can stick a pizza in the oven and heat up some beans in the microwave, but... I wanted to contribute while we're staying at Evermore. I didn't want to be useless in the kitchen."

I gawked at her. "You've been cooking with Mum?"

Sloane nodded, cheeks pink. "Yeah. And, uh, she taught me how to make jerk chicken with rice and peas. She said it's one of your favorites."

Fi giggled, her eyes darting back and forth between us..

"Oh my God," I said, shaking my head in disbelief. "That's why! Every Tuesday, I'd come home, and it was always jerk chicken for dinner."

"I wanted to surprise you," Sloane admitted, grinning sheepishly. "I thought maybe I could make it for dinner tonight. For all of us."

I was still trying to piece together the mental image of Sloane in my mother's kitchen, standing over a hob, probably looking at ingredients like they were a foreign language.

"You? Cook? Jerk chicken?"

Fi didn't tease, she just smiled warmly. "That's a really sweet thing to do."

Sloane grimaced, rolling her eyes. "Ugh, Fi, you're pushing it, calling me sweet."

Before I could say anything else, movement at the end of the driveway caught my eye. Jasper and Eva were leaving their cottage, Jasper slipping into the driver's seat of his truck with a nod in our direction while Eva waved at us.

Sloane raised an eyebrow. "So, there's the famous Jasper I've heard so much about."

Fi nodded eagerly. "I can't wait for you two to meet."

I smirked. "Yeah, I think you'll get on. Maybe we should invite him over tonight? What do you think, Sloane? Up for cooking for him too?"

Sloane hesitated. "Uh, sure. Why not?"

I reached for my phone, quickly typing out a text. I sent it off with a sigh, thinking about the night before. I cringed inwardly. I hadn't seen Jasper since last summer, and instead of saying hello like a normal person, I'd been too caught up in my own drunken awkwardness and probably come off as really rude. Hopefully, he didn't think I was deliberately being like that, *or worse,* that I was too wasted to care.

My phone buzzed. Jasper had texted back.

I grinned at the girls. "He's in."

Sloane's face paled. "Oh, God. I actually have to cook now."

"You've got four hours," I teased. "Plenty of time."

Sloane leapt up, a mix of panic and determination in her eyes.

"Four hours? I'm already behind schedule!" Then, as if she had only just remembered, she gasped. "Oh god! Fi! You're a vegetarian!"

I snorted and Fi shoved my shoulder lightly.

"Don't worry about that! I'll make some tofu to go with the rice," she said, her voice reassuring.

Sloane nodded, then bolted into the house.

For a while, Fi and I lay back, the sun dipping lower, setting the sky ablaze with gold. I tried to silence the hunger gnawing at me with a bag of crisps, but the distant crashes and muttered swearing from the kitchen became impossible to ignore.

"We should check on her," Fi said with a grin.

Inside, the kitchen was chaos. Pots and pans everywhere and somehow, a spring onion was lodged in Sloane's hair.

"Honestly, thank God for Eva keeping this kitchen so well-stocked," Sloane muttered, wiping her brow. "I've already dropped a whole bottle of soy sauce on the floor."

I spotted the pile of kitchen roll soaked with brown liquid and burst out laughing. "You're doing great," I assured, and began tidying up behind Sloane as she moved around the kitchen in a frenzy.

Fi took a seat at the breakfast bar, absentmindedly twisting her hair with magic, though it resisted her efforts. She sighed dramatically.

"I can control the elements," she muttered. "But I cannot get my hair to cooperate."

Finally, after what felt like hours, the kitchen was clean, the food was safely in the oven, and Fi's tofu was grilling away on the stove. The air smelled rich with roasted garlic and caramelized onions, the warmth of it curling into the humid summer evening.

Sloane collapsed into a chair with a dramatic groan, slumping forward like she'd just run a marathon. I reached over, plucking a stray garlic clove shell from her shoulder, and flicked it into the bin with a lazy wave of my fingers.

Fi stood up, stretching with a satisfied sigh. "I'm going to make us a pitcher to go with the meal."

I groaned. "More alcohol?"

Sloane immediately brightened, pushing

her hair out of her face. "I could use a drink."

Fi began gathering an assortment of herbs and odd liquids from the cupboards, setting them on the counter with quiet purpose. Sloane watched warily, one eyebrow creeping up. "I thought you meant, like, a vodka and Coke..."

I patted her shoulder, grinning. "You'll get used to Fi's kitchen magic. Just trust the process. If it looks like it shouldn't go together, it'll probably be the best thing you've ever tasted."

Fi worked methodically, her hands sure and practiced as she crushed herbs between her fingers, releasing their sharp, fresh scent into the air. The rhythmic clinking of glass and the swirl of colours in the pitcher felt almost hypnotic, like a spell being woven right in front of us.

As I watched her, excitement started bubbling up in my chest. *Sloane and Jasper were finally going to meet.* I twirled a strand of hair around my finger, barely containing myself. "I think you're going to love him, Sloane. You'll get on so well."

Sloane glanced up from her phone, giving me a smirk like she saw right through me.

"I'm sure I will." Her voice was dry, amused.

I checked my watch, and immediately felt a jolt of panic.

"Oh my God, is that the time? I need to get ready!"

I shot up from my seat, nearly knocking my chair over, and sprinted out of the room, their laughter trailing behind me.

Twenty minutes later, I was just about to head back into the kitchen when movement at the bifold doors caught my eye. Jasper was stepping inside, the last light of the evening casting his broad frame in subtle hues, making the edges of his silhouette glow.

For a second, I just watched him. It had been weeks since I'd last seen him properly, Fi was already across the kitchen, a wide smile lighting up her face.

"Jasper! I haven't seen you in forever!" She threw her arms around him, squeezing tight.

He hugged her back, laughing. "The last time must have been two weeks ago," Fi went on, her words spilling out with excitement. "You were just leaving your house as I arrived, remember? You're never there when I visit your mum!"

I reached for one of Fi's drinks on the counter, taking a generous gulp, hoping it would settle the sudden flutter in my stomach. It was sweet, but not in an artificial way, fruity with a slight floral note, chased by the slow, creeping warmth of alcohol. Beneath it all, there was something else, something earthy and strange that lingered on my tongue.

"Sounds about right," Jasper said, his voice snapping me out of my thoughts. "I've been helping out more on the grounds around here. I'm probably on a lawnmower or attacking hedges with the strimmer when you've been over."

Fi grinned and gave his arm a light punch, then froze, her eyes widening as she squeezed his bicep playfully. "Ooh, Jaspy! Look at you! Been lifting some weights, have you?"

A blush crept over Jasper's cheeks as he shoved Fi back teasingly.

Then his gaze lifted and found mine.

His face brightened, and before I could overthink it, I was smiling too, stepping toward him.

"Hey," I murmured, my voice softer than I intended.

Guilt tugged at me, settling low in my chest.

"About last night, I think I was more drunk than I realised. The fresh air must have hit me on the way back."

Jasper laughed, brushing his hand against my arm in an easy, familiar way.

"It's all good. It's nice having you back. Classic Sasha, making an entrance."

Our eyes held for a second, maybe two.

Then I remembered Fi and Sloane were in the room.

I cleared my throat, spinning around. "Sloane! Come over here! I want you to meet Jasper!"

Sloane made her way over, and the two of them exchanged an awkward handshake-hug hybrid, both shifting slightly, unsure of the movement.

Fi snorted at the interaction.

"I've heard a lot about you, Sloane," Jasper said, smiling kindly. "I—"

I cut him off before he could even finish.

"Guess who's cooked dinner?"

Jasper opened his mouth, but was cut off again.

"Sloane!" I announced, practically buzzing with pride. "She doesn't usually cook, so it's a big surprise. She's been learning, from my mum, of all people!"

Jasper turned to Sloane, looking impressed.

"Sloane's brilliant. She's going to university to study social work, near Wychbold Cove, just twenty-five minutes away! She's there for three years, so she's going to be around here a lot. You two are going to get on so well, Jasper! Sloane's such a laugh!"

Sloane waved a hand in the air, cheeks

pink. "Let's just wait until you try the food before you start singing my praises, yeah?"

I laughed, undeterred and turned to Sloane.

"Jasper's great too! You have no idea, he's such a good son to Eva, helps her out all the time with Evermore. And he even does lifeguarding on the side."

As I glanced back at Jasper, I caught Fi's amused expression from across the room. Heat crept into my cheeks. *Had I really just spent the last few minutes hyping them both up like an overenthusiastic parent?*

I cleared my throat, laughing lightly. "Anyway... how long until dinner's ready?"

Sloane shot up. "It should be ready! Let me serve it before you start writing me a letter of recommendation."

Fi chuckled, and I joined her at the table, setting out plates while Jasper leaned against the counter, checking his phone. A flicker of curiosity passed through me. *Who was he texting?*

I pushed the thought away, focusing on the meal.

When I took my first bite, warmth flooded through me.

"Sloane! This is amazing! It tastes just like my mum's!"

The others murmured in agreement. Sloane looked pleased, though she downplayed it with a shrug.

Between bites, I noticed Fi watching me, her eyes flicking to the drink in front of Jasper. A glance exchanged with Sloane.

They were up to something.

A look of bewilderment crossed Jasper's face as he sipped the cool liquid. "What is this?" He asked.

"Jasper, we don't question Fi in the kitchen." Sloane piped up, casting an amused glance at Fi who nodded in approval.

They were *definitely* up to something.

But for now, I let it go.

I took another sip of my drink, leaned back in my chair, and let the laughter and warmth of the evening wrap around me like a spell.

6

It was early on Wednesday morning, and I woke up hungry.

Sliding out of bed, I skipped down the stairs two at a time, already thinking about breakfast. Banana fritters. Perfect. The thought alone made my stomach grumble. I could already taste the crispy edges, the soft, sweet centre, the warmth of cinnamon lingering on my tongue.

It was a recipe I'd learned from one of my aunties, Mum's sister, on one of our many trips to Jamaica when I was little. A firm favorite for our Wednesday morning breakfasts as a family growing up. The memory of those mornings flickered in my mind, Mum standing by the stove, flipping fritters with the kind of ease I still hadn't mastered, Dad sneaking pieces before they'd even cooled, me giggling as my fingers got sticky with sugar. A tiny pang of homesickness stirred in my chest, not for a place but for a time.

The recipe had been passed down from their mother, my grandmother, who had sadly died when I was two. I'd only met her once, not that I remembered it. Sometimes I wished I did. I wondered if she would have liked me. If she would have thought I was anything like Mum.

I'd always loved cooking. There was something grounding about it, the rhythm of chopping, the scent of spices blooming in heat, the way a simple mix of ingredients could turn into something rich and comforting. Dad used to say it was something I'd definitely picked up from Mum's side of the family. I'd never met his mum, but he always joked that the most exotic thing she ever made was curry from a jar, and even then, it was just a korma.

Leaning against the kitchen island, I scrolled through playlists on my phone, searching for something that fit the morning. I landed on one called Summer of Magic and smiled when Everywhere by Fleetwood Mac floated through the Echo speaker.

Perfect.

The scent of fresh sunflowers reached me before I noticed them, standing bright and cheerful in a vase on the kitchen table. Eva must have been by this morning. The sight of them made me smile.

The post was piled neatly on the sideboard nearby, and as I flicked past letters addressed to Mum and Dad, a slightly creased postcard caught my eye at the bottom of the stack.

I grabbed it.

Germany. The first stop on Mum and Dad's tour.

A smile tugged at my lips as I read the brief but loving message, Mum's familiar handwriting looping across the card. I traced my thumb over the ink before pinning it up on the corkboard above the sideboard, placing the image of the Theatine Church in the middle. Hopefully, by the end of the summer, it would be full, all twenty-one destinations my parents were visiting.

I shook my head, half in awe, half in exhaustion just thinking about it. As much as I wanted to travel, I'd definitely need more than one night to explore a city as historical as Munich. I wanted to walk its streets, touch its history, feel its heartbeat beneath my feet.

But for now, I was perfectly happy spending my summer right here.

Right. Breakfast.

I made my way over to the fruit bowl just

as Fi appeared, bursting into the room like a shot of espresso.

"Sash!" she squeaked, as if I didn't live in the same house as her. "Pleaaaase tell me it's banana fritter Wednesday!"

I laughed, holding up the bunch of bananas in my hand.

Fi clapped her hands together and immediately started flitting around the kitchen, rummaging through cupboards for cinnamon and nutmeg. She grabbed a few other random ingredients at the same time, and I gave her a suspicious look.

"What are you making now?"

Every morning so far, she'd brewed a different herbal tea and tried, enthusiastically, to get me and Sloane to ditch our usual coffee. It wasn't working.

Fi rolled her eyes. "Today's tea is Essence of Summer, Sasha. But don't worry, you can have your caffeinated poison. I give up trying to get you to come to the light."

"So dramatic," I laughed as I smashed the bananas with a fork, their texture soft and yielding beneath my touch. The oil in the pan began to shimmer, the heat radiating upwards in waves. Beside me, Fi hummed under her breath as she poured hot water over a blend of lavender, lemon, and strawberry. The steam wafted into the air, floral and citrusy.

"What the hell?"

I turned to see Sloane standing in the doorway, looking like she'd just crawled out of the depths of a horror movie. She was still in her oversized Ghostface T-shirt, last night's makeup smudged around her eyes, her hair an impressive mess.

"Who ordered Mary Berry this morning?" she grumbled.

Fi giggled. "Good morning, sunshine!"

I smirked as Sloane trudged straight to the coffee machine, pressing the buttons with the urgency of someone in desperate need of caffeine.

"Don't talk to me until after my first coffee," she muttered.

I let her be, flipping the fritters in the pan as she sat at the breakfast bar, zoning out, lost in her own thoughts. I knew this version of Sloane well, the half-present, half-dreaming one that always surfaced in the mornings. It was like watching someone slowly return to themselves.

Eventually, when the warm black liquid had made its way into her bloodstream, and I set a plate of banana fritters in front of her, she started looking more human.

Sloane picked up a fritter, took a bite, and chewed thoughtfully.

"I'm seeing Joe today," she said suddenly, a mischievous expression crossing her face.

Fi let out a little squeak, and my eyes almost bugged out of my head.

A stifled smile played on Sloane's lips.

"Who on earth is Joe?" I asked, narrowing my eyes.

"I met him at that party on the beach last week." She grinned. "It was just after you left Sash, and Fi was like a moth dancing by that bonfire. I don't think she saw anything but the flames all night."

Fi shrugged, mouth full of fritter.

"We've been texting all week," Sloane continued. "He's nice, I think. He wants to take me out somewhere."

Fi squeaked again, but I frowned slightly.

"What, Sash?"

"Nothing..." I said slowly, "I just know your usual taste in guys, and I don't think any of them have ever fallen anywhere close to the nice category."

Sloane grimaced.

"I'll give you that one," she admitted. "But I don't know... this one seems different."

I snorted. "Okay, babe."

She rolled her eyes, but the smile tugging at her lips betrayed her.

"We'll see." She pushed her empty plate forward and stood up, stretching. "I need to go get ready. What are you two up to today?"

"We're going to see Briar and Linus at the shop," I said, and Fi nodded enthusiastically beside me.

"Mum and Dad have been dying to see Sasha," Fi added. "They really want to meet you too, Sloane!"

"I'll come next time, I promise," Sloane said, wiping her mouth on her T-shirt.

Fi grimaced. "That's disgusting."

Sloane just grinned before bounding off upstairs. Thirty seconds later, the shower turned on.

I shook my head, gathering the dishes. "Come on, let's clean up and get going. She's not going to be back until late."

∞ ∞ ∞

A few hours later, we wandered arm in arm up the high street toward The Alchemy, the warm cobbled streets holding the heat of the day beneath our feet.

"They get so busy now at this time of year," Fi gushed, practically bouncing beside me. "There's so much magical presence around lately. People are really getting into it, Sash."

I glanced at her, her curls catching the sunlight like strands of honey. "Is that a good thing?"

"Well, yeah," she said, as if it were obvious.

"I mean, Dad says a lot of the people who come into the shop don't actually have powers, but the more people who are interested in this stuff and open their minds to it, the better. Normal, everyday humans can practice the basics of witchcraft and manifestation. And just knowing that they aren't going to be completely scared of us is comforting, too."

I hummed in response, though something about it still left me uneasy. I wasn't like Fi, I didn't carry my magic like a badge of honour. It had come to me suddenly, and even now, it felt like something I wasn't supposed to have. Like I'd borrowed it from another life, one that had never been meant for me.

Even if I wanted to practice more, there was never a right time. The risk of my parents walking in on my homework writing itself was always too high. So I saved my magic for Evermore, like locking away a part of myself until summer arrived and I could finally breathe again.

Fi had taken me to her house the week after we'd been to the beach together, and Linus had sat me down, his voice warm and patient as he explained things I'd never thought possible. That was when I learned I was a Novus, a witch born to non-magical parents.

I had known then that I couldn't tell Mum and Dad. As much as they loved me, and as much as I loved them, they were practical, logical people. The kind of people who'd spent their lives writing stories that explained the world. Magic wasn't something they could fit between the lines. And I didn't want to be something they had to explain away.

The bells above the shop door chimed as we stepped inside, the scent of candle wax and aged paper hit my senses. The air was thick with something warm and electric, the hum of old magic woven into the floorboards.

We nearly collided with Linus, who looked as striking as ever. Today, his half-moon spectacles were bright red, matching his trousers, and his black shirt was patterned with golden stars, as if he had plucked the night sky and stitched it onto fabric.

"Girls!" he crooned, arms outstretched. "Where's the other one?"

"She's on a date," Fi sing-songed, a wicked grin pulling at her lips.

"Ooh," Linus smiled, eyes twinkling. "How exciting! I remember my first date..."

He trailed off mid-sentence, his gaze flicking toward Briar. She was behind the counter serving a broad and statuesque woman. The woman was chatting animatedly, her arms nearly knocking countless items off the sides as she gestured throughout her story.

"Oop, I had better go and rescue your mother," Linus chuckled, scurrying off.

I smirked to myself at the idea of this being Sloane's first date. *As if.*

Before I could say anything, the door opened again. A tall guy, about our age, stepped inside, his gaze darting around like he'd just walked into another world. He ran his hands across his shaved head, and when he squinted into the room, his crystal-blue eyes reflected the flickering candles around the shop.

I nudged Fi, watching as her jaw went slack.

"He looks like he needs help," I whispered, giving her a gentle shove forward.

Fi snapped her mouth shut, straightened her skirt, and twirled a strand of hair around her finger as she sauntered over.

What a flirt.

I shook my head, stepping aside as the woman at the counter finally finished her conversation and bustled past me out the door. Briar was now bent over the counter, frowning at something.

She looked up, her face softening. "Sasha, dear," she said, curling her long finger in a beckoning gesture.

I stepped forward, and she pulled me into a one-armed hug, the scent of sandalwood and lavender clinging to her sweater.

"How lovely to see you, sweetheart," she said warmly. "Do me a favor and write down these numbers for me, will you?"

She handed me a pen and a scrap of paper.

"Twenty-four, fifty-seven, and... ninety."

I jotted them down, the ink bleeding slightly into the parchment.

"Thank you, love. They're page numbers," she explained, tapping the paper. "I'm gathering some information for a friend of mine about being Bound."

"Being what?" I asked, the word sending my thoughts straight into dangerous territory. For a moment, I pictured one of Briar's friends tied up in bondage and grimaced, shaking my head to rid myself of the mental image.

"Bound, darling," Briar said, completely unaware of my entirely inappropriate train of thought. "It's a very strong connection. An invisible string tying two people together, love, friendship, any kind of relationship, really."

"Oh. Cute." I smiled. "Are you and Linus Bound?"

She shook her head, chewing thoughtfully on the end of a pencil. "No. Not that it diminishes our relationship in any way," she mused. "We are very much in love, and that's enough for us. A lot of people aren't Bound at all. And some who are Bound aren't even in love."

She tilted her head, considering something.

"It's quite an all-consuming feeling," she added after a moment, her voice quieter now. "It can be people's downfall. I knew a couple once who were Bound. She was married when they first met. They tried to fight it for years, but nothing could keep them apart in the end. It's beautiful, really... albeit a bit sad for her first husband."

I wrinkled my nose. "That is sad. So if you never meet your... Bound person, then you'll always be missing your soulmate?"

"Oh no, darling. This is something entirely different from soulmates. When you first meet the person you are Bound to, a connection is made, if you never meet that person then a connection is never formed. Not everyone is Bound for someone else and if you never meet your person then you would never know. But if you are lucky enough to be one of those people and you meet the person with whom you are connected to then those feelings are the strongest they will be, you are connected and stay connected, it's really quite lovely..."

Her voice drifted as an elderly man

shuffled up to the counter, clutching a bundle of herbs.

"Hello, Artimus!" Briar chirped, winking at me.

Taking that as my cue to leave, I glanced around for Fi. She was still talking to the tall guy, all fluttering eyelashes and absentminded hair twirls.

I brushed past her, squeezing her hand as I leaned in. "I'm popping to the café next door," I murmured.

She barely reacted, too engrossed in her conversation.

I smirked and pushed the door open, stepping out into the street, the light of morning between the buildings stretching my shadow long against the cobblestones.

$$\infty\infty\infty$$

The moment I stepped into the café, my eyes briefly caught on the "UNDER NEW MANAGEMENT" sign hastily taped to the window and a wave of disappointment settled in my chest. That was the second set of owners to take over in the last three years.

Before them, a family had run the place, and I fondly remembered their daughter,

Mei, who was the same age as me and Fi and one of Fi's good friends. I had crossed paths with Mei a handful of times, but they had moved away when we were all fifteen, something to do with the missing children in the area. My thoughts wandered to the last time that Fi and I had dropped in for milkshakes, the memory of Mei's wide grin lingering in my mind. It had been a rainy summers afternoon, the three of us squeezed into our favourite corner booth, sipping pale pink milkshakes through colourful, swirly straws. That was the summer before Mei's family left Wychbold Cove.

I surveyed the new interior.

The jewel-toned wallpaper was gone. So were the old, cosy booths where we used to squish together and gossip about school.

Now, the space was stark white. Sterile. Lifeless.

Even the menu had changed, now offering drinks that seemed tailored to serious, joyless businessmen in stiff suits.

I let out a sigh, my fingers curling around the cool metal of the counter as I ordered a salted caramel latte, paying extra for the syrupy shot.

Maybe some places were meant to change, I just wished this hadn't been one of them. I settled onto a high, uncomfortable stool at the end of the counter and waited for Fi to arrive.

7

*T*en years old

The next four summers unfolded in pretty much the same way. We spent our days sprawled in the sun-dappled garden and splashing about in the pool. At night, we curled up in the glow of fairy lights, the scent of popcorn clinging to the air as we whispered through old films, our laughter muffled under blankets. We had sleepovers that blurred into mornings, the first rays of dawn slipping through the curtains as we lay tangled in the haze of half-sleep. And then there were the nights we pressed our noses against the cool window glass, spying on Jasper and his friends as they laughed and played football. I loved every second I spent here, in this little pocket of magic that felt untouched by the outside world. And all I ever wished for was to bring Sloane with me. Everything here was so bright, shiny and... magical. Even back then, I knew

Sloane needed a little more magic in her life.

One afternoon during the first week of summer, our stomachs still full from Eva's homemade lemon ice cream, its tart sweetness still lingering on my tongue, I sat at the edge of the woods next to Fi. The trees whispered overhead, shifting lazily in the summer breeze. Fi was showing me her crystal collection, laying each stone out with careful reverence, her fingers dusted in a fine layer of earth.

I had never seen so many stones in varying shapes and sizes, let alone in so many colours. Some were rough and jagged, others polished so smooth they gleamed like glass in the sunlight. A few glittered when I turned them in my hands, tiny flecks of gold or silver catching the light like trapped stardust. One stone in particular called to me, it was dark blue, deep as the twilight sky, with swirling ribbons of white and gold that twisted through it like ocean currents. It was smooth, warm from the sun, and when I curled my fingers around it, it fit perfectly into my palm, as if it had always belonged there. It reminded me of the shore at Wistow Bay, the way the waves carved patterns into the wet sand, the golden light stretching across the water at dusk.

"That one's sodalite," Fi said matter-of-factly, brushing a strand of hair from her freckled face. "Mum told me it's good for accessing your intuition... whatever that

means." She wrinkled her nose. *"You can keep it if you like."*

She smiled at me, and I glanced down at the stone one last time before slipping it into the front pocket of my dungarees, where it clinked softly against the brass button.

"Fi..." I hesitated, running my fingers over the fabric of my pocket before looking up at her. She was turning a bright green stone over in her hands, watching the way the light bounced off its surface.

"Yeah?"

"Do you have anything that would help Sloane with her family?"

Her smile faded slightly.

"I talked to her last night," I added, shifting so I could see her better.

Fi set the green stone down and met my gaze, concern flickering behind her stormy blue eyes.

"Oh yeah? How is she?"

I had told Fi so much about Sloane over the years, filling her in on all the things I couldn't quite say aloud to anyone else. Every time I spoke about her, I saw something change in Fi's expression, a sadness that shone behind glassy eyes.

An empath. That's what Briar had called her once, after Fi had cried over a bumblebee that had drowned in the pool. It meant she felt things deeply, felt other people's pain as if it were her own. I saw it now in the way *she shifted, bracing herself for whatever I was about to say.*

I sighed, tilting my head back to watch the sunlight drip through the canopy of leaves. The wind stirred them gently, making them dance in a slow, lazy rhythm.

"Not great," I admitted. "It's her first summer working at the garage, and she hates it."

Fi wrinkled her nose. "What's she doing?"

"Filing papers. Making tea and coffee for the customers," I said, frustration curling at the edges of my voice. "She sounded miserable. The only reason we even got to talk was because her foster parents were passed out drunk on the sofa."

Fi didn't say anything right away, but I could see the way her fingers tightened around a small, rose-coloured stone in her lap.

"That sucks," she finally murmured, and I nodded.

"Yeah. She says the garage smells like sweat and cigarette smoke, and the customers are awful. She has to be there all day, and then when she gets home, Marcus is there too."

Fi frowned. "Marcus? That's her foster brother, right?"

"Yeah," I muttered, jaw tightening. "He's awful. He acts like he already owns the place just because he's older. He bosses her around at work and doesn't lift a finger when they're at

home. Sloane said she feels completely alone, especially with me here."

A lump formed in my throat, thick and aching. I swallowed hard, forcing it down. It didn't feel fair, this split between our summers. I was here, where the world was peaceful and fun, where I could wake up knowing I was safe and wanted. And Sloane was stuck there, in that house that smelled like old beer and grease, working a job she hated, with no one looking out for her.

Fi reached out and squeezed my arm, her touch grounding. "She'll be okay," she said softly. "She's tough, right?"

"Yeah." The word felt fragile on my tongue. "She is. I just... I wish she was here."

Fi didn't reply, but she sifted through her pile of rocks, her fingers brushing over each one until she settled on a pale green stone with flecks of brown and gold.

"It's jade," she said, rubbing a bit of dirt off its smooth surface. "It's supposed to strengthen relationships and bring stability. Tell her to hide it somewhere in the centre of the house."

She placed it in my hand, and I rolled it between my fingers before tucking it into my pocket beside the sodalite.

"Thanks, Fi. You're the best." I grinned, just as Eva's voice carried through the evening air, calling us in for dinner. We packed the stones away, bundling them into the soft, colourful

drawstring bag, and made our way up the hill toward the house, the scent of cottage pie drifting toward us.

∞∞∞

The weeks that followed unraveled like a nightmare.

Even Sloane, who I trusted like a sister, never knew what happened to us.

The following Wednesday we had spent all day in the pool and as dusk drew near we had run down to the rose garden, giggling wildly. But as we turned the corner, the laughter died in my throat.

The ground was littered with petals. Hundreds of them, plucked and torn apart, their velvet-soft remains scattered like bloodstains across the grass.

We froze.

"Why would someone do this?" My voice was barely above a whisper.

Fi didn't answer. She stood at the centre of it all, staring at the ruined flowers.

"They were watching us."

A chill licked down my spine. I followed her gaze, tracing the invisible line that led from the garden straight to the pool.

"*That is SO creepy.*" *I gasped, glancing in her direction.*

Fi was concentrating, eyes fixated onto the petals on the ground. Her fingers were twitching, her mouth moving with silent words.

"*I can't do it.*" *She sighed.*

Fi's magic wasn't fixing this and I could tell by the drop in her shoulders how disappointed she was. She leant down and started gathering up the discarded petals, putting them into a neat pile at the foot of the bush. I stooped down to help and once we had tidied the mess as best as we could I grabbed Fi by the hand and with one last glance through the gap and towards the pool, I pulled her back up to the house.

We didn't speak about it again, I pushed the thought to the back of my mind.

If only I had known then what I know now.

Maybe I would have told someone.

Last night mum and dad were watching some random program about some guy who was a stalker. He was following this girl and she didn't have a clue. So today I snuck into that big house on the corner through the woods and watched some girls there playing in the pool. I felt just like the guy in the program, it was so cool. My hiding place was the best too. Probably shouldn't have fucked those flowers up though. Then I remembered that the guy in the program kept like souvenirs from that girl so I took a load of the petals. I don't really know what I'm meant to do with them but it's still pretty cool.

8

The sun spilled through my pale curtains, bright and insistent, turning the room a shade of honey and pulling me out of sleep. I stretched lazily, rolling onto my side, eyes still heavy with last night's dreams. Outside, the world hummed, bees buzzing amongst the buddleia, a soft rustling of leaves in the breeze, the distant cry of a seagull.

I blinked myself awake, sitting up slowly, only to wince at the sight of my floor. Clothes were scattered everywhere, a mess of fabric draped over the chair, half-folded piles slumped against my dresser. A mess I had ignored for too long. The rest of my room was still relatively tidy, but the sight nagged at me, a reminder of the washing I had been putting off.

Still, this room was home. It held so many memories, so many moments frozen in time. My gaze drifted over the familiar walls, lingering on the little marks and scuffs, the faded remnants of old posters. A smile tugged at my lips as I remembered Fi collapsing backward off the bed, both of us breathless from laughing too hard. I couldn't even remember what had set us off, only the ache in my ribs, the way our laughter fed into each other's until we could barely breathe. It was always like that with us, one spark and we'd go up in flames, unstoppable, helpless to the joy of it.

I shook off the memory and dragged myself out of bed, padding across the warm wooden floor. I scooped up the scattered clothes, tossing them into my laundry basket, feeling a small satisfaction in restoring order. Then I made my way to the dresser, pulling out a running set, a bright orange cropped top and matching cycling shorts. The snug fabric stretched over my body as I slipped them on, the colour bold against my sun-kissed skin. It had been too long since my last run.

Catching my reflection in the mirror, I sighed at the wild halo of curls framing my face. They were in open rebellion. I grabbed a brush and some gel, slicking my hair into a ponytail, smoothing the edges with careful precision.

My eyes roamed my messy dressing table and I sighed, my brain had clearly been too consumed by thoughts of a certain tall, tanned man living across the lawn, and I had neglected my poor bedroom.

Scattered bottles lay on their sides alongside tangled jewellery and half-used tubes of lip balm. I pressed my lips together, then started putting things back in their rightful place. The act of tidying soothed me, as if controlling my space could somehow quiet my mind.

As I went through my morning skincare routine, my thoughts drifted back to what Briar had said yesterday about people being Bound.

Bound.

The word lingered. *Was I? To someone? A stranger in another city? Another country?* The thought unsettled me in a way I couldn't quite name. I imagined some invisible thread tying me to another soul, an unseen force guiding me toward them. The idea of it felt too big, too final. I shook my head, pushing the thought away. Some things were better left unknown.

Once my skin was glowing and my room felt fresh with the morning air coming through the open windows, I grabbed my washing basket and headed downstairs. The house was quiet, and a note on the counter caught my eye, Sloane's messy scrawl.

Left early with Joe. See you later. X

Joe. The elusive "nice guy" who had managed to win her over. I arched a brow, intrigued.

I tossed my laundry into the machine, did a few quick stretches, then set my watch for my run. Grabbing a bottle of water, I slipped out through the bifold doors and into the warmth of the morning.

As I jogged past Eva's house, I noticed the curtains were still drawn. Unusual. She was always up before me.

I rounded the far end of the cottage and slipped into the woods, the cool shade of the trees a welcome relief from the sun. I jogged in the direction of the lake. I wouldn't be passing it today, though—the long grass wasn't the most suitable running terrain. Instead, I made a left through the woodland and onto a well-ran-through public footpath. It was familiar beneath my trainers, the rhythm of my steps steady. I passed an elderly couple walking their boxer dog, its squashed face dripping with a comical amount of drool. I grimaced but smiled politely as they waved.

By the time I returned, sweat clung to my skin, but my mind felt clearer. Running did that, untangled the knots in my thoughts, reset something inside me. I slowed to a stop on the back patio, stretching out my sore muscles, eyes drifting toward the pool.

The water shimmered, catching the sunlight like scattered diamonds.

There was a time when Fi, Jasper, and I spent whole days here, splashing until our fingers wrinkled, Eva chasing us down with bottles of suncream. Last year, I spent more time lounging by the pool than in it, but I hadn't gone in yet this summer.

"Pool day," I said out loud.

An hour later, I was stretched out on a sunbed, pleased with my setup. A hot pink towel, a book I had been meaning to start, a cool box filled with ice, water, fresh fruit, and ice lollies. A tube of suncream *(don't worry, Eva, factor 50)* lay next to the lounger. The sun pressed against my skin, warm and intense, seeping into my bones.

Fi had emerged earlier, a bundle of nervous energy. The guy from The Alchemy had texted her and asked her out. She left glowing, excitement practically buzzing off her.

I settled deeper into the lounger, letting my bright green bikini straps slip down my shoulders to avoid tan lines. Just as I turned the first page—

A jet of ice-cold water smacked me

straight in the face.

I gasped, book slipping from my hands.

"What the fuck?" I spluttered, wiping the dripping liquid from my nose. More water fell from the sky, just for a few seconds before trailing off and landing on the side table next to me. I scrambled up, scanning the garden until I spotted him.

"Jasper!"

He was standing grappling with the hosepipe, the water pressure clearly too high. I ducked as the hose went skyward again, the water narrowly missing my lounger where my book lay. I jogged toward the house and turned the tap down a little. At the change in pressure, Jasper looked up, spotting me and waving. I rolled my eyes and marched over to where he was standing.

"Jasp, you literally just got me in the face."

"Oh." He faltered, eyes flicking to the wet streaks on my skin. "Sorry. This hose is different from ours."

I narrowed my eyes. "Don't blame the hose. You had the water way too high. Why were you even watering the plants? Where was your mum?"

"She was in bed. Feeling sick. But she was stressing about the flowers."

Something tugged at my chest. "Is she okay?"

"She's just tired. Coughing a little. I called Dr. Philips, he's coming this afternoon."

I pressed my lips together, worry settling in my stomach. Eva never got sick. "Hmm, I'll go check on her later, I'll let her sleep for now."

"I've checked her." Jasper met my eyes, a hint of concern shining in them. "She'll be fine."

I shrugged; I had no intention of leaving Jasper to it. I knew it had just been him and his mum for most of his life. His father had left them when he was a baby, and although he visited every now and then, the relationship between them was strained. But I wasn't a child anymore, and Eva was like a second mum to me. I felt bad for Jasper to an extent, he was so intent on being the man of the house, and even though I understood, he didn't have to be such a control freak all the time.

"Just don't get me wet again, I'm trying to read," I huffed, turning my back and walking back to my sunlounger.

As I walked across the lawn, I felt his eyes on me. Suddenly, I was aware of my bare skin, the way my bikini clung to my body.

I tried to pay attention to my book, but my gaze kept drifting to where Jasper was. The way his arms flexed, his jaw sharper than last summer. His body was leaner, stronger now, and I liked his hair longer too. It suited him like that, tied up on top of his head. His usual mousey brown mop of curls was now highlighted with flecks of gold from the sun, complementing the short beard he had grown perfectly. I gave up, closing my book and putting my headphones in.

I didn't know why I suddenly felt so... off-kilter.

It was just Jasper.

But then again, I couldn't deny how good-looking he was, and I couldn't deny the way it gave me a slight buzz every time he held my eye contact.

I shifted my body, a heat developing between my legs. This Is What Falling In Love Feels Like by Jvke played in my ears. Maybe a nap would be nice. Maybe I would dream about Jasper. I felt the warmth of the sun on my face as sleep threatened to take me.

"SASH!"

My eyes snapped open. Jasper stood over me, shirtless. His abs were inches from my face.

I yanked out my headphones. "What?"

"Your cool box is open. Everything's melting."

I looked down, watermelon slices swimming in melted ice.

"Oh." I slammed the lid shut.

Jasper smirked. "Okay, well, I'm done now, I'm heading to a mate's house."

A mate? A girl mate?

I forced a shrug. "Have fun."

I didn't watch him leave.

∞ ∞ ∞

It was getting chilly when I woke up from my nap. A breeze rolled in off the ocean, carrying the briny scent of salt and seaweed, the distant cry of seagulls again threading through the quiet. The towel slipped from my shoulders, pooling around my waist as I stretched, shaking off the drowsiness clinging to my limbs. The sky outside had softened into dusky pastels, the last traces of sunlight melting into the horizon.

I sighed, pulling on a black and gold kaftan over my bikini, the gauzy fabric whispering against my skin. Sliding my feet into my Birkenstocks, I gathered my things together.

Just as I stepped into the house I heard the front door slam and Fi strode into the kitchen, her cardigan slipping off one shoulder, her expression stormy.

"Good date?" I asked tentatively, placing my things down on the counter.

She shrugged, lips pursed. "Who knows?

Maybe I'm too weird for dating."

"That makes two of us," I said, offering her a sympathetic smile.

Fi slouched into a chair, picking at an imaginary piece of lint on her sleeve. She looked small for a moment, lost in thought, but I wasn't about to let her spiral.

"Right!" I straightened up, tossing my damp towel into the washing basket. "We aren't doing this. It's hot girl summer. Let's make cocktails."

Fi's face lit up instantly. "Midnight Margaritas!" she sang, already perking up.

"Put the lime in the coconut and shake it all up!" we chorused together, dissolving into laughter.

"I'll get the coconut!" Fi announced, dashing into the pantry.

I pulled down two glasses, hesitated, then reached for a third.

"I wonder when Sloane will be back," I called over my shoulder. "Should we make her one?"

"Oh, she's here," Fi replied, emerging with a handful of limes. "I saw her come through the front door just as I was making my way up the drive. She was with a guy. They must've gone up to her room."

"Charming." I giggled, grabbing a fourth glass and pulling out a pitcher. "Shall we knock on her door and see if they want to join us?"

"Yeah, definitely. I'll go ask in a mo!"

As we busied ourselves with the drinks, the tang of alcohol filled the kitchen, the rhythmic clinking of ice against glass breaking the stillness. I worked on slicing the limes, dragging the wedges along the rims of the glasses before dipping them into sugar. The motion was automatic, my mind drifting to Sloane.

I'd missed her these past few days. But I understood. She was finally free, free to make her own choices, to live without fear or restraint. If I had to lose her to a guy for a little while, I could live with that.

Whether this Joe was something real or just a summer fling, I knew Sloane would always come back. She wasn't the kind of person who disappeared completely.

"Where do you want to sit?" Fi asked, carefully placing a lime slice on the rim of my glass.

Before I could answer, the distant roar of a motorbike cut through the quiet.

My head snapped up. A single beam of light carved through the darkness, illuminating the front of the house for a brief second before vanishing.

I frowned, stepping closer to the window. "Maybe we could sit—"

A sudden, heavy banging on the front

door made us both freeze.

Fi and I exchanged a look, the kitchen's soft glow suddenly feeling too warm, too bright.

The knocking came again, sharper this time.

"You go," I whispered, nudging Fi toward the door. "Take a weapon."

She arched a brow at me.

I shrugged. "I've watched enough horror movies to know the person answering the door should always be armed."

Fi exhaled through her nose, grabbed the kettle off the counter, and strode into the hallway.

"What exactly are you planning to do with that?" I snickered, following close behind.

"Shh." She cracked the door open, peering around the frame.

"Is Sloane here?" a deep voice demanded. There was something familiar about it.

"Who's asking?" Fi replied, kettle still in hand.

"Her brother." Came the response.

My stomach dropped.

"Marcus?" I pulled the door open wider.

Sloane's foster brother stood on the doorstep, breathing heavily, his face flushed as though he'd run the whole way here. His usually sleek brown hair was wind-tousled, strands falling into his sharp green eyes, which glowed in the dim porch light. His black motorbike leathers gleamed under the moon, the helmet dangling from his fingers.

"Sasha." His gaze locked onto mine. "Where is she?"

"She's upstairs." The words left me automatically before my brain caught up. "What are you doing here?"

"Is she alright?" His voice was edged, impatient.

Fi and I exchanged another glance. His urgency felt out of place.

"I think so?" I said carefully. "Why do you care? And what are you even doing here?"

A voice called from upstairs.

"What's going on? What was all that banging?"

Sloane appeared at the top of the stairs, hair mussed, cheeks flushed, her top on backward.

I barely had time to register the scene before Marcus did.

His eyes darkened.

His jaw clenched.

His mouth opened like he was going to say something, then snapped shut as another figure stepped into view behind Sloane. A guy. Joe. His hand found her waist, a small, protective gesture.

"Marcus?" Sloane's voice was thick with disbelief. "What are you doing here?"

"That seems to be the question of the night," Fi quipped, ever the diplomat. She held out her hand to Marcus as if this were some polite social call. "Hi, I'm Fi. Come on in."

Sloane came down the stairs as Marcus stepped inside, shutting the door behind him. The silence that followed was heavy, thick with things unsaid. Even the candle on the console table seemed to crackle louder than usual.

Finally, Joe broke the tension. "Why are you holding a kettle?"

Fi looked down at the kettle like she'd forgotten she was still clutching it. "Protection. From him." She jerked her chin toward Marcus before holding out her hand again. "I'm Fi."

Joe took it, lips quirking. "Joe."

"Sunny, can I talk to you?" Marcus spoke, his voice quieter now.

Sloane stiffened. "I've told you not to call me that."

He didn't respond.

She exhaled sharply. "Fine. Come on, then." She led him toward the snug, shooting Joe a quick, reassuring look before disappearing through the door.

As it clicked shut, I turned back to Joe, studying him properly. He was tall, golden-skinned, with hair like sun-bleached silk.

But it was his eyes that caught me, dark blue, striking, yet somehow unreadable.

I smiled. "Joe, do you like margaritas?"

In the kitchen, Fi and I handed Joe a margarita before pulling up seats across from him. The shine of the overhead lights cast soft shadows over the counter, the scent of lime and tequila still lingering in the air.

"Alright, Joe," I said, propping my elbows on the table, studying him over the rim of my glass. "Interview time."

Joe chuckled, leaning back like he was settling in for a game. Then, with a dramatic shift, he straightened, clasping his hands together as if we were about to conduct a formal interrogation. "Please continue, ladies."

Fi and I exchanged a glance. A willing participant. *This was going to be fun.*

For the next ten minutes, we fired questions at him, his intentions for Sloane, his future career plans, hobbies, family values. He answered each one with an easy confidence, but I kept an eye on his expressions, looking for any flicker of hesitation. He liked surfing. Wanted to travel after college. Lives with his parents and one brother. I clocked the way his fingers tightened around his glass at that one. *Interesting.*

The real laugh came when he admitted, almost sheepishly, that his dream girl was someone soft, sweet, and in need of taking care of.

Fi nearly choked on her drink. I snorted.

"You'd better give up that illusion," I warned, shaking my head. "Try to take care of Sloane, and she'll drop-kick you across the room."

Joe grinned, unfazed. "She's amazing." His voice was quiet, but full of something I couldn't quite put my finger on. *Admiration? Awe?*

I tilted my head, watching him. Was he the type who liked a challenge? Or was he really seeing Sloane for who she was, jagged edges and all?

The margaritas left a warm buzz in my veins, making everything feel a little softer. I stretched, letting my limbs go slack, sinking deeper into my chair.

"Alright, Joe," I declared, swirling the last of my drink. "You pass. Have your wicked way with our friend."

"Oh, I intend to," he said, winking as he downed the rest of his glass.

Fi groaned, covering her ears. "Ew! TMI!"

We were still laughing when the mood shifted.

Sloane stormed back in, her presence like

a gust of wind through the room. Behind her, Marcus followed, his movements measured, controlled, but his jaw was tight, his shoulders rigid.

I sat up a little straighter.

Sloane dropped into the seat beside Joe, her body language full of defiance. And then, almost instinctively, her hand found his knee.

Marcus' eyes followed the movement.

The tension in the room thickened, pressing against my ribs.

Fi cleared her throat, cutting through the silence. "Marcus, where are you staying?"

He shrugged in response.

Fi, never one to let an awkward moment fester, breezed past it. "It's late. Stay in the pool house."

Her eyes looked over to me for approval and in return I glanced at Sloane.

Sloane's eyes rolled in her head. "Whatever." She stood up and made her way over to the pitcher of margarita and poured herself a glass.

I got up and joined her, talking under my breath.

"Only if you're okay with it."

Sloane took a gulp of her drink and turned to face me.

"It is what it is." She grumbled. "Can't exactly send him back out there, it's dark and there's nowhere for him to stay nearby."

"Fi," I said, spinning around. "Let Marcus into the pool house, there's fresh bedding."

Fi dutifully got up and motioned for Marcus to follow her, which he did but not without a backwards glance at Sloane, who looked away.

"I'm going back up to bed," Sloane huffed out. She started to make her way towards Joe but I grabbed her arm, pulling her back.

"We love him by the way." I whispered in my friend's ear. Sloane's shoulders visibly dropped as some of the tension left her body. She gave me a grateful smile before taking Joe's hand and leading him back out of the room.

I dropped back down into my chair, draining the last dregs of my cocktail.

My gaze flickered to the window, to the house next door. Eva's cottage was dark, but I focused on Jasper's bedroom window, searching for that familiar glow.

It wasn't there.

His light was still off.

He wasn't home.

I exhaled slowly, trying to ignore the odd sinking feeling in my chest. It wasn't like I was waiting for him. It wasn't like it mattered.

I needed to go to bed.

That was way too much excitement for

one night.

9

*T*en years old

The following week, we had mostly forgotten about the rose petal incident. It was a breezy Wednesday morning, and I slipped on my favorite summer dress before heading downstairs for breakfast. The fabric was soft against my skin, light and airy, perfect for the warmth of the season. It was pale blue, with little yellow flowers stitched delicately around the hem, a gift from Dad on our last trip into town together. I remembered the way his eyes had crinkled at the corners when he first saw me in it.

"Sunbeams dance in your eyes when you wear that," he had said, his voice full of quiet admiration.

Being a writer, he was always so good with words. Mum liked to say compliments were his specialty, a natural gift he had. According to her, that's how he won her over in the first place.

I'd heard the story of how my parents met more times than I could count, but it never got old. Dad had a way of making you feel like you were the only person in the world when he spoke to you, and apparently, that's exactly what happened to Mum the night they first met.

It was at some party thrown by a mutual friend, one Mum hadn't even wanted to attend. She wasn't the kind of person who enjoyed big social gatherings, but for some reason, that night, she felt like she had to go. She never could explain it, just an unshakable feeling, like something was waiting for her.

Dad, on the other hand, was in his element, gliding from conversation to conversation, blending in effortlessly. But then, he saw her.

"She was wearing this simple dress, leaning against the back of the room, trying to fade into the crowd," he always said, his voice turning wistful. "A wallflower in a room full of roses. But to me, she was the most beautiful flower in the garden."

Of course, he didn't just stand there and admire her from afar. That wasn't his style. He walked straight up to her and, with that confident yet disarming smile of his, said the words that changed everything.

"You have the most incredible smile. The way it illuminates every feature on your face,

it makes me feel like I'm exactly where I'm supposed to be."

Mum always rolled her eyes at this part of the story, claiming she had been ready to brush him off. But there was something about the way he said it. He wasn't being cheesy, wasn't trying too hard. He was just... seeing her, in a way no one else had.

"Well," she had replied, half-smiling, "I'm not sure about that."

Dad had only laughed, reaching for her hand as if it was the most natural thing in the world.

"Then I'll have to show you."

And just like that, they had been pulled into their own little world. They talked for hours that night, the rest of the party fading away into nothing. No grand gestures, no sweeping declarations, just two people who saw each other, really saw each other. That was the night it all began, and I loved hearing about it every time.

Wednesday mornings were always one of my favorite parts of summer. Since the beginning, Mum and Dad had promised we'd always have a big family breakfast once a week, no matter how busy they were.

As we gathered around the large oak table in the kitchen, I ran my fingers lightly over the delicate lace table runner. It had scalloped edges, intricate and carefully stitched, something I was almost certain Eva had found at a car boot sale. It suited the kitchen perfectly, adding to the warm, welcoming atmosphere.

The table was laden with food: freshly baked pastries, crispy bacon, and a plate of Mum's scrambled eggs, the kind she always made with diced peppers and tomatoes, just like her own mother had taught her. She had been showing me how to make them recently, a quiet tradition being passed down between us.

Mum picked up a croissant, peering at me over her thick tortoiseshell glasses as she took a bite.

"So, sweetheart, tell me, what are you and Fi up to today?" She licked a stray flake of pastry from the corner of her mouth, a quick movement before she settled back comfortably in her seat. Her dark curls were twisted up as always, pinned into place with a single pencil. Stray tendrils had already begun escaping, and I knew she'd end up stabbing a few more into her hair before the morning was over.

I swallowed a mouthful of eggs before answering. "Not sure yet, but we might explore the woods a bit more today. If that's okay?"

Mum's brown eyes softened. "Of course, hun. Just make sure you tell Eva where you're going and check in often."

I nodded, and we spent the next half-hour chatting, about their writing, about how Eva managed to keep the house and gardens so *pristine, about all the random little things Fi had woven through her hair lately.*

After breakfast, I wandered down to the bottom of the garden, waiting for Fi. I sat cross-legged in the grass, absently twisting daisy stems together into a chain. The air smelled fresh, carrying the distant scent of the sea, and the wind played lightly with the hem of my dress.

I was five loops in when I felt a presence next to me.

"All right?"

I glanced up, straight into Jasper's sun-kissed face. The summer always suited him, his skin turning a shade darker, his mousy brown curls lightening at the tips, his hazel eyes flecked with warm amber.

I swallowed, my stomach doing that weird fluttery thing it had been doing around him lately. "Yeah... just waiting for Fi."

"Cool."

He dropped down beside me with a soft thud, close enough that our knees almost brushed. I was suddenly hyperaware of every inch of space between us, or rather, the lack of it.

For a few minutes, we sat in companionable silence. Jasper plucked daisies and passed them to me, and I threaded them through my chain, my fingers working automatically.

"No Spider-Man dolly today?" I teased, my voice light.

A flush crept up from beneath his collar, settling high on his cheekbones.

"I was eight," he grumbled, shooting me a look.

I giggled, nudging my knee against his. He knocked his back against mine in response, and I smiled, pleased at having gotten a rise out of him. His fingers darted out, poking me in the ribs in retaliation. I yelped, grabbing his wrist instinctively, but the second we touched, he jolted back as if I'd burned him.

Our eyes met, and for a moment, something unspoken passed between us. A question neither of us was quite ready to ask.

"Jasp!"

The moment shattered. Jasper scrambled to his feet as Eli rounded the corner of the garden wall.

"There you are, mate," Eli said. "Your mum said you were out here." His gaze flicked between us, something unreadable in his expression before it smoothed over. "The lads are playing football at the rec. You coming?"

Jasper hesitated for half a second before nodding. "Yeah… yeah, let me grab my jumper."

Without another glance in my direction, he turned and walked away.

I exhaled sharply, rolling my eyes. "Boys."

"What are you grumbling about over there?"

Fi's voice rang out, and I turned, grinning as

she appeared through the garden gate.

"There you are!" I jumped up, looping the daisy chain over her head.

"Sorry, I had to harvest some white sage before it went bad."

"Sage can go bad?"

"It's aura can," Fi replied, as if it were the most obvious thing in the world. Her green eyes glinted knowingly in the dappled sunlight. "Come on, let's go. I've found the perfect spot for our den."

We set off into the woods, weaving between towering oaks and willowy birches, the scent of earth and pine filling the air. The ground beneath our feet was soft with fallen leaves, and the occasional snap of a twig underfoot echoed through the stillness. As we walked, birds rustled in the canopy above, their songs mingling with the distant hum of the waves beyond Evermore.

Eventually, we arrived at a clearing where the grass grew tall and wild, tickling our knees as we waded through it. The whole space shimmered in the midday glow, golden sunlight spilling through the treetops in scattered beams. Off to the right stood a magnificent tree—its branches first reaching high toward the sky before curving downward, sweeping low to the earth as if bowing in greeting. The deep green pines tickled the ground, concealing the space beneath like a secret waiting to be discovered.

Fi led me toward it, her movements quick and eager, and with a flourish, she pulled back a branch. Behind it lay a hollowed-out cavern beneath the tree's great limbs, the dense foliage turning the space into a hidden trove, nestled at the heart of the woods.

"Fi, this is incredible," I breathed, stepping forward and lifting my hand to catch the thin shafts of sunlight that pierced through the pine needles. The soft light danced over my palm, warm and fleeting.

"I know, right?" Fi's grin widened as she rummaged through her ever-mysterious bag of trinkets. A moment later, she pulled out a pair of tiny fairy cakes, each one topped with a dusting of hundreds and thousands. She handed one to me, her eyes twinkling with barely concealed mischief.

"Try this," she said, biting back a smirk.

There was something about Fi's expression that should have warned me, but curiosity got the better of me. I took a bite, the sugary frosting melting on my tongue, and swallowed. Suddenly, laughter burst out of me, uncontrollable and wild.

Fi took a bite of her own, and within seconds, she was doubled over, clutching her stomach as she howled with mirth. The two of us collapsed onto the forest floor, gasping for breath, our giggles ricocheting through the trees.

"What..." I wheezed, my sides aching. "What did you..." Another uncontrollable laugh escaped before I could finish my sentence.

Fi held up a hand, gulping down air before finally managing to speak. "If you simmer ginseng into butter while reciting the Risus incantation and then bake it into a cake, it stimulates the part of your brain that produces laughter." She beamed, her face still flushed with amusement. "Mum helped me with them this morning."

"That's..." I tried to steady my breathing, still shaking with residual giggles. "That's amazing."

We spent the next hour transforming the hidden space into our den. We swept the ground clear using fallen branches, brushing aside pine needles to reveal the soft earth beneath. An old tree stump became our dining table, and we pulled up tufts of grass to pad the thick branch we claimed as our seat. Around the edges, we wove leaves and dried shrubbery, creating a cosy, enclosed nook that felt like it had been waiting for us all along.

Fi, always the enchantress, produced a collection of crystal suncatchers and tiny glass beads from her bag, hanging them from the lowest branches. When the wind stirred, the glass chimed softly, catching the light in a way that made the entire den feel alive. She lined up tiny vials of mysterious liquids and powders in the natural crevices of the tree trunk, each one a mystery to me.

I reached out, running my fingers along the edge of a suncatcher. It spun gently at my touch, refracting flecks of rainbow light across my skin.

"This is perfect," I murmured, stepping back to admire our work, already imagining all the hours we would spend here, laughing, practicing magic, escaping into our own world.

Fi, however, wasn't finished. She swept her gaze up toward the higher branches, her brow furrowing. "We need flowers," she declared. "We can weave them through the gaps to make it feel more magical. Come on, there's a wildflower meadow just past those trees."

She reached into her bag and pulled out a small wicker basket, one far too large to have possibly fit inside the satchel. I arched a brow, but I knew better than to question the workings of Seraphina Fox.

The meadow stretched out before us in a breathtaking expanse of colour, violets and buttercups, clusters of delicate Queen Anne's lace, and wild poppies that swayed gently in the breeze. We spent the next twenty minutes carefully selecting flowers, gathering handfuls of each type. As we worked, Fi named them one by one, explaining their uses in her family's craft, some for healing, some for luck, others for dreams. Her voice was full of reverence, as *if each petal held a story only she could read.*

Meanwhile, I entertained myself by making the flowers float, my powers stronger now than when I had first tried. I could almost juggle three at a time, making them drift lazily around my head like a slow, weightless dance. Magic was becoming easier, more natural.

By the time we made our way back, the light had begun to shift. The sun was disappearing behind a wall of dark clouds that had seemed to appear out of no where. A hush had settled over the clearing as I glanced upward at the twisted canopy above, squinting at the waning light. The vibrant warmth of the afternoon had faded into something dimmer, something quieter.

We approached our tree, and I reached for the branch that served as our door—

—and froze.

Fi sucked in a sharp breath beside me, her basket slipping from her fingers, landing with a dull thud on the earth.

The den was destroyed.

Branches lay snapped and scattered, the once-soft grass now trampled into the dirt. Deep, erratic gashes marred the tree's trunk, its bark stripped away in jagged wounds. Every decoration we had carefully placed, every suncatcher, every vial, lay shattered on the ground. Crystal shards glittered in the dying light, their beauty reduced to ruin.

And strewn across the wreckage, half-buried in the soil, were dark, withered rose petals.

My breath caught in my throat. The sight of them sent a shiver down my spine, cold and sudden. I knew these petals. I had spent my summers playing between the very bushes they had come from. I would have recognised them anywhere.

"Oh my god," I whispered. "It's..."

"Eva's roses," Fi finished for me, her voice barely above a breath.

A prickling sensation crept up my arms. The woods, once so full of life, now felt unnervingly still. The silence pressed against us, thick and waiting. My heart pounded so hard I could hear the rush of blood in my ears.

Fi's fingers trembled as she bent to retrieve her fallen basket. My own gaze darted across the clearing, searching for movement, for a presence unseen but surely nearby.

Was someone watching us?

Slowly, I took a step forward, my breath shallow, my pulse thundering. My hand reached back instinctively, finding Fi's. Her grip tightened around mine, cold and urgent.

"Sasha, I don't like this..." Her voice was barely a whisper, laced with fear.

"I know." My eyes never stopped scanning the shadows. "Let's go."

And then we ran, through the trees, past the tangled undergrowth, our legs burning and our lungs heaving, until the familiar outline of Fi's cottage came into view.

Only when we were inside, the door firmly shut behind us, did we finally allow ourselves to breathe.

I followed them again today. They went to the woods near the meadow and started building a den. They are so childish, I built better dens than that when I was way younger. I heard that one with the ratty blonde hair say about getting some flowers to decorate it and I thought of something so funny. I ran out and fucked up the whole of their stupid den, literally just broke all their shit. I still had some of those petals in my pocket so I chucked them about too. I was so fast and then I went and hid again. When they got back they were so freaked out. They looked for me but they couldn't find me, my hiding place was so good. I'm getting really good at this. It was so funny though, they're such fucking idiots. I bet they'd be so scared if they actually met me.

10

I woke to a soft knocking sound, distant at first, filtering through the haze of sleep. The room was warm, sunlight spilling through the curtains in amber slats, casting patterns across the duvet. I stretched, feeling the satisfying pull of my muscles, then rolled over, fumbling for my phone. The screen lit up nearly 10am. A rare luxury, a morning where I hadn't been jolted awake by an alarm or some half-remembered dream.

A text from Mum was waiting for me, a little notification of her absence. I tapped it open, a photo of a croissant, perfectly golden and flakey, taken at some Parisian café.
Arrived safe! Wish you were here! was all it said. I could practically hear her voice in my head, breezy and affectionate, as though she weren't thousands of miles away.
The knocking came again, firmer this time, tugging me fully into wakefulness. I

rubbed my eyes with the heels of my hands, my limbs still heavy with sleep.

"Come in!" I croaked, my voice rough from disuse.

"Only me!"

Fi's golden waves tumbled around the door before the rest of her followed, the scent of vanilla and something herbal trailing in with her. She moved with effortless grace, her pajama set, a silky turquoise with lace trim, catching the morning light. The delicate vine tattoo on her thigh peeked out from beneath the hem of her shorts as she skipped across the room and dove into bed beside me. The mattress dipped beneath her weight, the sheets rustling as she burrowed into the blankets. Only her emerald eyes and the wild halo of her hair were visible, peeking out from beneath the covers.

"Sloane and Marcus are in the kitchen having some sort of heated debate," she mumbled, voice muffled by the thick blanket. "Did I do a bad thing inviting him to stay?"

The crease between her brows deepened, a flicker of worry behind her eyes. I could tell she'd been stewing on it, the way she always did when she was afraid she'd made a mistake.

"They have a complicated relationship,"

I said, choosing my words carefully. "He's never been as awful as his parents, and sometimes I feel bad for the guy. After all, he was raised in that house too." A frown tugged at my lips. "But Sloane is a tough gal. If she had an issue with it, she would've told you herself. Don't worry about it. Maybe she just needs to get some things off her chest."

Fi studied me for a moment, then sighed, rolling onto her back to stare at the ceiling.

I hesitated, pressing my lips together. My heart thudded a little harder against my ribs. "Fi..." Now was as good a time as any.

She rolled back over, her sharp green eyes locking onto mine, waiting.

"I think I kind of fancy Jasper."

The words left my mouth before I could second-guess them.

Fi pulled the quilt down just enough to smirk at me. "It's about time you figured that one out, Sash. Pretty sure you've been in love with him for years."

"What?! I have not!" My heart kicked into a full gallop, heat creeping up my neck.

Fi's smirk widened.

I scrambled for some kind of counterargument, but my mind betrayed me, flipping through memory after memory like an old film reel.

Jasper, laughing on the beach, his hair wild from the sea breeze. The way his eyes crinkled at the corners when he smiled. The way my pulse stuttered, just slightly, whenever he was near, though I'd always told myself it was nothing.

Every time I saw him, it ended in some painfully awkward encounter where I walked away feeling like a complete twat. He probably thought I was pathetic.

"Okay then." Fi scoffed, rolling her eyes.

Panic prickled at my skin. Had I always felt this way about Jasper? Surely not. It wasn't like we even got on particularly well anymore, not like when we were kids.

But then... I thought of all the times I'd casually asked Eva where he was, pretending not to care. The way I paid attention to every little thing he did or said, even when I swore I wasn't listening. The way my breath caught in my throat when he got too close, the faintest brush of his hand against mine sending an electric shiver up my spine.

Oh God.

Fi was right.

"Why didn't you tell me?!" I shrieked, my voice coming out higher than intended.

"I thought you knew!" Fi laughed, jumping up out of the bed. "It's your brain! Or heart, I suppose."

I groaned, yanking the covers over my head. Maybe I could just stay here for the rest of the summer, curled up in my cocoon of shame. The girls could bring me food and water, keep me alive while I wallowed in self-pity.

I was just strategizing how I'd make my exile work when, suddenly, the blanket was ripped off me, exposing my very oversized and very holey Eagles T-shirt, the one that used to belong to Dad before I claimed it as pajamas and refused to give it back.

"Come on!" Fi laughed, standing victorious with the covers in her arms.

"That's all three of us with romance brewing now," she said. "I think it's time we did some proper magic. I could use a distraction, and maybe it'll prompt Sebastian to actually text me back." She winked, reaching out and grabbing my hands, tugging me upright.

I sighed but let her pull me to my feet.

"Let's go check on Sloane," Fi continued. "We've got supplies to gather."

∞ ∞ ∞

Two hours later, after coffee and a leftover fritter each, we were dressed for the day and heading through the woods.

The air was crisp, and as I breathed in

deeply, the earthy scent of pine and damp leaves clung to my lungs, filling me with an odd sense of calm. We walked side by side, the soft crunch of our feet on the path the only sound breaking the midday quiet.

The gardens of Evermore had given way to the dense woods beyond, and the towering trees cast long, graceful shadows that seemed to dance with the fading light. The atmosphere felt serene, the kind of stillness that wraps around you like a familiar, comforting blanket. I felt a cool breeze sweep across my skin, making the hairs on my arms stand on end, the sensation both refreshing and grounding.

Sloane broke the quiet, her voice slicing through the silence with a tentative edge.

"I was in town with Joe the other day," she said, her words a little hesitant. "We went to grab a coffee, and... I saw all those posters. The missing children." She glanced at Fi, her gaze flicking nervously to the ground. "They were everywhere, some of them so old they were falling apart."

My stomach clenched at the mention of the posters. I had noticed some new ones amongst the older ones too. I tried not to let them get to me, but they always did. The faces of smiling children, frozen in time, their wide, innocent eyes staring out at the world, a silent plea in their gazes. Some were forgotten, others fresh with the weight of loss, their parents' desperate pleas printed in bold beneath their faces. It was a grim reminder of how fragile safety could be, even in a town like this. The weight of it lingered with me long after I tried to shove the thought aside.

Fi sighed deeply, her breath shaky and laden with years of unspoken sorrow. "It's been happening since I was a kid," she said, her voice quiet, barely more than a whisper above the rustling trees. Her eyes were fixed ahead, her steps steady, but there was an air of sadness around her that made my chest tighten. "The police... they're stumped. Every time, it's the same thing. A kid disappears, no sign of a struggle, no clues. They vanish without a trace."

I swallowed, my throat dry. The unease that had settled in my stomach was growing, twisting with each word.

"A few have been found," Fi continued, her voice barely more than a murmur. "But it's never good when they are. It's always within days of them going missing, but even by then..." She hesitated, her face distant, as if remembering something she wished she could forget. "By then, they're too drugged or traumatized to tell anyone what happened. Some don't even remember anything at all. It's like they're lost even when they're found."

Sloane frowned, her brow furrowing as she tried to make sense of it all. "But why? Why is it happening? Hasn't anyone been caught?"

Fi shook her head, her expression somber. "A few people, here and there. But they never talk. It's all a mystery. The best guess anyone has is trafficking. We're close to the docks, after all. Easy to move people in and out without much notice."

The word "trafficking" hung heavy in the air, a cold weight that made my throat tighten and my stomach churn. I could hear the resignation in Fi's voice, the way the words tumbled out, defeated, like she had long since given up on finding an answer.

"They've tried everything," Fi went on. "The police, I mean. They've set up stings, most recently at Wistow Bay. They tried to intercept whatever's going on, but it never works for long. They might stop it for a while, but another child always goes missing eventually. It's like… it never really stops."

The woods around us felt darker now, as if the trees themselves were leaning in, listening, absorbing the sorrow in the air. I couldn't bring myself to look up; I kept my gaze fixed on the ground, where the uneven trail twisted beneath our feet. The weight of it all felt suffocating, and I didn't know what to say. *What could anyone say to make it better?*

Sloane's voice cracked through the silence again, her words thick with disbelief. "How do people in the town live with it? I mean, seeing those posters, knowing that it keeps happening?"

Fi shrugged, but the movement was hollow, empty. "The town's numb to it," she said. "The media covers it for a few days, but the story never spreads more than a hundred miles out. It dies out fast, like it's old news. People stop asking questions after a while."

The hollow resignation in her voice sent a shiver down my spine. I tried to push away the image of those missing children, their faces haunting the back of my mind, their silent eyes staring at me from the posters. I wanted to forget, to stop thinking about it, but the thought wouldn't leave me.

I glanced at Fi, whose gaze had turned inward, her eyes lost somewhere far away, and then at Sloane, who still looked troubled, her lips pressed into a thin line. I felt the pull of the silence, but it felt far from comforting now. It felt heavy, oppressive, like the forest itself was holding its breath.

Just then, we broke into a less dense patch of trees, and the light of the sun poured down, warming the air around us. The change was immediate, like a breath of fresh air after being submerged underwater. I inhaled deeply, the cool air filling my lungs, and for a moment, the tension that had built up between us seemed to lift.

"Fi, what are we actually doing?" Sloane asked, stepping over a large fallen branch. I glanced at her, trying to hide my amusement at the bewildered look on her face.

Sloane had been giving Fi the side-eye for the whole walk, watching her fill her basket with various "supplies" with a raised eyebrow. That same look was back now, even as Fi strode ahead, her determination renewed.

"A love ritual," Fi hummed, plucking a few stems of some lavender-like plant from the ground, her voice light and distracted.

"Excuse me?" Sloane spluttered, and I couldn't help but laugh at the confusion in her voice. "I'm not even a witch… and I'm not looking to cast a spell on him."

Fi shot a smile over her shoulder, her eyes twinkling. "Apart from me not particularly believing you, none of that matters anyway. Its's just a little light spellcasting, to ensure we stay safe and strong on our respective romantic journeys."

"Fine." Sloane rolled her eyes inwardly but smiled back, resigned to whatever Fi had planned.

Eventually we reached a clearing, and my eyes roamed over the sunlit space.

Something about it felt oddly familiar, like a memory I couldn't quite place. My eyes settled on a large drooping willow tree, and a sudden wave of unease swept over me. My breath caught, and the air around me seemed to thicken. My mind flashed back to a day I didn't want to remember. Wilted petals seemed to invade my thoughts, and the familiar feeling of fear crawled over my skin like a phantom touch.

"Sasha?" Fi's voice cut through the tension, pulling me back to the present. I blinked, shaking the unsettling memory away, and turned toward her.

"I was just telling Sloane that anything in nature with five petals or five stems can be used in magic," Fi continued, oblivious to the unease that had gripped me moments before.

"I gathered some dianthus flowers from the garden this morning; they'll be an important addition to the ritual."

Fi started unpacking in the centre of the clearing, her movements fluid and practiced. The faint rustling of her bag as she rummaged through it felt oddly loud in the stillness, but it was a welcome sound. The air smelled sweetly floral, and the heat from the late afternoon sun cast dappled light across everything around us. She set up a pile of twigs surrounded by a ring of small stones, their rough edges worn smooth over time.

Fi pulled some yellowed with age parchment from her bag and tore it into long strips. She rolled the strips up and placed them carefully between the gaps in the twigs that formed the makeshift campfire. A soft breeze ruffled her hair as she moved.

I noticed a flicker of excitement in Sloane's eyes as Fi rummaged through her bag again, pulling out a large wooden bowl, a small pestle and mortar, and a box of long matches. There was a sort of anticipation in the air.

"Sloane, you take this," Fi said, handing over the pestle and mortar to Sloane. She placed a large rose quartz in the centre of the fire, the soft pink stone catching the sun's rays and glowing warmly.

"Could you grind these bits together?" Fi's voice was gentle, but there was an undercurrent of determination. "Nothing fancy, just into a sort of chunky paste." She handed over a bunch of brightly coloured stems, their vibrant hues almost too vivid against the dark green backdrop of the woods. "Dianthus is for affection, salvia nemorosa is cleansing, and these..." Fi threw a small bag of sunflower seeds across to Sloane. "Are, of course, for harmony."

Sloane set to work, her brow furrowing in concentration. She leaned over the marble bowl, and I could smell the spicy fragrance of the herbs as they ground together under her hands. The scent was both sharp and warm, like cinnamon, and it seemed to settle deep in my chest.

Fi spoke, her voice thoughtful. "Aphrodite's favorite colour was green, did you know that?" She wasn't really asking for an answer; it was more like a piece of knowledge she was just sharing. "You would assume it would be red or pink, being as she's the goddess of love and all. I like to think it's because she's so intertwined with nature."

The idea of green, vibrant and alive, seemed to resonate with me. It felt like the right colour for a goddess who embodied the growth of things, the flourishing of emotions.

Sloane finished her duty and passed the bowl back over to Fi who then handed each of us a piece of parchment and a pen. She busied herself, tipping the ground-up herbs into the wooden bowl with a fluid motion, like she had done a thousand times before. The substance looked like a colourful powder, flecked with bits of leaves and petals. Fi added three drops of essential oil, each one a clear, precise drop that smelled of roses, soft and comforting.

"Rose oil will help our journeys to be smooth," she said, sprinkling a small amount of some sort of herb over the top. "And just a little touch of valerian, obviously," she added, winking at me knowingly, although at this point I was sure the confusion on my face mimicked Sloanes.

Fi set the bowl down beside the fire and took a match from the box, twirling the thin wood between her fingers. She bent down and tossed the match onto the pile, then flames licked upwards, catching the ripped parchment with ease and taking hold of the twigs and kindling next.

"Right, girls, come sit around the fire with me." Fi's voice was filled with excitement. The heat from the fire swirled around us, mixing with the rays of sun that still cut through the trees, warming my face.

"Perfect weather for it," Fi continued, her smile lighting up her face.

"Love is definitely not a cold emotion. You know what they say, 'A life without love is like a year without summer.'" Her eyes sparkled with the joy of the moment, her happiness contagious.

"On your parchment I want you both to write out your intentions for the summer, what you would like to receive from the goddess and specifically what you would like to leave behind from this moment onwards."

I stared at the blank page in front of me, feeling the soft paper beneath my fingertips. I wrote his name and then paused, not knowing what exactly it was I wanted to come of all of this, deciding all I really wanted was to know Jasper's true feelings, I started writing. *Maybe just maybe, this would give me the clarity I so desperately needed.*

The words came easier as I continued, each line feeling more like a release. But then the question Fi had posed echoed in my mind, what *did* I want to leave behind?

That one was easy. The memories of the past, the ones that still haunted me, kept resurfacing in ways I couldn't control. The smell of his breath, the way my body had trembled with fear, it was all so vivid, so clear, even after all these years.

I squeezed my eyes shut, trying to push the memories away, but they were relentless. I could still see his hands, still hear the stifled sobs I had fought to suppress. It was only as the drop of a tear hit the page in front of me, smudging the ink as it fell that I realised I was crying for real. I quickly wiped my face with the back of my hand, my fingers trembling.

The words on my page grew more frantic, more desperate, as I wrote and wrote, spilling all my pain and my fear into the thick paper. By the time I finished, the page was soaked with emotion, ink blurring at the edges. I glanced up and saw that Sloane and Fi had already folded their papers, their faces unreadable.

"Good!" Fi's voice cut through the air, the excitement real but with an edge of strained enthusiasm. She tossed the small square of parchment into the wooden bowl. We all did the same.

"Now, the flames will take our intentions and put them back out into the universe," she said, her voice filled with belief. "Grab each other's hands and try to let the heat seep into your heart chakras." She held her palm flat over her chest, her gaze steady. "Try and feel it right here."

Fi proceeded to tip the contents of the bowl into the fire.

I reached out and grabbed Sloane and Fi's hands, feeling the warmth of their skin, the steady pulse of their hearts beneath my fingers. As the flames danced before us, I let the heat from the fire sink deep into my chest, feeling the magic, the power, and the connection that wrapped around us like a blanket. The fire blazed brighter, the orange flames turning to red, then shifting into a rich, vibrant pink. I looked to Sloane, wanting to see if she felt it too, but her eyes were lightly shut, her expression serene.

We stayed there for a while longer, the air thick with emotion. We spoke about the guys in our lives, the ones who danced around our hearts, teasing us with possibilities. But for a brief moment, it wasn't about them. It was about us, our friendship, our magic, our bond.

Fi handed around a small tub of fresh strawberries, the sweet aroma making my mouth water. We ate, laughing, until our stomachs ached from both the fruit and the joy. Finally, we packed up, our hearts full and content.

"You know, I sensed something coming from Sloane during the ritual." Fi's voice was a soft whisper as we walked toward Evermore, her eyes dancing with intrigue. Sloane was a bit further ahead, her thoughts clearly somewhere else.

"What kind of something?" I asked, curiosity rising in my chest.

"Magic, obviously!" Fi trilled, her eyes gleaming with mischief.

"Absolutely not." I laughed, shaking my head. "Sloane? Never. She's way too practical for that."

"It's called Practical Magic for a reason," Fi teased. "No, but seriously, there are plenty of serious and practical people who are magic. Not everyone is as sunshine-y as me. We'll have to wait and see, won't we?" She finished with a wink, skipping ahead to grab a small pine cone off a tree.

I frowned after her, the seed of curiosity taking root in my mind. Fi's intuition had always been uncanny, the way she seemed to know things before they happened. But Sloane being a witch? That felt like a stretch. Still, there was a part of me that wondered... maybe Fi was right.

We walked through the front door, the scent of fresh air and the salty tang of the ocean drifting in with us. We headed for the kitchen, still laughing as we teased Fi about actually wearing shoes for once, if you could even call the light strappy sandals she had on "shoes." Her laughter rang through the space, bright and unfiltered. But the moment we entered the kitchen, the mood shifted. Our eyes landed on Marcus, sitting at the breakfast bar with a beer in hand. His presence, always imposing, seemed to fill the room in an unexpected way, the air thickening with something unspoken. The moment he saw us, his head snapped up, his gaze darting between the three of us before settling on Sloane.

"Right... I'm going for a shower," Sloane muttered. She turned and left abruptly. An awkward silence fell over the room.

Marcus was the one to break the tension.

"Beer?" he asked, his voice almost too casual, lifting the bottle in a half-hearted gesture toward Fi and me.

"Sure!" Fi chirped, her usual cheerfulness returning. She moved to the fridge, grabbing two bottles and handing one to me.

I could feel Marcus's eyes on me, a weight pressing down from across the room. With a quiet breath, I slid into the chair across from him, the leather creaking slightly as I sank into it.

"Why are you here, Marcus?" The words came out sharper than I intended, my voice carrying an edge of curiosity. "Don't you have work at the garage?"

He shifted uncomfortably in his seat, his broad shoulders tensing, but he didn't look me in the eye at first. Instead, he kept his focus on the bottle, his fingers wrapping around it in an almost desperate grip. When he finally spoke, his voice was quieter, with a hint of hesitation that was so unlike him.

"I, uh... had a bit of an argument with my

parents the morning after Sloane left..." He paused, and I saw his eyes drop to the bottle again, like it was easier to focus on it than the conversation. "I quit."

"You quit?!" I exclaimed. The thought of Marcus walking away from the garage, his parents' garage, shocked me. We'd always assumed Marcus would be working there forever, taking it over when his parents eventually drank themselves into an early grave. I couldn't imagine him doing anything else. "So what are you going to do all summer?"

Marcus started ripping at the label on his beer bottle, his fingers working furiously, the sound of paper tearing scraping at my nerves. His usual stoic, almost impenetrable demeanor was slipping, replaced by something raw and fragile. There was a vulnerability in his posture, his shoulders slumped just enough for me to notice, and it unsettled me. I wasn't used to this version of him, the one who looked like he might break at any moment.

"I have no idea." His voice softened, sounding smaller than I'd ever heard it. "I've got plenty of money saved up... don't really spend it on anything. But I won't be going home. Not anytime soon anyway. Maybe I'll grab a hotel in the city or something."

"Oh, Marcus, you can't do that!" Fi's voice

broke through my thoughts, filled with her usual empathy. I could see it in her eyes, the concern bubbling up like a tide. "Why don't you stay here? No one's using the pool house, and I'm sure Sloane won't mind. You're her family after all... kind of... I mean...." She trailed off, her eyes darting frantically to me. The realisation of the true nature of Sloane and Marcus' relationship coming back to her.

Thankfully the sound of footsteps came from behind us and Sloane walked back into the room, her eyes narrowing when she saw the two of us sitting across from Marcus.

I felt my chest tighten, a twinge of guilt sinking deep. I knew I needed to support Sloane, to stand by her, she was my best friend, but seeing Marcus, the usual tough guy, looking so defeated made me feel torn. My gaze shifted to Sloane, and I could almost feel the heaviness of her stare as she processed Fi's words. The muscles in her jaw tightened as she looked from Fi to Marcus, and I knew there was a storm brewing in her thoughts.

"Won't mind what?" Sloane's voice was guarded, the words crisp and calculated.

"If Marcus stays for the summer in the pool house," Fi repeated quietly. "He had an argument with your parents after you left and quit his job..."

I watched Sloane's expression harden, like a steel door slamming shut.

"His parents." She said between clenched teeth.

She could never claim those people as her family, and I knew it. Her eyes flicked back to Marcus, but this time, they softened just slightly when she really took him in, though her features remained tight. It was like the smallest crack in her armor, and I wasn't sure how to interpret it.

"It's fine, honestly," Marcus said, his voice almost apologetic. "I'll just grab a hotel for a bit..." He started to stand, his hand sweeping across the counter, the crumpled paper from his label gathering in his palm with one quick motion.

"No," Sloane said firmly, her voice cutting through the room with an unexpected sharpness. "Stay. It's not like we'll see you much anyway. Besides, I'll be busy with Joe most of the summer."

I watched Marcus's eyes narrow at the mention of Joe, the subtle twitch in his jaw betraying something more. A flicker of jealousy? Hurt? I couldn't be sure, but it was there, barely perceptible, but enough to make the room feel colder. The silence stretched between them, thick and heavy, like the space was shrinking with every passing second.

"Fine," Marcus muttered, his voice tight and strained.

"Fine," Sloane snapped back, her eyes locking with his in a way that made the air feel charged. I could feel the weight of the moment between them, the standoff lingering like a storm cloud.

Fi looked between them, trying to read the room, but it was clear neither of them was going to back down. The tension was almost suffocating, and I couldn't help but notice how the small sounds, the clink of the bottle, the creak of the chair, seemed louder in the silence.

"Is that okay, Sasha?" Marcus's voice softened, and I caught the quiet plea in his eyes, the weight of his uncertainty pressing on me.

I took a slow breath, glancing at Sloane. Her eyes were still fixed on Marcus, her expression like stone, but I nodded. "Sure... if Sloane's okay with it, then I am." My gaze lingered on my best friend, who looked like she could set fire to him with nothing more than a glance.

"Okay... well... thanks. I'll keep out of the way." Marcus said, his voice quieter now. He gave one last, uncertain look at Sloane before he turned and walked toward the bifold doors and towards his new home for the summer.

11

Rifling through the top drawer on my altar, I cursed under my breath. I knew I had a beautiful turquoise stone in here somewhere, somewhere beneath all the clutter. Years of pocket money spent at The Alchemy had meant the little bureau in the corner of my room was a little overstuffed. It was my favorite part of my room, a small mahogany unit with a fold-out desk tucked into the corner by my window. The surface was always adorned with pillar candles, crystals, and trinkets, each one holding its own little piece of meaning. The sweet, earthy scent of incense sticks always filled the air, and I had enough options to match any intention I was setting. It was a place of calm I'd carefully cultivated over the years. The flickering candlelight danced along the edges of the room, casting soft shadows, and I could almost taste the tranquility in the air.

"Gotcha!" I grinned as a flash of bright

blue greeted my eyes. I pulled the smooth stone out of the drawer. On my run this morning, I'd decided to put together a small care package for Eva before heading over to check on her, and turquoise, with its healing properties, seemed like the perfect choice. I'd spent the 45 minutes jogging through the woods with my mind sifting through ideas for what to add to the hamper.

It had taken years for me to feel comfortable leaving my altar out in plain sight and practicing some of my rituals in the open. I'd never shared my secret with anyone except for Sloane, and of course Fi. Keeping magic a secret was hard, especially since my parents had no idea about my powers. I'd hidden them from them for as long as I could remember, masking the little unexplainable things that happened around me. At first, I thought Fi was crazy when she told me that I was magic too, but eventually, I believed her. The strange events, like books containing information on what happened to be in my head at that moment in time falling off shelves when I was nowhere near them, or candles flickering to life with a single thought, started to make sense. As I grew older, the signs became impossible to ignore, as if the universe was knocking on my door, waiting for me to answer.

It wasn't until I learned the truth about

my grandmother that everything started falling into place. I found out that my grandmother had been a witch in Jamaica, practicing a form of magic called Obeah. This magic had deep roots in the traditions of enslaved Africans brought to the Caribbean in the 1800s. The excitement that flooded through me when I found out about her past was overwhelming. For the first time, I felt a real connection to my powers, as if they had a purpose, a history that stretched far beyond me. My mum had never practiced magic, never spoken of it. To everyone else, she was a practical, no-nonsense woman. I suspected she either didn't know about her own lineage or had chosen to leave it behind, maybe out of fear or a desire for a simpler life. But discovering my grandmother's story in an old journal, abandoned in an old suitcase in the attic of their house in Jamaica, had opened something inside me, a door I didn't even know was there. Knowing my magic came from somewhere gave me a sense of identity I hadn't known I was missing. I wasn't just a girl with strange powers. I was part of something bigger, a lineage stretching back generations. Even though the magic seemed to have skipped my mum, I was determined to explore this part of myself, to understand where I came from. In a way, it made me feel whole, like a missing piece of me had finally been found, and the world suddenly made a little more sense. Every flicker of light, every spark of magic, felt like a whisper from the past, reminding me of who I was and what I was capable of.

I bounced down the stairs, stone in hand, and entered the kitchen, where I saw Fi sitting on the floor of the back patio with the door open. It wasn't as sunny today, thick grey clouds threatened in the sky. I was just about to greet her when I noticed a small porcelain bowl in front of her feet. The plastic tub of table salt sat beside it, and inexplicably Fi had her finger in the bowl, swirling the clear liquid clockwise. I paused for a moment, the scent of salt faint but grounding, watching her as she muttered something to herself, eyes closed in concentration.

She looked peaceful, dressed in a long white dress. I wasn't sure if it was pajamas or not, but either way, it was lovely. The open back revealed her dainty swan-wing tattoos, barely visible beneath the cascade of delicate beach waves in her hair. I didn't want to disturb her just yet. She was clearly concentrating, her brow furrowed in the way it always did when she was deep in thought. Instead, I went over to one of the lower cupboards and pulled out a wicker basket. I placed it on the counter, the texture of the wicker smooth beneath my fingertips. Opening the fridge, I grabbed a bottle of sparkling water and added it to the basket, along with the turquoise stone, feeling its cool surface against my palm once more.

Suddenly, a beam of light danced across the countertop, startling me. I lifted my head, looking toward the glass doors to see Fi standing there, smiling at me. As my gaze swept past her, I noticed the clouds had completely disappeared, and bright blue skies and golden sunshine filled the day, warming the room instantly.

I couldn't help but raise an eyebrow, letting out a laugh.

"Doesn't that go against the laws of magic or something?" I teased, my voice light, though a part of me was curious.

Fi shrugged nonchalantly, "I mean, I love each season, but I told Sloane I'd take her out today, and nice weather would help."

I smiled back at her. I knew she was up to something, but like I'd said before, Sloane could hold her own.

"Well, do you have a bit of time before you head out? I'm trying to put together a little hamper for Eva to help her feel better. I'm heading over there today to check up on her and see if I can help with anything." Before

I even finished my sentence, Fi started gathering bits and bobs from around the kitchen, her energy infectious.

"Of course! I'd love to. I'll make her some of my special lavender bread."

I grinned at her, I had been hoping she would say that. I had so many fond memories of Fi's famous bread. Even when we were young, Fi had known her way around the kitchen. I thought back to when we were about seven. I'd been bedridden with a nasty midsummer cold, and Fi had shown up with a fresh loaf of bread, still steaming hot from the oven. She had cut me a thick wedge and slathered salted butter on top, and in just a few hours, I felt loads better. Sure, I was still sniffling for a few days, but I was up and running through the gardens again the next day, right beside Fi, as if nothing had happened.

"Perfect, thank you so much, Fi! I've got some turquoise and a bottle of fizzy water, and I thought I'd throw in some flowers to brighten her room up too. Who knows if Jasper's thought of any of that." I rolled my eyes.

"Oh! Pour a bit of this in the water," Fi said, rummaging through her bag and pulling out a small glass vial filled with a mauve liquid. "It's violet tonic I put together a while ago, good for the sniffles."

We set to work gathering the contents for the hamper. Fi focused on her baking, the sweet scent of lavender filling the air, while I, under her direction, ran to Briar and Linus' cottage garden to gather the flowers and herbs she had suggested. The wind had picked up slightly, carrying the scent of wildflowers and fresh earth. I paused by Eva's roses, watching bees buzz from bloom to bloom, their tiny bodies dusted in golden pollen. I smiled, watching them for a moment, the peacefulness of the scene soaking into my bones. Then a wasp darted past, nearly landing on me. I flinched, remembering how Sloane had once been stung by one. I had never been stung myself, but I couldn't forget the sound of Sloane's pained cry when it happened.

Back then, she had rushed home, tears streaming down her face, hoping for some comfort from her foster parents. But instead of comforting her, Mallory and Rory had laughed at her, calling her a baby for making a fuss over "just a sting." I remembered Marcus, smugly talking over her, recounting what he'd learned in science class about treating stings. He had said, "You have to remove the stinger, clean the area with soap and water, then apply something cold." Their parents had fawned over Marcus, praising him for being so clever. Meanwhile, Sloane had stood there, tears running down her face, her leg swelling and turning red. I could still hear Mallory's ridiculous comment about how Sloane wouldn't have gotten stung in the first place if she had been a better student.

I rolled my eyes at the memory of Marcus always stealing the spotlight. The anger simmered in my chest as I thought of Sloane's foster parents, always so cruel, never giving her the kindness she deserved. They had belittled her, while building Marcus up. But Sloane had always been resilient. Even as a child, she had used the information Marcus boasted about to treat her sting, and I was proud of her for it.

Shaking my head, I tried to push the frustration away. I wished I could have done more for her back then, given her the support she needed.

But as I resumed walking towards Fi's parents cottage, I vowed to always be the kind of friend Sloane could count on, no matter what.

On my return to Evermore, the scent of warm salted honey filled my nostrils. I walked through the open doors to see Fi carefully arranging a few final sprigs of lavender on top of the freshly baked bread. I laid the flowers I'd gathered on the counter and carefully tied them together with a long piece of lilac ribbon. Once I finished, I held the stems upside down, letting the ribbons cascade gently to the buds and leaves. The perfect floral swag to hang in Eva's room, I thought. It would definitely brighten her day. After wrapping the bread in beeswax paper and assembling the basket, I took one last look in the mirror, ran my hand through my wayward locks, and set off down the garden path to Eva's house.

∞ ∞ ∞

Walking up the path to the bright red door, I extended my hand, already knowing Eva mostly left the door unlocked during the day. The safety of Evermore's grounds made it feel like nothing could touch us here. Resting my hand on the smooth bronze knob, I made to turn it when, once again, the door flung open from the inside.

Fortunately, with the lack of alcohol in my system this time, I managed to stop myself from stumbling inside. I straightened my posture quickly, scowling internally as I realised exactly who was standing in the doorway. Jasper's flecked eyes glinted with amusement, locking onto my flushed face.

"Are you completely incapable of making

it through doorways on two feet?" he teased, his voice thick with laughter. He raised one eyebrow, the smirk playing on his lips like he was thoroughly entertained.

I refused to dignify him with a response and pushed past him with my nose in the air. *Was there no end to the ways I could embarrass myself in front of him?* My mind briefly drifted to last summer, when everything between us had felt so easy, so normal. There hadn't been that swirl in my stomach, the flush of embarrassment, or the feeling that I might be an utter fool every time he looked at me.

I could hear his boyish chuckle from behind me as I made my way up the stairs to Eva's bedroom. Knocking lightly on the door, I waited until I heard Eva's soft croak telling me to come in.

"Hi Eva, how are you feeling?" I asked, stepping into the room and making my way to the end of her bed. I hadn't been up here too many times over the years, but when I did, it always felt like home, cosy and familiar. The pine furniture had been painted in a rainbow of colours, each corner of the room holding memories of Eva's creativity. The bed was covered in a patchwork quilt made from Jasper's baby clothes, lovingly sewn together by Eva herself. I ran my fingers over the warm, smooth surface of the quilt, tracing the familiar patterns, before turning my attention back to Eva's tired face.

"Hi, honey. I'm alright. Terrible cough though. I'll be fine, just need some rest for a few more days." Eva smiled sleepily at me, her eyes half-lidded, but trying to keep the warmth in her gaze.

"It's not just a cough, mum." Jasper appeared behind me, his presence unmistakable. I glanced over my shoulder, catching sight of him leaning against the doorframe, his grey t-shirt stretching tight over his bulging biceps. God, he looked good. My eyes snapped away before I started drooling. "She has pneumonia." His voice was steady. "I picked her up some antibiotics this morning, a week's worth."

At his words my full attention was back on Eva.

"Jesus, Eva. Pneumonia?" I felt sick. I'd heard terrible things about the illness.

"Honestly, pet, I'll be fine. I'm a tough old bird, and I feel much better since the first tablet." Eva smiled reassuringly. "Now, what have you got in your little basket?" She gestured to the items at my feet, and I jumped up, removing the floral swag and hooking it over the brass handle of the top sash window.

"It's a mixture of flowers and herbs,

all chosen specifically for their properties, most of them for healing or calming," I explained, pulling out the bread next. "Fi made you a batch of her lavender bread. Oh, and she sends her love."

Eva's eyes softened. "Oh, bless her. What an angel. I absolutely love that girl's lavender bread. Send my love back, won't you?"

I smiled and nodded. "I've also brought you some turquoise and some tonic." I placed both items gently on Eva's bedside table.

"Good job you brought your magic stones and potions along. Who needs modern medicine and antibiotics when you've got bread to cure you?" Jasper teased from the doorway, and I scowled across the room at him.

"Stop that, Jasper. It was a lovely thing the girls have done for me, and you know there's truth behind it all." Eva hushed him, and he rolled his eyes in response. The small lady let out a large yawn, settling further down into her bed.

"Look, I'll take the bread down and bring you up a slice with butter, and a glass for your tonic. Then you get some rest." I busied myself, grabbing the items, ready to leave, when Eva interrupted me.

"Sasha, darling, come back round for

dinner on Wednesday. I'm sure I'll be feeling much better by then, and Jasper here is an incredible cook."

I gave Jasper a skeptical look, and he just shrugged in response. "I'd love to, Eva. Thank you," I said, smiling.

Once downstairs, I made my way over to the cupboard, pulling out a plate and cutting a large wedge of the bread. When I turned toward the fridge, I saw Jasper standing there, arm outstretched, holding the butter toward me.

"Thanks," I mumbled, glancing up at him. "Weren't you on your way out?"

Jasper looked down at the watch on his wrist. "Oh yeah, I am... actually, I'm late."

"You know you don't have to hang around just because I'm here. I can be trusted with your mum," I snapped, the irritation bubbling up.

Jasper grinned, his eyes glinting with that infuriating amusement. "Of course, what on earth would she do without your bundles of foliage to help her?"

"Look, there's a lot you don't know. You don't always have to be so cynical," I shot back, feeling my heart sag. How could I possibly entertain any idea of a future with a guy who thought I was such a joke? I stormed past him, throwing the butter back into the fridge. I'd been stupid, thinking he would feel the same way about me. Grabbing the plate of bread, I turned on my heel, ready to leave.

But just before I made it out the door, I felt a large, warm hand envelop mine. I froze, slowly turning my head back around to see Jasper's hand on me.

I looked up, my gaze meeting his, and the air between us thickened. His brown eyes narrowed, and I watched the muscles in his jawline tighten. We were close, too close. *Was this... tension?* My breath slowed, everything around me falling away until all that was left was him.

"Listen, Sash, I'm sorry," he said, his voice low. "You know I don't mean it. I really am grateful for all of your help, not just today, but for all the times when I've not been around throughout the summer. Mum is lucky to have you... we both are."

My breath caught in my throat, and my heart thudded hard against my chest as I felt his thumb lightly trace my wrist. The only response I could muster was a soft nod, the prolonged eye contact severing the link between my brain and mouth.

"You're, um, still holding my hand," I said after a beat, my voice barely above a whisper. His gaze flickered down, and he released my wrist with a sigh.

He maneuvered past me, grabbing his

jacket from the bannister, and I watched every movement of his. I felt a pang of disappointment as I made my way past him and back up the stairs.

You're still holding my hand?! I scolded myself silently. *Get it together, Sasha.*

"Sasha?" Jasper's voice broke through my internal chaos. I spun around halfway up the stairs, meeting his chestnut eyes again.

"Yeah?" My voice came out in a squeak.

"Dinner's at seven."

12

Ten years old

A couple of weeks had passed since the den incident, and the summer had been uneventful since. There were a couple of times when I felt like I was being followed, but nothing ever came of it. Fi and I hadn't had any more strange occurrences either.

I was really looking forward to this week in particular because I had been invited to spend a few days at The Alchemy. The shop was busy with tourists during the summer weeks, and Fi had been spending some time helping Briar and Linus out. I missed her when she was gone. Jasper didn't quite cut it as a bestie, even though I did enjoy his company when he wasn't being an annoying boy.

Fi had asked her parents if I could go with her to help out, and they had agreed. She'd come racing over to Evermore to tell me the good news. We were even going to earn some pocket *money, my first real job!*

I dressed in my smartest clothes, a pale green dress with a Peter Pan collar, and Eva had tied my hair up in a couple of space buns so it was out of my face. The soft cotton of the dress brushed against my skin as I kissed my mum and dad goodbye, my heart fluttering with excitement. I ran to Fi's house, feeling very grown-up to be heading off to work.

When we arrived at The Alchemy, Linus had shown me how to sort stock. Fi had been manning the till for a few months now and had been stationed there while Briar helped customers and Linus went into the office on a business call. The cool air in the back room smelled of herbs, wood, and incense. I loved the feeling of being surrounded by crystals, dried flowers, and old books. It was all so magical.

Linus had shown me how to unpack the boxes and sort the items inside into differently labeled crates ready to be moved into the main store when stock ran low. I was having the best time, the gentle hum of the shop's bustle providing a calming background to my work. I wondered if this was how Sloane felt while she was working at the garage, although sorting out crystals, herbs, and dreamcatchers was probably much more fun than car parts. I sighed at the thought of Sloane. I missed her so much during the summer, no matter how much fun I was having. It wasn't right; Sloane should be here. Her foster parents didn't even want her around, using her like free labour, no pay, no care.

"Are you hungry?" Fi's voice pulled me from my thoughts, her warm tone always a comfort. She peered around the corner into the stockroom.

I looked up, placing the last crystal from the current box into the crate labeled 'Large Amethysts.' A sharp scent of lavender and sage filled the air as I tucked the small stone into its place.

"Starving!" I smiled, my stomach growling in agreement.

"We can go to Chaihu." Fi brushed her tulle skirt flat, trying to remove the creases that had formed from sitting at the counter all morning. "Mei will probably be there; she's always helping out during the summer."

I jumped up, eager for a break. I had only met Fi's friend Mei a couple of times, but she was always really friendly. Fi was homeschooled, so she didn't have many friends around here, but Mei's parents owned the café next door to The Alchemy, and Fi and Mei spent their days hanging out when their parents were working.

We pushed through the doors to Chaihu Coffee ten minutes later. The bell jingled as we stepped inside, and I took a deep breath, the warm, earthy smell of coffee mingling with the scent of fresh pastries. The rich aroma seemed to hug me, and I could feel my muscles relax as the cosy atmosphere washed over me. The décor was eclectic and inviting, comfortable sofas in corner booths and mismatched chairs scattered around quirky tables. The walls were a deep, comforting red, and the subtle ochre ceiling made the room feel like a warm embrace.

A mix of people were scattered around the shop. Businessmen tapped away at their laptops, while a couple with a baby in a pram cooed over their child, sipping tea from delicate china and chunky mugs. A younger boy sat in the corner, scribbling in some kind of book, his concentration fierce. He glanced up as we walked in but quickly returned to his writing, the intensity of his focus almost palpable.

We made our way to the counter, and my mouth watered at the sight of all the food on display. Traditional Chinese delicacies were nestled beside everyday English grub, a mouthwatering combination that made my stomach churn with hunger.

Mei stood behind the counter, her face lighting up when she saw us approaching.

"Fi! Sasha!" she beamed, peering at us from beneath her straight black fringe. "You okay?"

"Hey Mei!" Fi and I said in unison, and the three of us laughed, the sound of our voices filling the air like music.

We ordered some food and took a seat at

a nearby table. The sofa sank beneath me, its emerald green fabric soft and inviting. I tucked my feet underneath me as I sank into the cushions, the smooth texture comforting against my skin. We devoured our sandwiches and sipped brightly coloured milkshakes that Mei had made for us. The sweet tang of fruit danced on my tongue, the cold drink refreshing in the warm café air.

Mei, having been given a break by her parents, sat on a floral armchair and chatted animatedly about the latest drama from her band practice. Mei was amazing at the drums, and I couldn't help but admire her talent. Her band had played a few sets at charity events and were looking to book their first paid gig. However, the lead singer was acting like a diva, insisting on choosing the setlist himself.

"How annoying, Mei." Fi rolled her eyes as Mei finished speaking. "Hopefully your parents can talk to his parents and sort it out."

"Yeah, that's what I'm hoping for." Mei shrugged. Suddenly, there was a crash behind us, and we all jumped.

The boy who had been writing in the corner was standing behind our sofa, a tray in his hands. His movements were stiff, and he looked furious. A river of brown, fizzy liquid spilled onto the floor, dripping between the cracks of the wooden tiles. My stomach clenched, and my breath caught in my throat as I studied his face. It was bright red, not from embarrassment, but from sheer anger. A vein bulged on his forehead, and his knuckles were white as he gripped the tray.

"Don't worry!" Mei chirped, offering him a friendly smile. She jumped up from her seat, her light footsteps quick as she straightened the little apron around her waist and rushed to grab a cloth.

"Looks like my break is over, guys." She winked at us before bending down to clean up the mess.

Fi giggled, but I couldn't shake the feeling in my chest. The boy scowled, slamming the tray onto the nearest table, then spun on his heels, muttering something under his breath.

For some reason, his reaction made my breath hitch in my throat. I couldn't take my eyes off him as he stormed across the café, snatched up his book, and made his way toward the door. The weight of his presence seemed to linger in the air long after he left. He pushed open the door, but just before disappearing into the street, he turned and caught my gaze. His icy blue eyes locked with mine, narrowing into a frown. I felt the electricity in the air, a tension that pressed in on me. And then he was gone, the bell chiming as the door swung shut, the sharp sound almost jarring after the silence he left in his wake.

"What on earth was his problem?" Fi's voice cut through the haze of my thoughts, her words laced with confusion.

Mei stood up, the mess now clean. "He comes in here quite a lot," she shrugged. "He's always writing in his diary thing. He doesn't really say much, but I do think he's a bit weird."

I swallowed, running my hands over my arms, the hairs on the back of my neck standing on end.

"I didn't like him." Fi whispered, her voice low and hesitant. "Bad vibes."

I nodded, agreeing, something about the boy's angry, icy eyes seemed to haunt me. For the rest of the day, my mind kept replaying the look he had given me, as if it were personal. I had to shake my head multiple times to stop thinking about him. By the time Briar and Linus were locking up the shop and walking us back through town to their cottage, I was beginning to feel more at ease.

We spent a few more days working at The Alchemy that week. Even though we enjoyed amazing food and chats with Mei every lunchtime at Chaihu, the strange boy hadn't returned, thankfully.

Despite all the fun I was having, and the laughter we shared, I couldn't shake the feeling that I was being watched. They say intuition is a powerful thing, and I now know that more than ever. But at ten years old, the idea of *intuition was a foreign concept to me. I don't ignore my feelings anymore, if that summer taught me anything, it was that my gut is always right.*

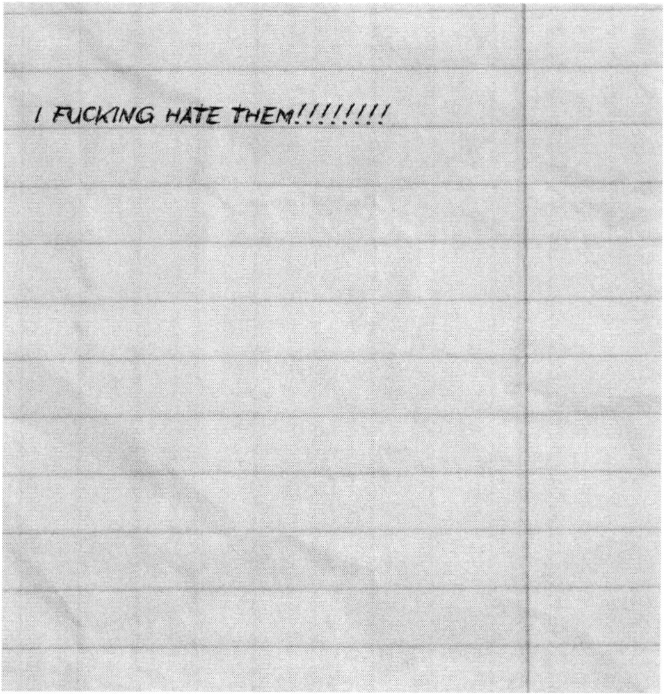
I FUCKING HATE THEM!!!!!!!!

13

I walked up the lawn back to Evermore, Jasper's words still echoing in my mind.

"Dinner's at 7."

A flutter of butterflies stirred in my stomach, and a warm heat spread across my chest. I scowled at myself, just 10 minutes ago I was snapping at him and feeling intense irritation at his constant sarcasm and goading of me. But one hand on my wrist, his body so close to mine I could almost feel the heat coming off it and a few gentle words and I was simping after him like a bitch on heat. I shook my head. All those years of seeing him only as Eva's annoying son, and now here I was, imagining ripping his clothes off.

I rounded the corner of the pool house, and a sudden chill crept over me, my heart sinking a little. The thought slipped in, uninvited, that he might never feel the same way. Apart from that one brief moment, he hadn't really given me any indication that he did. Maybe that was just him, trying to make up for being a sarcastic prick. A warm flush washed over me again as I fought to push the doubt away.

Suddenly, someone stepped out from the shadows of the building. A bright light flickered, blinding me for a second, before it revealed a figure. I jumped, startled, not expecting to come face to face with anyone, let alone a man, in my garden. The light flickered again, and there he was, Marcus. He ended his phone call and shoved the device into his back pocket.

"Alright?" he asked, clearly surprised by my reaction.

"Yeah, sorry," I said, placing a hand on my chest to steady my frantic heartbeat. I couldn't seem to shake the way the air felt heavy in my lungs. "You made me jump, that's all. You came out of nowhere."

"I was just on the phone," Marcus explained, shifting uncomfortably. "I, uh, got a job. I don't expect to stay here forever or anything. I know you aren't my biggest fan, but I'm going stir-crazy. All I've ever really known is working, it keeps me sane."

I shifted my weight from one foot to the other, trying to find the right words. The grass beneath me felt damp through my flip flops.

"That makes sense…" I trailed off, unsure what to say next.

"I spoke to a few garages around town," he continued, sounding a little more at ease now. "One of them liked me and what I could do. They're letting me work there on a temporary basis. I don't have a plan, but if you're okay with it, I'd like to stick around for a bit."

I had no idea what made Marcus want to stay in my pool house, but he wasn't causing any trouble, and Sloane seemed fine with it. I'd check with her again, but otherwise, I didn't mind.

"That's fine, Marcus," I said, my voice steadying as I turned to leave. "But if Sloane has an issue or you cause any problems, then you're out, okay?"

Marcus nodded, his gaze lingering on me longer than necessary, as I made my way toward the main house. The tension in the air hung around me like a heavy fog. I glanced back once I reached the kitchen. He was still standing there, watching me. His stare felt almost like a weight pressing against my chest, but I forced myself to look away.

I pulled the kitchen door open and went inside. Sloane and Fi were sitting at the breakfast bar.

"Oh my god, Sasha!" Fi squeaked, jumping up in excitement. "There you are!"

I looked between them. Fi looked ready to burst, practically glowing with excitement, but Sloane seemed more uncomfortable, her fingers nervously twisting the hem of her cropped cardigan. The contrast between them obvious.

"What's going on?" I asked, suddenly nervous.

"Sloane's a witch!" Fi exclaimed, her voice bubbling with joy as she clapped her hands and pulled Sloane into a hug from behind.

"She is…?" I asked, my pulse quickening. I turned to Sloane, whose expression was quiet, almost embarrassed.

"Apparently, everyone's a witch," she muttered, her voice barely above a whisper.

I felt a wave of shock spread through me, *Sloane, too? What were the odds?*

"How do you know?"

"You know how I am with my intuition about people," Fi shrugged. "I don't know how I know, I just do. It's more than a feeling, it's knowledge, but I don't know where it comes from. Like the first time I saw you, Sasha, I just knew. Same with Sloane, though hers was harder to figure out. That's why I made her light the Deprehensio Candle."

"You've always had good intuition about

people," I mused aloud. The warmth of the light spilling into the kitchen made everything feel cosy, but the weight of what Fi had just said hung heavily in the air. "I wonder if it's a magic thing."

Fi looked down at her hands, which were splayed out on the counter. Her silver rings left dark indents on her fingers as she toyed with them.

"I don't know," she said slowly. "I could ask my dad about it. It's like an aura or something. A change in the atmosphere. I can sense the magic around someone. It's gotten stronger as I've grown older. Sometimes, when I'm walking down the street, I can hear it, like a hum in the air that gets louder as the person gets closer. I mostly ignore it now, it's like background noise."

"I wish I could ignore this," Sloane muttered, her voice laced with frustration.

"Isn't being a witch a good thing, Sloane?" I turned to her, noticing how she was staring miserably at her hands, absently toying with the handmade bracelet around her wrist. I felt a wave of empathy stir inside me, the anxiety in the air swirling. I pulled a stool over and sat beside her. Fi seemed to eventually read the room and sat next to Sloane, gently taking her hand in hers.

Sloane sighed, the sound heavy and tired.

"Yeah, I mean, obviously, I grew up with you around, Sash. I was always kind of jealous of your powers and the things you could do. I loved hearing the stories from your summers here, but I always felt left out. You two were in some club that I never thought I'd be a part of." She paused, her hands shaking as she pulled a hair tie off her wrist and yanked her silky, jet-black hair into a ponytail.

"I guess it's just a shock. Like, who am I? Were my biological parents witches? How do I even have these powers now? It just leaves me with even more questions. I have no idea where I come from, and why they didn't want me."

Tears pricked at the corners of my eyes. I glanced at Fi, and I saw her eyes were filled with the same sadness. I couldn't help but ache for Sloane. She was so strong, so capable, that it was easy to forget the pain she carried. But the truth was, she'd been through so much. I couldn't give her the answers she longed for. I could never give her what she truly needed.

I pulled Sloane into a hug, and Fi did the same from the other side. We sat there for a while, wrapped in silence, knowing that sometimes, words weren't necessary.

Fi broke the silence first. She sat up and looked at us, her eyes bright with realization.

"You do know what this means, don't you?"

I straightened.

"We're technically a coven."

"We are?" Sloane sniffed.

"Well, yeah," Fi continued, her tone light but serious. "What other reason could there be for us three to have been brought together like this? Call it fate, the power of the moon, feminist movements, or kismet. But we're meant to be together. We're a family now."

Sloane sat up, the weight seeming to lift from her just a little.

"Thanks, girls," she said, wiping a tear off her cheek. "You're all the family I need."

I watched as realisation suddenly crossed her face, her spine straightened as a smirk tugged at her lips.

She stood up, the chair screeching against the marble tiles as she threw her hands in the air, addressing an imaginary audience.

"I'm a motherfucking witch!"

∞ ∞ ∞

Apparently, forming a coven wasn't just as simple as saying we were a coven.

According to Fi, we needed to be united into a coven bond.

She spent the next morning flitting between her house and The Alchemy, popping up here and there, running back and forth up the lawn carrying baskets of items while Sloane and I watched bemusedly from the patio furniture.

We were sipping our coffee and discussing our love lives. I was filling Sloane in on the day before at Eva's house, the tension with Jasper, and the fact he was going to be cooking me dinner.

"What's he making?" Sloane asked.

"Absolutely no idea," I mused. "I didn't even really know he could cook."

"I don't know if Joe can cook either. Maybe I should text him." And with that, Sloane's head dropped back into her phone. That was where she spent most of her time now, when she wasn't with Joe, that was.

"Right!" Fi appeared, startling us. Sloane's phone bounced off the floor, and she scrambled to retrieve it, brushing dust off the screen and scowling in Fi's direction.

"Sorry," Fi winced, offering an apologetic smile at Sloane. "I'm ready though. Just in time, it's pretty much sunset. Follow me!"

We linked arms as we walked through the gloaming, our strides in sync, a striking trio cloaked in black. It was no surprise for

Sloane, whose wardrobe lived in shadows, but for myself and especially Fi, it was an unusual choice, making our unity feel almost fated. Together, we were a vision against the dusky backdrop, walking with purpose toward the woods.

I, tall and elegant, moved like a whisper between my friends, my mocha skin even more radiant from the golden weeks of summer. I wore a cropped black t-shirt with a high neck, its simplicity offset by a flowing calf-length skirt and heeled ankle boots that clicked softly on the path. A wide-brimmed hat sat perfectly atop my head, casting a mysterious shadow over my winged eyeliner and bold red lips, completing my effortless allure.

Fi skipped lightly on my left, the hem of her floor-length maxi dress swishing around her ankles. The dress, with its low neckline laced delicately with a cream ribbon, floated around her in the soft breeze. The bell sleeves, nearly grazing the earth as she moved, gave her an ethereal air. Her hair, loose and free in beachy waves, framed her face, and her freckles, darkened by the summer sun, danced across her upturned nose. With no makeup save for her long, fluttering lashes, Fi was a breath of warmth and wildness, as natural as the woods we were heading toward.

On my right, Sloane strutted with confidence, her petite, curvy frame wrapped in a short black faux-leather mini skirt and thigh-high boots that hugged her legs like second skin. Her fitted jumper clung to her, highlighting every curve, while a tilted trilby cast a shadow over her piercing gaze. Her inky, straight hair brushed her chin, sharp and precise, while her lips were painted in a dark, seductive crimson, completing the image of a woman who moved through the world with quiet, magnetic power.

I glanced to my left, then to my right, my smile spreading wide as we disappeared through the trees. The three of us, draped in dark elegance, were more than a sight, we were a force to be reckoned with.

The sun was low as we emerged into the clearing that Fi had been setting up all day.

I gasped, looking around in awe. Sloane seemed to be doing the same.

The floor had been cleared of all debris, and hundreds of snapped twigs lay in the shape of a pentacle. Any smooth, flat surface was adorned with some sort of candle, pillar candles in all different heights, tea lights in coloured holders, and long taper candles sat in empty glass bottles. The flames illuminated the area, and I marveled at the different coloured glow coming off each of them. Crystals covered the clearing, on the floor, in branches, and hung by twine, their jagged glass surfaces picking up the disappearing light from the low-lying sun and casting dancing rainbows across the open floor space. Jars and bowls of different herbs and powders that I couldn't identify were placed around the area, most gathered in one spot near where I assumed Fi would conduct the ritual, the rest seemingly placed purposefully where they were needed. It looked so magical. Fi waved her hand over toward an old radio sat atop one of the stumps, and suddenly "Harbinger" by Kiki Rockwell started slowly wafting out through the trees.

"Fi, this is breathtaking," I said, the words tumbling out of my mouth as I took in the otherworldly scene in front of me. Sloane nodded in agreement.

Fi grinned, clearly happy with her day's work.

"Okay, places please, girls!" Her hands gestured out in front of her.

Sloane and I moved to the individual candles at the bottom points of the pentacle and stood, waiting for instruction. Fi took a place at the topmost point.

She bent to light a smudge stick of sage leaves, the smoke rising up and disappearing through the trees. She held it above her head and began, "Magic, we call upon you as three peers. There shall be no lead to this Coven, we are souls of equal measure and would like to be bound together as such."

A low humming broke through the music, and I noticed a movement to my left. A beautiful copper-sounding bowl lay on a bed of leaves, its rod moving around the rim of the bowl by itself.

"Thank you," Fi continued. "The pentacle represents good and pure and white magic, it surrounds us in its protection and its light and love. The circle stands for wholeness and unity, and together they are used to focus and direct our energies."

She stepped lightly into the middle of the circle and placed the burning sage down into the centre. She then returned to her original position.

"Sasha," she turned to face me, the tallest of the trio. "Do you come to bind yourself to this coven? Do you bring yourself and nothing else, and offer to the coven all that you are?"

I took a breath, a warmth filling my body, my skin feeling electric, and the tips of my fingers tingling and vibrating with energy. Inexplicably, I realised I knew exactly what I had to say:

"I come to bind myself to this coven. I have purified my sense of purpose, bringing myself and nothing else, and I come to offer the coven all that I am and all that I will be."

The hum from the sounding bowl grew louder, the rod spinning faster and faster against the edge.

"Sloane," Fi continued, raising her voice over the sound of the bowl. "Do you come to bind yourself to this coven? Do you bring yourself and nothing else, and offer to the coven all that you are?"

I turned my head and looked at Sloane. I watched as the telltale signs of magic took over her body, the same way it had with me. I could see Sloane's fingers twitching as the energies coursed through her veins.

"I come to bind myself to this coven, I offer the coven all that I am and all that I will be. May we be bound together in magic and life."

Again, the sounding bowl picked up speed. The sound permeating from the bowl was almost deafening at this point.

"I too bind myself to this coven," Fi shouted above the din. "I offer the coven all that I am and all that I will be. With the addition of myself, that makes three!"

At Fi's final word, all noise stopped dead, and the rod clunked lifelessly into the bottom of the bowl. The silence that followed left a ringing in our ears.

Fi reached down beside her and, one by one, provided each of us with a little bowl of powder and a small dagger.

"Moonstone," Fi told us. "It encourages us to embrace change and joyfully embark on new beginnings."

I blinked at the sight of the blade but swallowed down my fears. I trusted Fi, and although the glinting metal caused unwelcome memories to flash through my mind, I knew I wasn't in danger.

Once Fi had taken her place back at her original candle, she reached for her dagger. Sloane and I followed suit.

"I offer my blood with the cut of my knife," Fi lightly dragged the blade across her palm, a slither of red blood seeping through her skin. "May my blood be yours for the rest of my life."

She nodded to us to do the same. I watched Sloane copy the movement without hesitation, then placed the knife against my own skin and paused to gather the courage to go ahead. Closing my eyes and sucking in a breath, I winced as the blade sliced across my palm. Dropping the dagger onto the ground, I lifted my hand, watching the red liquid pool. I had never had an issue with blood, but the slight sting and the knowledge that I had made the incision myself was making me feel a bit faint. I took a deep breath to calm myself, my nerve returning.

Together, we lifted our hands over the bowls of moonstone and squeezed a few drops of blood into the powder. Then slowly, Fi lifted her bowl and gently poured the substance onto the flame in front of her.

There was a flash of light from Fi's candle. The flame grew, large and white and flickering in the light breeze. She looked at me as though gesturing for me to me to do the same.

I poured my bowl over the candle, and the bright flame rose up again. It danced for a second before subsiding, the flame also white.

Finally, Sloane raised her bowl and tipped the contents over her flame. There was another flash, but this time, it was darker. The flame grew like before but much larger, a spark crackling and popping as the fire turned dark black, and a plume of smoke made its way up into the atmosphere.

I turned my head to look at Fi, whose face was still, eyeing the flame curiously. Sloane had also looked up to check Fi's reaction, her eyes darting between her friend and the dark flame bobbing in the wind before her.

Fi drew in a breath, snapping her gaze away from Sloane's flame. She reached out her hands toward us, and we took them, each of us holding the spare hand of the other.

"I take who you are, and I give you me. We bond together, so mote it be." She vowed. Her head nodded at us to join in.

"I take who you are, and I give you me. We bond together, so mote it be!" We all chanted in unison.

One by one, the flames extinguished. The air was thick with the smell of burning herbs and melted wax, a lingering scent of sage and something sharper, like ozone after a storm. A strange silence settled over us, heavy and charged, and for a moment, all we could hear was our own breathing.

Suddenly, a sharp searing pain blossomed on my back, right between my shoulder blades at the nape of my neck. I gasped, my hand flying to the spot instinctively, feeling the heat radiate from my skin.

"Ow!" I hissed, my fingers brushing against something hot and slightly raised. I glanced at Fi and Sloane, who were wincing in pain as well, their hands mirroring mine, clutching the same spot on their backs.

"What... what just happened?" Sloane asked, her voice tight with discomfort. She turned, trying to get a better look at her friends. "Is it just me, or do you guys feel like you're burning?"

She hurried over to me and pulled down the tight collar of my top to look. Her eyes grew wide.

"Sasha," she whispered. "You have a mark... like, a symbol. Right here."

I twisted around trying to see over my shoulder, but it was impossible.

"What? What kind of symbol?"

Fi stepped behind Sloane and did the same. "It's not just Sasha. You have it too, Sloane. And I think I have it as well."

I moved behind Fi, pulling her long hair out of the way to get a better look. Sure enough, a dark, almost black sigil was burned into the skin at the nape of her neck, surrounded by a fainter ring. The skin was raised and red, like a fresh burn, but the lines were precise and intricate, almost like a tattoo that had been etched into our flesh in an instant.

Fi's eyes were wide with a mix of fear and excitement. "I've heard about this," she said, her voice barely above a whisper. "It's a mark, a sigil. It means the ritual was successful. This... this is our coven's symbol. It's been branded onto us."

The three of us exchanged glances, a mixture of awe and appreciation passing between us. We had known the ritual was powerful, we could feel that much, but none of us had expected this, a literal physical mark of our bond, burned into our skin. My fingers graced the edge of the sigil on my neck, feeling the heat and the strange, almost magnetic energy pulsing beneath my fingertips.

"Does it hurt like a bitch for you guys too?" Sloane asked.

"A bit," I admitted, wincing as the pain flared again. "But I guess this means it worked. We are connected now. For real."

Fi nodded, a small smile tugging at her lips despite the pain. "Yeah," she said softly. "We're a coven. Connected. Forever."

I took a deep breath, the reality of what we had just done settling over me like a blanket.

Fi squealed. "We're a coven!"

We all cheered, and I pulled them both into a hug.

"I love you guys!" I gushed, breaking away and looking at them both. "My hand fucking hurts though too."

We laughed, each of us falling to sit on the ground. Our eyes swept the scene before us, hearts full of magic and love, and minds full of the bond we had just made with each other.

∞∞∞

That night, as I lay in bed, the forest floor still vivid in my mind and a buzz of wine humming through my system, my thoughts drifted back to the ritual and everything that had happened. I couldn't quite believe it. We were a coven now. The weight of it pressed in on me, and I still couldn't wrap my head around it, the power I had felt as I was bound to Sloane and Fi. I was tethered to them, to these two incredible, magical women, for life. I would do anything for them, I realised.

Just as I was about to drift into the depths of sleep, a memory tugged at the edges of my mind. The sight of a dark flame flickering between two bright ones. Fi's expression as she watched that candle burn, a mix of fear and something I couldn't quite place. I wondered what it meant. But I was too tired to dwell on it now, and so, with a soft smile, I let sleep take me.

14

*T*en years old

At this age, things don't tend to worry you for long, and the angry look that had shone in the boy's eyes at the coffee shop was already becoming a distant memory, like a shadow fading in the midday sun. The heat of the day pressed down on us, the air thick and heavy, but the light breeze that fluttered through the trees offered a brief moment of relief.

We had spent the morning in the pool, our skin still tingling with the aftermath of chlorine, but by the time lunchtime came, we'd been shooed out and told to dry off and dress for Eva's feast. The scent of fresh-cut grass mixed with the warmth of the summer sun as we lay at the top of the hill in Evermore's garden, our stomachs full from tuna and cucumber sandwiches, paired with the sweet tang of homemade lemonade.

"Sooo hot," Fi moaned, fanning herself with her hands, the slight whoosh of air doing little to cool her flushed face.

Jasper rolled over beside me, stretching his arms out like he was trying to find a cooler patch of grass.

"We need shade," I said, squinting up at the sky, the sun almost too bright to look at directly, but there was no mistaking how fiercely it bore down on us.

I pushed myself up, my legs stiff and sticky from the heat, my sandals scraping against the ground. I scanned the area, searching for some sanctuary from the burning sun, my eyes landing on the rose bushes at the bottom of the decline.

The ground between the rows was darker, the long shadows stretching across the soil like fingers reaching for the coolness of the earth. I pointed. "Over there."

Jasper propped himself up on his elbows, squinting at the distance. "Worth a shot," he said with a shrug. The three of us sluggishly trudged towards the flower beds, the heat clinging to our skin like a second layer, sweat trickling down my back in tiny rivulets.

When we finally reached the shade the relief was instant. We sat for a while whilst Jasper entertained us by reciting ridiculous and often rude rhymes and songs he had learnt at school. Fi was often completely bewildered and Jasper roared with laughter at her complete innocence and often misunderstandings of the words involved. Being completely honest there were a fair few I didn't understand either but I wasn't going to admit that and I often breathed a sigh of relief at Fi requesting explanations for some of the words I had no idea of the meaning of.

At one point, after Fi had asked yet another innocent question, Jasper laughed so hard that he tumbled backwards, landing under an especially large and thick rose bush.

"Jasper!" Fi exclaimed, her voice sharp with concern as she tugged at his foot. "Be careful of the thorns."

Jasper barked a laugh again. "It's fine!" he gasped, "I've been around these— OUCH!"

Fi's face lit up with a smug smile, the corners of her mouth twitching as if she couldn't wait to say I told you so. But Jasper sat up suddenly, holding a pen in his hand, his expression bewildered.

"This just stabbed me in the back!" he said, frowning as he brought it closer to his face. "Hubbard's Beer and Wine Distillery," he read aloud. "How the hell did this get here?"

Fi shrugged and my face must have looked as blank as my mind felt because he continued.

"It's a place that makes alcohol in the next town over. A girl in my class, her dad works there," Jasper explained, twisting the pen between his fingers. "It's crap, apparently," he added as an afterthought, as if remembering something. "She says he always says the pay is shit and the hours are long. Whatever that means."

He clicked the pen a few times, the repetitive sound cutting through the air. "Whose pen do you think it is?"

I didn't know. My brain was too preoccupied with the strange sense of curiosity I felt. I found myself wondering who this girl in Jasper's class was and how Jasper seemed to know so much about her father.

"I have an idea," Fi piped up suddenly. "Let's be detectives!"

"Detectives?" I repeated.

Fi stood up, hands on her hips, and a look of intense seriousness on her face, her chest puffed out like she was about to deliver an announcement to an audience. "The Case of the Mysterious Pen." She gestured with grand flourishes, her fingers moving in the air as if writing the title in invisible ink.

Jasper groaned, but I couldn't help but laugh, the heat of the day dissipating just a little in the wake of her enthusiasm.

"Three World Famous detectives come together for one time only to find out who the suspicious pen found in the rose garden belongs to, and to return it to its rightful owner," Fi continued, her voice full of mock gravitas.

"You watch too much TV," Jasper muttered,

rolling back onto his back.

Fi's nose wrinkled as she shot him a look. "I watch basically no TV, thank you very much. I just have an imagination, Jaspy."

I snickered as Jasper groaned, covering his face with his arms, but there was a lightness in the air now, something easy between us.

"Detectives Seraphina, Sasha, and Jasper interrogate and interview the suspects in order to get to the bottom of the mystery. No stone shall be left unturned!" Fi concluded with a bow, as if performing a final flourish.

"I'm in," I said, my voice eager. "It sounds better than sitting here and melting anyway."

"That's the spirit, Sash!" Fi grinned, her eyes sparkling. "Jasper, you game?"

He sat up, removing his arms from across his face and looking around, slightly bemused.

"Fine." He shrugged, a little curiosity lighting up his face. "I am curious as to how it got here."

The first person we asked was Eva. She was in the kitchen of her and Jasper's cottage, her pillar box red hair a beacon through the window as we approached the house. Her movements were quick and light as she busied herself with something at the counter.

"Mum," Jasper started, holding up the pen like it was evidence. "Is this yours?"

Eva squinted at the object being held an inch from her eyes.

"Hold it closer, Jasper, why don't you?" She

took a step back, finally getting a better look. "A distillery," she tutted, shaking her head. "No, not mine. Chance would be a fine thing!" she added with a wink, showing us she was just joking.

"Your dad will be taking a break now, Sasha," she said, glancing up at the kitschy cuckoo clock hanging above the door. "Go ask him."

We nodded and turned to leave.

"Where did you find it anyway?" Eva asked as we were halfway out the door.

I glanced back at her just as Jasper called out, "The rose garden!" The look on her face was quick but noticeable, a flash of something, confusion, maybe, but just as fast, it was gone, replaced with her usual cheerful demeanor.

Fi and Jasper were already heading up the bank and I jogged a little to catch up to them.

Jasper broke the silence, his voice light but full of thought. "Your dad likes a drink in the evenings. Bet it's his."

"Oh," I nudged him as we entered the kitchen. "Enjoying the game now, are you?"

Fi snorted and high-fived me behind Jasper's back, and I grinned.

"No," Jasper faltered, the tips of his ears turning pink. "I just want to know who the bloody pen belongs to."

"We're just teasing," Fi giggled, squeezing his arm. "Pleasure to have you on board, Detective Jasper!" She saluted him as he rolled his eyes.

"Hello kiddos!" Dad's voice came from the living room, warm and familiar. He was bent over, furrowing through a basket he'd pulled out from a sideboard cupboard.

"Lost a pen?" Jasper asked, holding it up.

Dad stood, taking the pen from Jasper's outstretched hand, and turned it over, inspecting it just as Jasper had. "I haven't lost it," he said, studying the writing on it. "Hubbard's. Very puzzling. Where did you find it?"

"In the rose garden," I replied. "It was right under one of the bushes. We're detectives, solving the mystery."

Dad's eyes narrowed as he studied the pen, his expression thoughtful.

"You know your mother and I have written a fair few mystery books in our time," he said, looking up at us. "You've got to follow the clues. The pen isn't dirty, so it can't have been there for long. That narrows it down to anyone who has been in the house over the past couple of days. It's from a distillery, and while that might just be a coincidence, it's a good place to start. Do you know anyone who's been there or works there?"

"A girl's dad in Jasper's class," Fi piped up, earning a snort from Jasper.

"Ah, interesting stuff," Dad replied, handing the pen back to Jasper. "Any chance she's got a little crush on you, mate?" he teased. "Maybe *she's been hiding in the rose bushes, watching you in the pool."*

I froze. A cold feeling crept down my spine. Someone had been watching us. My stomach tightened, and I glanced at Fi. Was she thinking the same thing? But she was too busy snickering at Jasper's reaction.

I turned back to Dad, forcing a smile as he ruffled my hair before retreating to his study. The conversation continued, but I wasn't really listening anymore.

"Who else should we ask?" Jasper's voice cut through my thoughts.

"No one," I snapped, my voice too sharp. "There were workmen here last week, changing the taps or something. It was probably one of theirs."

I felt their eyes on me, but I didn't meet them. I could sense Jasper and Fi's curious glances, but I didn't want to say more.

Before either of them could say anything, Eva breezed back into the room, her presence like a sudden breeze that swept everything else away.

"Ah good, you're all here," she said cheerfully. "Much too hot to be out there. I just caught your Mum, Sasha, and she said you can buy a film on the TV to watch for the afternoon. I'll make popcorn."

Fi and Jasper whooped and dove for the sofa, shoving each other out of the way for the best spot, but I couldn't shake the unease that had settled in my chest.

I grabbed the remote, forcing a smile as I scrolled through the options.

Ten minutes later, Harry Potter and the Philosopher's Stone was playing on the TV, but I couldn't concentrate. The crunch of popcorn in the background, the laughter of Fi and Jasper it all seemed distant.

"Imagine needing a wand to cast all your spells," Fi giggled as Professor McGonagall appeared on screen, disguised as a cat.

Jasper scoffed. "Rather than doing it in your head, you mean?" His hand reaching into his bowl of popcorn and shoving a handful into his mouth.

I glanced at Fi, pleading with her silently to stop talking, but she continued seemingly forgetting that Jasper had no idea that she was a witch.

"Well, yeah, there's no way a twig could help you channel your magic, it's obviously in your mind-" Fi retorted.

I coughed loudly at this point staring at daggers in her direction. Both of them looked over at me, confused, as I stared straight at Fi. Jasper raised an eyebrow, a piece of popcorn frozen halfway to his mouth.

Fi stopped mid-sentence, her eyes widening as the realisation seemed to dawn on her.

"You two are so weird," Jasper muttered,

clearly deciding whatever we were talking about wasn't important enough to stick with. He turned his attention back to the movie.

I settled back into my chair, the warmth of the popcorn no longer comforting. My eyes flicked back to the pen, sitting abandoned on the coffee table. Our mystery seemed forgotten by the others, but I couldn't let it go.

Where had it come from?

The chill returned, a cold weight pressing on my chest. Had someone been watching us again? This time it felt deliberate. I looked at Fi, but she didn't seem worried, so I tried to push the feeling away.

Still, as the credits rolled and the movie ended, the discomfort lingered in my bones. Something was wrong, and I couldn't shake the feeling that the mystery wasn't over yet.

Those stupid fucking girls made me lose my pen today. I stole it from mum's work when she took me there last week. It was another souvenir and it was special. I'm so good at stealing things now, no one even pays any attention to me so it's easy. It wrote so good too. I was watching them out by the roses again when they started running in my direction so I had to leg it and I didn't realise I'd dropped it until I was over the fence. Now they're wandering round playing detectives trying to find out who's it is, I'd love to stab a pen through their fucking faces.

15

We sat in the clearing where the ritual had taken place just days before. I was perched on a fallen log, its bark worn smooth beneath my fingers, while Sloane leant against a weathered tree stump, arms draped loosely over her knees. Fi paced the clearing's edge, her hands twisting together, her movements restless as the wind.

Her rust-coloured, wide-legged trousers skimmed the earth as she walked, gathering leaves and twigs in their fabric. I still couldn't fathom how she went barefoot without a second thought, treading over stones and brambles as if the ground had never once hurt her. When she stepped squarely onto an upturned twig, I winced in sympathy, but she didn't so much as blink.

Her long hair was piled into a haphazard bun, strands escaping in tangled plaits, a single feather jutting from the side. At the nape of her neck, just visible beneath the curve of her hair, her new sigil tattoo stood bold against her skin. The redness had faded now, leaving only stark black lines, intricate and certain, as if they had always belonged there.

"…And he still hasn't called me back," Fi moaned.

I tuned back into the conversation, glancing over to see that Sloane wasn't really paying attention to Fi's complaints either. She picked up twigs, snapped them between her fingers, and tossed the discarded pieces back to the ground. Her dark brow was furrowed, and she had a serious case of resting bitch face going on.

I studied her for a moment, she was in black cycling shorts and an oversized sweater with a skull printed on the back. White crew socks and trainers finished the outfit.

"Well, don't call him again," I said, looking away from Sloane and back to Fi's pacing. "If he's interested, he'll reach out. He's probably just busy, working or something."

"He is clearing out his mum's house," Fi mumbled. "She passed away a few months ago, which is awful, of course. But, like, it's not hard to pick up the phone."

She plopped down onto the ground,

picking a leaf off her cream knitted bralette before turning her eyes to Sloane.

"Are you okay, Sloane?" She seemed to have picked up on the tension coming off her, too.

Sloane sighed. "I was thinking..." She hesitated before continuing. "My flame. It was black."

I stilled. I had been wondering when she'd bring this up.

"What does that mean? You two had white flames."

Fi moved to sit beside her. "There are two kinds of magic," she said, taking Sloane's hand. "Light and dark. It's not always like in the movies, though. Light witches aren't always good, and dark witches aren't always bad. It's basically genetics, lineage, that kind of thing."

"So my parents were probably dark witches?"

"Not necessarily." Fi stuck a twig in her bun and scratched her head. "Could've been your grandparents, or even further back. There are people called Novus, witches born to non-witch parents. That's what we thought Sasha was for years until she found her grandma's diary. Her parents never practiced witchcraft at all, didn't even acknowledge its existence. The only reason we know she isn't a Novus now is because it's in her bloodline further back."

I smiled softly, watching the desolate expression on Sloane's face.

"I'm sorry, Sloane," I said, moving to sit with them and taking her other hand in mine. "I know it's always been hard for you, not knowing who they were."

"It's not like Mallory or Rory ever told me anything about them, if they even knew," she grumbled, referencing her foster parents. "And now I find out my real parents might have been evil witches who passed some dark magic shit on to me. Perfect."

"It's really not like that, Sloane." Fi interjected. "Honestly, there are some amazing dark witches in history. You know, I haven't seen my dad for ages, he's always been at the shop when I've been home, but he's really knowledgeable about all this stuff."

She got to her feet.

"When you meet him, you can ask him. But I promise, it's not a bad thing. Your kind of magic is very strong, one of the oldest kinds. And it doesn't mean you're 'evil,'" she said, using air quotes around the word. "My mum's sister, my aunt, and her husband were mixed up in dark magic. I never met them, but Mum and Dad say they were two of the best people you could ever meet."

I watched as Sloane looked up at Fi and sighed.

"Thanks, Fi," she breathed. "It's just hard not knowing. And I'm new to all this magic stuff. I don't even know where to start or what I'm supposed to be able to do now."

"Right," Fi said, grabbing our hands and pulling us up. "Follow me!"

Sloane and I smirked at each other but did as we were told, trailing behind Fi until we reached the meadow nearby.

Fi motioned for us to sit, and we both sank into the soft green grass.

I blinked up at the sky. The sun was strong out here, no clouds in sight, the heat pressing down on us. I wondered if Fi had anything to do with the weather today. I wasn't sure I'd ever see a clear sky again without questioning it.

"Watch this," Fi grinned. She stood in front of us, angled so we could still see her face, and raised her hand, palm outstretched.

I glanced at Sloane, who just shrugged.

Fi closed her eyes, lips parting slightly.

For a moment, nothing happened.

I kept my eyes on her, waiting for any indication that whatever she was trying to do was working.

Then, something soft grazed my fingers.

I startled, breath catching, and glanced

down. A small white rabbit sat beside me, its fur bright against the green, its nose twitching as if it had been here all along, waiting for me to notice.

I lifted my gaze, following an unseen thread of quiet magic, and saw Sloane staring straight ahead, her expression caught between wonder and disbelief. Hidden among the grass, barely rustling the meadow's golden hush, at least seven pairs of round, unblinking eyes watched us.

Fi opened her eyes, a slow, knowing smile unfurling across her face. Without hesitation, she melted into the buttercups, the yellow petals folding around her. At once, the rabbits moved, tiny paws pressing into the earth, ears flicking forward, a hush of soft bodies weaving through the grass.

Ten of them, maybe more, bounded toward her, drawn by something unseen. She reached out, stroking the space between their ears with careful fingers, and one, small and pale like a fallen cloud, hopped straight onto her lap.

"How did you…?" Sloane trailed off.

"Animal summoning," Fi said with a smile. "One of my favorites. I always get bunnies, although once, when I was eleven, a doe and her fawn came to me."

"Wow," I breathed. "I want to try."

Fi thanked the bunnies surrounding her,

and one by one, they hopped away, disappearing into the tall grasses.

"Just envision what you want to achieve, Sash," Fi told me. "Magic is about intention. If you believe you can, then that's half the battle."

I got to my feet, copying what she had done moments before. I held my hand out and shut my eyes.

I filled my mind with creatures, delicate-winged butterflies, drowsy bees, foxes slipping like shadows through the underbrush, badgers trundling through the earth's embrace. I imagined them drawing near, their curious eyes locking with mine, tiny feet whispering against my skin, silken fur brushing past my legs like a fleeting breath of wind. A slow, shimmering warmth bloomed in my palm, unfurling like ivy up my arm and rooting itself deep in my chest.

A breeze, feather-light, kissed my cheek. Somewhere beside me, Sloane let out a startled gasp.

I opened my eyes, blinking against the sun's golden glare.

At least twenty birds surrounded me, their wings stirring the air like a living constellation. Some hovered just above, catching the light in flashes of iridescence; others flitted and swooped, painting arcs of movement through the sky. A few perched on the ground, heads tilted, watching.

Then, as if answering some silent call just like with Fi, a starling landed on my outstretched hand.

I lifted it gently, bringing it closer, studying the fine, glistening feathers, the quick rise and fall of its breath. In its small, dark eyes, I glimpsed something familiar, an echo of my own wonder, staring curiously back at me.

I glanced at Fi, who was grinning like a proud parent.

"Now what?" I mouthed.

"Thank them," she whispered back.

I looked at the birds around me and smiled.

"Thank you," I said softly. "Thank you for coming to me."

Their wings beat the air as they lifted off, flying away one by one.

"Incredible," I murmured. "Sloane, your turn."

Sloane hesitated before stepping forward. She took the same stance we had, closing her eyes.

I glanced at the sky, looking for movement. Fi was peering into the trees.

Nothing happened.

Sloane's eyes opened, and she shrugged. "Nothing."

"Are you picturing them?" I asked.

"I was trying," she muttered. "Maybe I'm just not in the mood."

"What about trying to think of something happy again?" I suggested, directing my question towards Fi.

"How many happy memories do you think I have?" Sloane muttered.

"It doesn't really work like that." Fi sighed. "Thinking of happy thoughts is great for beginners, it helps to get into the mindset of emptying your head and focusing on what you want. But it only really works the first few times, after that you really need to tap into your own intuition. Your mind needs to work out how to get to that point itself."

Sloane flopped back down into the grass. "I'm grumpy, I'll try again another time."

With that she pulled out her phone and started ferociously texting Joe again.

Fi and I exchanged a look but said nothing.

"Are we going to that beach party later?" Fi asked.

Sloane nodded, her fingers still going ten to the dozen.

"I can't," I said, excitement bubbling up. "I have dinner at Eva's."

"Oh yeah," Fi squeaked. "Jasper's cooking, isn't he?"

"Apparently so," I shrugged. "I'm actually really looking forward to it, I hope he makes dessert."

I winked and Fi fell about laughing.

"Come on, Sloane," I said, reaching for her hand as I stood. "We need to get ready!"

∞∞∞

I jogged up the steps to Eva's cottage at 6:50 pm, pausing briefly on the porch to compose myself. Tonight I planned to walk through doors like a normal person, not fall through them like a poorly coordinated bambi.

I rapped lightly on the door before easing it open. The scent of something warm and buttery drifted through the air. Jasper stood at the stove, a pair of oven gloves slung carelessly over his shoulder. His shirt, loose and white contrasted with the dark linen of his chinos and highlighted the muscles he'd been honing to perfection. A very attractive byproduct of his days spent in the garden. His long tousled hair shimmered with natural highlights, like strands of sunlight had woven themselves through it.

He glanced my way, eyes narrowing.

"What?" he asked, suspicion laced in his voice.

I realised I had been gazing at him with a big, dopey smile on my face. I rearranged my features.

"Nothing, sorry..." I trailed off. "I was just thinking of something else."

"Oh right—" Jasper began.

"Ah, Sasha!" Eva smiled, coming into the kitchen from the other room.

She looked better than I had seen her in a while. She had lost weight, her cheekbones more prominent, and her brightly coloured tie-dye jumpsuit hung a little differently off her shoulders. But she was up and about, and the colour was returning to her face.

"Eva!" I smiled, tearing my eyes away from Jasper. "You're up!" I hurried across the kitchen and into Eva's arms, pulling back to hold her at arm's length and study her face.

"You look fab!" I gushed. "But we need to top up this pink!" I fingered the front of her fading pink locks.

"I'll get the dye," Eva smiled. "Can you do it for me one night?"

"Absolutely."

I pulled out a chair at the kitchen table, which was set up with patchwork placemats, a jug of sunflowers, and a few mismatched candlestick holders, the flames flickering in the breeze coming through the slightly opened window.

My mind wandered, lost in the image of Jasper and I sitting at the table, his large hand holding mine, gazing into each other's eyes as he fed me some delicious bite of food, his fingers placing it in my mouth and lingering for a moment as my tongue lightly flicked over the tips.

"Sit down, Mum," Jasper's voice broke through my daydreaming, and I felt my cheeks grow hot. Now was not the time for that. I straightened myself up and brought my mind back to the present.

Eva clucked her tongue. "Okay, okay," she grumbled, giving me a wink. "He's so controlling."

Jasper rolled his eyes, and I grinned at the little woman.

Ten minutes later, we were all sitting down and digging in. Jasper had made an amazing prawn risotto.

"He went down to the fishmonger's and got the prawns fresh this morning," Eva beamed.

I was impressed. I had no idea Jasper could cook, but the food was delicious, and the Sauvignon Blanc I washed it down with created a comforting buzz in my chest. The conversation was light, touching on Eva's recent coach trip to some stately home and Jasper's weird new obsession with soil density.

"So what's the plan for after this summer, Sasha?" Eva asked, taking a swig of her wine.

I groaned. "This summer is never ending, Eva."

Eva laughed. "I'm afraid it will one day, my dear." She pushed her empty plate away and leaned back in her chair. "You did so well at school, darling. I thought you were planning on heading off to university at some point?"

"Yeah." I twirled my fork in what little was left of my food. "I am going to, the plan is still journalism, but like, I haven't done anything else with my life yet. Don't get me wrong, school back home and my summers here have been a dream. I am aware I am very privileged, and Mum and Dad have taken me on some amazing holidays in the other school breaks, but I want to travel. I want to see the world."

Jasper shifted in his seat next to me, and I glanced at him. He was watching me, but his eyes snapped down toward his plate as mine met his, the muscles in his clenched jaw twitching.

"That sounds lovely." Eva smiled. "I think it's a wonderful idea. Maybe a gap year and then back to your studies the September after?"

"Yeah." I turned my attention back to Eva. The air felt thick with the tension coming from Jasper. *Had I said something wrong?*

"I haven't spoken to Mum and Dad about it yet, but I think they'll be happy for me to travel. They did it when they were around this age."

"It's very important to see the world." Eva stood and began clearing the plates off the table.

"Leave that, Mum, I'll do it." Jasper jumped to his feet and took the plates from Eva's hands.

Eva tutted again. "I wish my Jasper had some ambitions to leave this town."

"Maybe I do." Jasper was loading the plates into the dishwasher. "But I start that job next month. Lifeguarding has been fine, and it has worked well around helping you out here, Mum, but this could become more of a career."

"What is it?" I asked. Eva was sitting back down at the table, rubbing her face with her hands.

"Mum, go to bed," Jasper said softly. "You've done well to make it this late."

"No stamina anymore!" Eva laughed, but her eyes looked tired. "I will go up if that's okay with you, Sasha. This old bird can't even make it to 9 p.m. nowadays!"

"Of course that's alright!" I jumped up and rounded the table to give Eva a hug goodnight. "It's been lovely, thank you so much."

"Oh, I didn't do much, darling, but you're welcome. It's always a pleasure having you here."

With a squeeze of Jasper's shoulder, she turned and left the room, the sound of her soft footfall padding up the stairs and fading into the distance.

I twirled the stem of my empty wine glass between my fingers.

"More?" Jasper asked, opening another bottle.

I held my glass up to him as he poured me some more of the pale liquid, which was now coursing through my veins.

"Shall we go to the other room?" Jasper had his back to me, putting the bottle back into the fridge. The air was tense again. I swallowed.

"Yeah, that sounds a bit more comfortable."

I made my way into the living room, settling into the large, soft yellow sofa, my body sinking into the brightly coloured cushions. I glanced around, there were colours everywhere. Eva was definitely a maximalist. The fireplace was painted in shades of orange, and the tiles inside were an emerald green. The bookcases on either side were full of books, plants, and photo frames. A young Jasper grinned back at me from one shelf, and on the other side was a picture of the three of us, me, Jasper, and Fi. We had been running down the hill at Evermore, our arms outstretched and heads thrown back in laughter.

"What are you smiling at?" Jasper had entered the room and was standing in the doorframe watching me, a bemused look on his face.

"I was just remembering the summer when we had about a hundred races down that hill." I nodded toward the photo, and Jasper's eyes followed. "We made Eva take photos and videos of every single one. She never got fed up with us."

Jasper sat down next to me, taking another sip of his wine and placing the glass on the side table.

"I think I would have gotten tired of us." He smiled.

"I thought you did get tired of us." I laughed self-consciously. "You couldn't wait to escape to your dad's or to Eli's house or wherever."

"Not true." Jasper's face suddenly looked serious. "I always thought you never wanted me around. You used to run off into the woods without me, or go to the lake, and I was never invited." He nudged me playfully in the ribs.

I studied his face. *Did he really think that?* I had always thought he never cared. I had always wanted him to come, but we couldn't do magic with him around. I recalled mornings when we would have to sneak off into the woods before Jasper woke up for the day so we could practice our spells and incantations alone. My heart sank a little at the thought of him feeling left out.

"I'm sorry," I said quietly. "That was never our intention. I, I... always wanted you around."

He smiled at me. We were close now, the soft sofa sagging in the centre and pushing us together. I looked up at him, his face inches from mine. My breath hitched. The anticipation rippled over my skin in waves.

Suddenly, he turned, picking up his wine and finishing the glass.

"More?" he asked, standing and making his way into the kitchen.

I let out a breath and finished my own glass. "Yes, please."

Jasper returned with the bottle, the pale liquid sloshing gently as he refilled both our glasses. He set the half-empty bottle on the floor with a quiet clink, then reached for the remote. A burst of tinny music filled the silence, the theme song of some soap I didn't recognise, its melody out of place in the dim hush of the room.

"What's this job anyway?" I asked, watching as Jasper settled beside me again. The space between us had widened, though I wasn't sure if he'd meant for it to.

"Oh." He ran a hand through his hair before answering. "One of the customers at the country club needs a groundskeeper. The guy he has now is getting older, and he wants to train someone younger to take over. It's a good job, full of benefits. And I've done enough of that work at Evermore over the years that I already know what I'm doing."

I shifted on the sofa, tucking my legs beneath me. Jasper's fingers had found a loose thread on one of the cushions, it was a deep red embroidered with a golden sun, and he toyed with it absently, twisting and pulling.

"You don't sound too thrilled," I observed, tilting my head. He didn't exactly exude excitement.

Jasper sighed, his shoulders rising and falling. "No, it'll be good. And it means I can stay local, be around Mum for longer. I don't know how she'd cope on her own."

"She'd hate to hear you say that, Jasp."

"I know." He gave the thread one final

tug, and it came free, unraveling between his fingers. "But what am I supposed to do? I'm all she has. I can't leave her." His voice softened, tinged with something almost resigned. "You talking about travelling earlier just made me realise how stuck here I really am. And after this summer... who knows when I'll see you again? You'll be off in Japan, or Bali, or wherever."

I took another sip of wine, the taste warm and heady on my tongue. I'd always known Jasper was loyal to his mum, that he wouldn't want to leave her. But I hadn't realised how trapped he actually felt.

"She'd want you to live your life," I murmured, glancing up at him.

"I know. It's just... hard."

Somehow, without me even noticing, we'd drifted back together. His leg pressed against mine, solid and warm.

Jasper hesitated, his hand hovering in the air for the briefest moment before it came down, resting on my thigh. The weight of it sent a shiver up my spine. His fingers didn't move, they just stayed there, steady. His eyes roamed my face, searching, waiting, as if checking to see if he'd overstepped.

I gave him a small smile, an unspoken reassurance.

The television droned on in the background. The 10 o'clock news flickered onto the screen, filling the space between us with sterile voices and flashing headlines. Jasper's eyes flicked toward it, then back to mine.

Gently, he lifted a hand, tucking a loose strand of hair behind my ear.

"Sasha," he breathed, his face tilting closer, his gaze dipping from my eyes to my lips and back again. "I—"

"BREAKING NEWS," the television blared, slicing through the moment like a knife. "ANOTHER CHILD HAS GONE MISSING, PRESUMED TAKEN FROM THE LOCAL AREA. THIS MAKES THE FIFTH CHILD THIS YEAR, AND POLICE REMAIN WITHOUT LEADS."

I snapped my head toward the screen. Jasper exhaled beside me.

"Not another one," he muttered, running a hand down his face.

"It's awful." My skin prickled, but I couldn't tell if it was from the news or the weight of Jasper's hand still resting on my thigh.

"I can't believe it's been ten years, and they're still disappearing." His voice was tight. "How are they getting away with this?"

I shook my head, unable to answer.

Jasper's jaw clenched. "I knew one of them."

I turned to him.

He stared at the television, lost somewhere in the past. "He was in my form class when I was fourteen. I didn't really know him that well, but... it's weird, you know? One day, someone's just there, every day, and then they're not."

Something cold curled in my stomach.

He kept talking, voice quiet, almost detached. "They never found him. His mum was all over the news, begging for information. She was on her own with it, his dad had died, and she'd remarried. Had another kid. But I don't think his stepdad really cared. Eventually, the posters came down. They always do. One missing face replaced by another."

"That's so sad." My chest ached for those children. For the parents left behind, lost in an endless cycle of hope and grief.

Jasper nodded. "His name was Silas."

The name hit me like a wrecking ball.

The room seemed to twist, the walls closing in. My fingers slackened, and my wine glass slipped from my grasp. I scrambled to catch it, my fingertips grazing the cool glass just before it tumbled. It landed with a soft clink, threatening to shatter the silence.

But it wasn't the glass that had my heart in my throat.

It was the name. The face. The nightmare that had never truly left me.

The memory surged forward, violent and unrelenting. His eyes, dark and furious, narrowed into slits. The snarl curling his lips. His hand clamping down on my arm, nails biting into my flesh. Pain. Real and sharp, even now.

My breath hitched. The edges of the room blurred.

"I—I'm sorry," I stammered, shoving to my feet. "I have to go."

"Sasha?" Jasper stood, concern knitting his brows. He reached for me, but his hand stopped midair, uncertain.

"I need to go," I repeated, pulse hammering in my ears.

The missing posters. The names. The ghosts plastered on every street corner.

Silas Burns.

Fourteen years old.

The same age Jasper had just mentioned. The same boy.

My legs moved before I could think. My jacket was thrown over my shoulders, my bag gripped in trembling hands.

"Sasha, wait, are you okay?" Jasper took a hesitant step forward, his worry thick in the space between us.

"Yes, yes," I lied, my voice brittle as cracked glass. "I'm fine. I'll… talk to you tomorrow."

I forced a smile, but it didn't feel right. His confusion was palpable, but I knew I couldn't explain. I was unable to unravel the terror sinking its claws into me.

I turned and fled.

The red door slammed behind me, the sound ricocheting through the night. The summer air hit my face like a slap, but I didn't slow down. My feet pounded against the pavement, my breath coming in uneven gasps as I hurried toward Evermore.

I could feel Jasper's eyes on my back, watching me disappear into the dark.

But I didn't look back.

The name echoed in my mind, over and over, growing louder with every step.

Silas Burns.

Whatever it meant, whatever Jasper knew, I would have to face it eventually.

But not tonight.

Tonight, I needed space. I needed air.

Above all, I needed to be alone.

16

Still disappointed from my behavior last night, I scowled at my reflection in the bathroom mirror. I'd essentially done a runner on Jasper all because I am still unable to shake the vivid images from all those years ago, and I was positive he was leaning in to kiss me. Was he? I stared at myself harder, smoothing down my curls, and shrugged. It didn't matter now, I supposed. After last night, I'd definitely blown it.Walking back into my bedroom, I let the door click softly shut behind me. I approached my altar. Maybe I should do some self care.

I struck a match, the sulfur sparking to life, and lit a fresh stick of incense. Wisps of bergamot-scented smoke curled into the air, weaving invisible threads of warmth and citrus. I inhaled deeply, letting the fragrance settle in my chest, coaxing some of the tension from my bones.

Reaching for my affirmation cards, I

closed my eyes and drew one from the deck, my fingers brushing the worn edges. When I flipped it over, the words stared back at me like they knew me all too well.

"Fear keeps me standing still. I choose to keep moving forward with courage."

I exhaled, rolling my eyes even as I set the card in its wooden display stand. The universe had a way of being a little too on the nose.

Rummaging through a small ceramic pot, I plucked out a smooth piece of rose quartz, its cool surface smooth against my fingertips. I placed it carefully in the designated space, watching how the light caught the pale pink hues.

"I wish," I murmured under my breath, my voice barely more than a whisper. My gaze drifted to a Self-Love spell jar I had crafted at the beginning of summer, the herbs and crystals inside settled like a tiny universe of hope. On impulse, I added it to the altar beside the quartz. Maybe its magic still had something left to give. Maybe, if I could find it in me to be a little softer with myself, some of that grace would extend to Jasper too.

I slugged down the stairs and walked into the kitchen, only to interrupt a make-out session between Fi and the guy from The Alchemy.

"Oh! Sorry!" I smiled sheepishly, feeling guilty for intruding on their moment.

"Sash!" Fi pulled back from the attractive guy in front of her, slightly flushed and grinning from ear to ear. "No, you're fine. Come meet Seb!"

I smiled back at her friend and headed over to the breakfast bar, taking a seat. I aimed a smile at the broad guy sitting across from me as he looked up through dark lashes.

"Hi, Sasha," he offered a polite smile. "It's really nice to meet you."

I could tell Sebastian was shy as I greeted him back. His bright blue eyes darted nervously around the room, and his large shoulders seemed hunched, as if he were trying to make himself smaller. He lifted his hand and rubbed it across his short, shaved hair. There was an uneasiness about him, a tension that made me wary, despite feeling a flicker of interest in his quiet demeanor. Meanwhile, Fi hovered nearby, clearly anxious for my approval, her eyes flicking back and forth between us.

"So, Sebastian," I began cautiously, giving Fi a sideways glance. "Fi tells me you're an artist?"

Sebastian nodded, fiddling with the edge of his coffee cup. "Yeah, I... I do some painting. Mostly abstract stuff."

"That's cool," I said, trying to sound encouraging, but I sensed my tone held a slight edge of skepticism. "Do you do any exhibitions or anything?"

He hesitated, his eyes dropping to the table. "Not at the moment. I, uh, mostly just keep my work to myself right now."

Fi jumped in, her voice a little too eager. "But he's so talented, Sasha! You should hear some of his ideas, they're amazing."

I smiled, though I could feel it didn't quite reach my eyes. "I'm sure they are," I replied, still studying Sebastian. I took in the contrast of his bright eye colour against the umber brown tones of his skin. He seemed to shrink further under my gaze. "Maybe sometime."

Fi's nervous energy was palpable. "He's not a big talker until he gets to know you," she said, wrapping her arms around Sebastian's shoulder and planting a kiss on the side of his face. His hand came up and stroked Fi's arm in response. As he glanced up at my friend, I could see genuine affection in his eyes.

"Yeah, I get that," I said, my voice softening slightly as I smiled in both of their directions. "I'm sure we'll get to know each other better."

Sebastian managed a small smile, but his unease was still clear. "I'd like that," he said quietly, his voice barely above a whisper.

I nodded, my own feelings still mixed. "Hey, why don't we have a barbecue this afternoon? Are you guys free? We could see what Sloane and Joe are up to too?"

I wanted to give him a chance for Fi's sake.

"That's an amazing idea!" Fi squealed with excitement. "We're free, aren't we, babe?" She looked over at Sebastian, who nodded back at her, his eyes shining with amusement at her giddy reaction.

"Perfect," I smiled back at her. "Say, 2 pm, back here?"

"Sorted, we'll be there," Fi said brightly, clearly pleased she was going to get a chance to show Sebastian off. She hopped off the bar stool, taking the aloof man by the hand. "We're just heading outside to sunbathe. I would maybe avoid the garden to the side of the house for the morning, if you catch my drift." She giggled.

I watched as the already flustered Sebastian seemed to concave inwardly at Fi's words and let out a burst of laughter at my friend.

"I understand," I winked exaggeratedly. "Enjoy both. Sebastian, it was a pleasure to meet you. I hope you know you've got your hands full with that one."

I laughed, nodding in Fi's direction, seeing a grateful look in her eyes.

Sebastian smiled at me as he took Fi's hand, and they disappeared out of the kitchen door together.

I let out a breath and absentmindedly rubbed the coven sigil mark at the back of my neck. He seemed nice, I thought, just shy, and maybe a little socially awkward. But Fi was smart and had the best intuition of anyone I'd ever met. I was sure she knew what she was doing. And if she didn't, then I'd be there for her if it all went wrong.

I was no stranger to dealing with the fallout of my friends' relationships. I'd been friends with Sloane long enough that I was a pro at picking up the pieces. I rummaged in the drawer for my favorite coffee pod, noting that our supply was getting a bit low.

"Alex Marsh," I muttered to myself, my body shuddering at the memory. I wrote 'coffee pods' in my scrawling handwriting on the whiteboard we used to communicate with Eva and flicked the coffee machine on.

My mind drifted back to that rainy afternoon when Sloane had shown up on my doorstep, mascara streaked down her cheeks, lips trembling, her hands clutched tight around her phone. It had only been three months, but to Sloane, the breakup had felt like the end of the world. She hadn't even needed to say anything when I opened the door; the look on her face had said enough.

I, always the calm one, had pulled my best friend inside without a word, offering the kind of hug that spoke more than any words could. As we made our way up to my bedroom, my thoughts had wandered back to all the times I had kept quiet about Sloane's now-ex-boyfriend. I'd never liked him, the way he'd always seemed too smug, his laugh insincere, and his habit of checking his phone whenever Sloane hadn't been looking. But I hadn't wanted to ruin things for my friend, not when she'd been so infatuated. Then hadn't been the time to bring it up either. This was about Sloane, not me.

Once we were upstairs, Sloane had collapsed onto my bed, burying her face in a pillow. I had sat beside her, rubbing small circles on her back, just listening to her cry. The soft murmur of voices from downstairs had drifted up, and soon enough, my mum had appeared, gently knocking on the door with a steaming pot of pepper pot stew in her hands. The warm, familiar scent of spices had filled the room, and I had given her a grateful smile. The stew was more than just food, it was comfort, something my mum always knew how to offer without words.

"Thanks, Mum," I had said as she placed the tray on the bedside table. She had given us a knowing look, the kind only mothers seem to have, and quietly left the room. Sloane had sniffed and sat up, her eyes red and puffy, but the smell of the stew had drawn her out of her shell just a little.

We hadn't even started eating when there had been another knock at the door. This time, it had been my dad, holding a DVD box set of Gilmore Girls like it was the Holy Grail. "Thought you might need this," he had said with a wink before backing out just as quickly. I hadn't been able to help but grin.

For the next few hours, we had stayed cocooned in my bed, bowls of stew in our laps, the comforting sounds of Lorelai and Rory Gilmore filling the room. Sloane had picked at her food at first, but slowly, as the episodes had rolled on, she had started to eat more, laugh a little, and cry a lot less. I had made sure not to push; I had let Sloane lead the conversation, only commenting here and there about how ridiculous her ex had been or how Sloane had deserved better, which she absolutely had.

By the third episode, Sloane had turned to me with a small, sad smile. "You know, maybe it's for the best," she had admitted, her voice shaky but a little stronger than before.

I had nodded, my chest swelling with relief. "I think so, too."

I smiled at the memory as I thought about how much I missed my parents.

I fired off a text to my mum and moved to sit at the breakfast bar when a flash of movement caught my attention out the window. Jasper. He was standing at the bottom of the bank, shovel in hand... topless. His defined abs glistened with sweat from the blazing sun, and his white t-shirt was tucked into the back pocket of his low-slung Levi's. I let my eyes trace him from head to toe, his mussed chestnut hair pulled up in a messy bun, and his tanned skin only serving to make him look like the cast of Baywatch. My mouth hung open, how was it possible that he was even more attractive every time I saw him? He wiped the back of his hand across his forehead, and I was sure things were moving in slow motion.

I hurried into the hallway and looked at myself in the mirror, my head tilted. I was in a set of white shortie pyjamas with a long matching cardigan hanging off my shoulders. They were my favorites; the contrast of the stark white made my skin look glowy. I squared my shoulders. I couldn't ignore him forever. Moving back into the kitchen, I opened the fridge and poured a tall glass of Fi's homemade lemonade, a peace offering for last night. Topping the pale blue glass with some ice cubes, I walked out the door and onto the patio. Sloane had her bedroom window wide open, and the sound of her music was drifting across the garden. It must have been close to 25 degrees out as I crossed the lawn toward Jasper.

"Hey," I began, a sheepish expression on my face. I extended the lemonade across to the tall man in front of me. "I, uh, sorry I ran out on you last night..." I trailed off, forcing myself to look up into his large brown eyes. Jasper gave a small smile, accepting the cold drink and taking a sip.

"Did I do something?" There was a vulnerability in his voice as he placed the glass down on the wall next to him.

"No!" My voice came out louder than I intended. "No... honestly, you were great. It was me, I just... you were great. I promise." I stared deep into his eyes, wanting to show how sincere I was. "It was lovely to spend time with you and Eva."

He smiled in response, but this time, it met his eyes. I reached up and went to smooth down my curls when his hand came up and stopped me from performing the self-conscious motion.

"Don't do that, you always do that."

As my hand lowered, he didn't let go, and we stood facing each other, fingers entwined.

"The food was lovely," my stomach flipped as I felt his thumb graze the back of my hand.

"I didn't know you could cook. Who taught you? When did you learn?"

Jasper's eyebrows rose, and a smirk played on his lips.

"I'm sorry, I'm babbling, I just feel really bad about leaving. I want to explain..."

He shook his head, a silent reassurance that no explanation was needed. His eyes darkened, they were a quiet storm, a fire flickered behind dark irises as they traced the contours of my face. They lingered, hesitating just a moment too long on my lips, and suddenly, the air between us felt charged, electric.

My heart pounded against my ribs, each beat a drumroll of anticipation. I was acutely aware of the space between us, of the way my breath came uneven, rising and falling in time with the unspoken tension stretching taut like a thread between us. I swallowed hard, my throat tight, as if that simple movement might steady the unraveling inside me.

I needed to pull myself together, Jasper was still watching me intently.

"So, um, we're gonna have a barbecue today... up at the house. The girls and Sebastian... maybe Joe too. You could come along? If you want to, that is." I looked up through my dark lashes.

"I'd love to." His response was short but sincere. A boyish grin spread across his lips, and my nerves settled slightly.

"I really did have a nice time with you last night, Jasper."

"So did I, Sash. Really nice... there was one thing that I was disappointed with, though." His hand reached down towards my chin as his finger slipped underneath it and angled my face up towards his. I watched the muscles in his jaw tense. My heart skipped in response.

"...What?"

Without warning, his mouth claimed mine, and everything inside me seemed to explode. Butterflies fluttered wildly in my stomach, their wings beating with frantic energy. His left arm wound around my waist, pulling me so close that I could feel the heat of him, the solid press of his body against mine, while his right hand tangled in the soft strands of my hair, gripping as if he never wanted to let go.

For a moment, I wasn't sure if I was still

standing or floating, my soul suspended somewhere above, unable to tether itself to reality. I was lost in him, in the sensation, in the perfect, dizzying intensity of this kiss,the kind of kiss that only exists in novels and films, the kind that makes time stretch and blur into something unforgettable.

My body responded without thought, electric and alive in ways I had never known. Static surged through me, prickling the surface of my skin, leaving a trail of goosebumps in its wake. Every inch of me seemed to hum.

From Sloane's room, the familiar strains of This Kiss by Faith Hill filled the air, and it felt as if the universe itself was in tune with the moment, echoing the rhythm of our hearts. I melted deeper into him, every breath drawing me closer, until nothing else existed but the two of us, lost in the intimacy of a kiss that felt like the beginning of everything.

"You have no idea how long I've been wanting to do that," Jasper said, his usual boyish charm replaced by a fire. He looked like a man possessed, and he seemed to be possessed by me. "And I'm fed up with waiting for permission."

I leaned back into him, drawn in like a magnet. He grabbed me again, and I could feel the swell of him against my stomach. My breath hitched in my chest, and I sucked in a sharp intake of air, trying to steady myself. His mouth found mine, and I couldn't help but respond, our tongues exploring each other with a hunger I hadn't realised I was feeling. I wrapped my arms around his neck, letting him lift me slightly onto my toes, the warmth of his body pulling me closer, if that was even possible.

His fingers brushed lightly down the side of my breast, and a shiver ran up my spine. God, I wanted him. I wanted all of him.

But then, a shrill noise shattered the moment, Jasper's phone, ringing out through the air. I pulled back just enough to watch him plunge his hand into his pocket and silence it, his focus still on me, before his fingers found their way back to my breast. His touch was slow, deliberate, running circles around my nipple through the thin fabric of my top, and it was almost too much.

Oh my God, Jasper.

I opened my mouth, but before any words could come out, my phone buzzed, breaking through the silence. My heart skipped a beat, and I pulled away properly, our chests heaving in the space between us. I fumbled for my phone, pulling it out of my cardigan pocket, and saw Eva's name flashing across the screen.

I glanced up at Jasper. He was frowning down at my phone, his brow furrowed in confusion.

"Hello? Eva?" I answered, my eyes staying locked on Jasper's.

"Darling…" Eva's voice sounded pained, like she was far away, her words trembling through the receiver. "Darling," she repeated, quieter this time, and I felt my chest tighten. "Not to worry you, I'm fine, but I can't seem to get hold of Jasper… I've had a bit of a fall."

∞∞∞

I barreled through the front door right behind Jasper, panic coursing through my body. "In here," came the weak reply from the kitchen. I followed Jasper into the bright yellow room, my breath catching in my throat at the sight of Eva slumped in one of the multicoloured dining table chairs. Her eyes flicked up to meet ours, and she managed a small smile. "Oh look at the pair of you, Sasha darling, you're still in your pajamas! I told you I was fine."

A greyish-blue bruise was already starting to form across her right cheekbone, and it trailed down toward her jaw. I felt a sharp sting in my chest, tears welling up in my eyes. I couldn't bear to see her hurt.

"Mum, what happened?" Jasper's voice was hard, almost angry. "Your cheek." He reached for her face, gently angling it toward him to get a better look, though the tenderness in his touch was at odds with the tone of his voice. He sighed deeply, running his hands through his hair as he stood back up.

I opened the freezer and grabbed an ice pack, the kind shaped like a strawberry for kids. Wrapping it in a towel, I handed it over to him. He pressed it gently against his mother's face, his worry showing in the way he carefully adjusted it.

"I just tripped back over the door frame coming in," Eva said, her voice soft and almost amused, though her eyes were tired. "That's all, love. I was just coming to get a glass of water."

"You should be in bed." Jasper's tone was more of a demand than a suggestion, and Eva raised an eyebrow at him.

"You seem to have things handled here." I could tell Jasper needed some time alone with his mum, without the weight of what had just happened between us hanging over him. I needed to give them space.

"Eva, I'll give you a call in a little while. And uh, Jasp... see you later?" I glanced up at him, offering a small, reassuring smile, but I could see the way his shoulders were slumped, the guilt weighing heavily on him.

He nodded silently in response, and I turned to leave, the ache in my chest still lingering. I hadn't even made it to the door when a warm hand gripped mine, pulling me back toward him. I didn't resist, my heart aching for him as I was pulled into the chest of the beautiful man I had just been tangled up with.

"I'm sorry, Sash," he said, his expression was pained. "I've only been out of the house for ten minutes, and this happens. This is why I can't leave her long term."

I could feel my own heart break for him, for the weight of responsibility he carried.

"I understand," I replied softly, giving his hand a gentle squeeze. "She's tough though, you know? She's just weak right now. Things will get better, and she'll be back to her normal self soon."

Jasper smiled down at me, his fingers once again slipping under my chin to tilt my face up toward his. He placed a soft kiss on my lips, and then let me go, his gaze lingering for a moment before he turned back towards the kitchen and disappeared from view.

A few minutes later I made my way back through the bifold doors into Evermore's kitchen, just as Sloane and Joe entered from the other direction.

"Hey, I was hoping to catch you guys!" I beamed at them, shaking my head to clear away the negative energy.

I watched Sloane tear her grey doe eyes away from the towering man to the side of her. Sloane had a habit of falling fast but I was sure I'd never seen the look that was currently on her face, she looked out of it, high on love... or lust I supposed. Afterall, it had only been a few weeks. Either way Sloane beamed back at me, giving me her full attention.

"We're having a barbecue today, around 2-ish. I caught Fi and Sebastian this morning... and Jasper said he'd come too." I smiled sheepishly, watching as Sloane's eyes widened in understanding, as a huge grin spread across her face.

"We'd love to!" Joe's voice boomed, making me jump. Everything about him was larger than life. He towered over Sloane, his massive frame easily two feet taller than her small one. His giant hand rested possessively on her shoulder, and his white-blonde hair was swept back, not a strand out of place. His unusually dark eyes glinted in his tanned face like two shining coals, and the confidence radiating off him was undeniable. He was definitely sexy, I thought, as I watched him playfully squeeze Sloane's ass.

Sloane giggled in response, she looked up at him, her eyes not leaving his for a second. "Definitely," she said, her voice a little dreamy. "We were just about to head into town. What can we bring?"

17

Ten years old

I glanced up at the ornate clock on the wall, its golden hands pointed squarely at six. Thursday evening. I was staying the night at Fi's house. Cross-legged on the thick, layered rug in the centre of her bedroom, I busied myself snipping glossy pictures from a magazine to add to the mood board we were making. Fi had darted off to fetch us a drink. She wanted to redecorate her bedroom, and her parents had given her the go-ahead, but as I slowly took in the room around me, I couldn't begin to fathom why she'd want to change a single thing.

The space was pure Fi, unapologetically her in every detail. It was the cosiest room I'd ever stepped into, warm and curious and full of life. The walls were a muted, dusky cream, soft and putty-toned, but barely visible beneath the layers of personality draped and pinned across them. Deep purple fabric hung from the ceiling like stage curtains, forming a theatrical border to the room. In the corners, the drapes tumbled all the way to the floor, while in the middle they were pulled back almost as though an invisible party were pulling them up to get a better look at the curiosities inside. Heavy brass hooks shaped like bees clasped the fabric in place, casting gentle shadows and folds as the fabric fell.

Where the walls peeked through the drapes, they were adorned with shelves, leafy green plants, and knotted macramé, each item a collected memory, a story woven through time by Fi and her parents. Gifts, treasured finds, and lovingly handmade pieces created a living collage of her life. Woven hangings, some purely decorative, others functioning as holders for potted greenery draped from yet more hooks. Her beloved baskets lined the walls like an ever-changing installation, though I noticed a few gaps where they'd clearly been put to practical use around the room.

Her bed, low to the ground, was a nest of blankets and cushions in rich jewel tones, emerald, sapphire, amethyst. Each pillow had its own texture: tassels, frayed edges and embroidered patterns that told their own little stories. Though scattered in what looked like careless abandon, I couldn't imagine a better arrangement, they were chaotic in the most comforting way.

The furniture was mostly dark wood, each piece with its own storybook elegance. The desk, wardrobe, and chest of drawers looked as though they belonged in a forgotten manor, yet somehow they fit perfectly in this cottage room. Above us, the ceiling was a constellation of dreamcatchers, twelve in total, swaying gently in the breeze from the open window. The thick lace curtains fluttered like moth wings, and between the dreamcatchers, bulbs dangled on cords of varying lengths, casting a warm, mellow light that made the whole space feel like a home.

I shifted the way I was sitting, unfolding my legs from beneath me with a slight wince as pins and needles sparked across my calves. My fingers traced absentmindedly over the rug beneath me, thick, soft, and rich in colour. This particular one was deep red with an intricate Bakhtiari pattern woven through it, no doubt one of Briar's many charity shop treasures. The floor beneath us was a patchwork of textiles: a tightly coiled hessian rug shaped like a blooming flower in a wheat-coloured weave, and another in a faded blue hue, adorned with swirling oriental dragons that looked as though they might ripple into motion under the right light.

I stood to stretch, reaching my arms above

my head and narrowly dodging one of the many dreamcatchers overhead. The beads and feathers swayed gently in my wake. Tugging at the hem of my cream cotton shorts where they'd ridden up, I smoothed the creases in my brown vest top, its thin straps twisted across my shoulder. Turning, I wandered over to one of the wall shelves and let my fingertips skim the surfaces, tiny crystals in dusky pinks, translucent whites, and sea-glass greens caught the low light and glimmered softly. I plucked up a pen from the shelf and carefully placed it back into Fi's homemade pen pot.

We'd made those pots one summer a couple of years ago, sculpting the clay with our clumsy hands. Fi's was a cheerful mess of colour and texture, lumpy, bright, decorated with sparkly gems and cheerful splodges of paint. Mine sat back at Evermore, pride of place on Mum's desk: neat, symmetrical, adorned with carefully cut stars and diamonds, painted in clean strokes of gold and blue. And yet... I liked hers more. Mine looked like it could've been made by anyone, but Fi's had a personality which was unmistakably hers.

I heard her footsteps on the stairs, light and quick, and padded across the room to open the door just as she reached it. She breezed in with the scent of wildflowers and something citrusy clinging to her, carrying two glasses of squash which she set down with a clink on the chest of drawers, nudging aside a stack of books and a little bundle of tied herbs in the process.

Her hair, as ever, looked as though it had been in a battle with the wind. Stray feathers poked from the wild bun atop her head, giving her the look of a half-transformed bird. She wore a mint-green and white striped dress, ankle-length and swishing softly as she moved. The bodice was ruched seersucker, fitting snugly, while the skirt fanned out in weightless layers.

"Fi, why are you even changing your room?" I asked, shutting the door behind her. "It's perfect. I don't think anywhere could be more 'you' if it tried."

She spun around dramatically, eyes wide. "Change it!?" She scoffed, flopping back onto the rug and grabbing the scissors from the floor. "I don't want to change it. I want to add to it."

She grinned up at me, her eyes dancing with mischief.

I laughed. That made more sense.

I sat down beside her, the scissors cool in my hands as I began to cut around an image of a golden tray set with purple gemstones on a velvet cloth.

"Girls, dinner!" Linus's voice echoed faintly from downstairs.

Fi groaned and rolled her eyes. "He could've

said that a minute ago when I was literally down there." She grinned, gathering up the drinks from the chest of drawers and waiting for me to open the door. Together, we headed down to the kitchen.

The table was already set in the familiar mismatched way Briar loved. She loathed anything that matched too perfectly, so the plates, bowls, and cutlery had been gathered over years of boot sales and treasure hunts through charity shops. I took a seat in front of a brown plate featuring cartoon pigs in wellington boots. A red-and-white napkin, slightly faded and creased, flew through the air and landed with surprising elegance beside my fork.

"Oops! Sorry, Sasha," Linus called cheerfully, winking. "Wasn't quite paying attention."

I grinned back at him. There was never a dull moment in this house.

"What film shall we watch later, girls?" Briar's voice chimed from the counter as she stirred something in a large mixing bowl.

"Not Harry Potter!" Fi giggled, casting a sly glance my way.

I burst out laughing, shaking my head at the memory of the near-disaster with Jasper at my house a few nights ago.

Linus eased into his chair with a dramatic sigh. "Ah, some joke we're not privy to, darling," he said to Briar. "Well, we'll see what we've got later."

Briar nodded and floated over to the table, placing a heavy wooden bowl down in the centre. Inside was the most vibrant salad I'd ever seen. Bright orange slices of roasted squash and buttery green avocado fanned out atop a bed of glossy spinach leaves. Pomegranate seeds glittered like rubies between chickpeas and crumbled feta, and a tangy balsamic dressing had been artfully drizzled across the top. My stomach growled as a generous portion was spooned onto my plate, the pigs on the porcelain vanishing beneath the rainbow of food.

"So," Linus asked, a spinach leaf clinging stubbornly to the corner of his mouth, "what's the plan for you two tomorrow?"

"Probably exploring," Fi said airily, popping a pomegranate seed into her mouth. "Jasper keeps saying we haven't explored all of the woods, and we want to prove him wrong."

I nodded, too absorbed in chewing to answer.

"We've been basically everywhere," Fi continued, her fork waving vaguely in the air. "But he says the boys at his school talk about this place called The Wishing Tree. I don't know what that tree even is, but if we haven't been there, then I'm going."

She was busy stabbing at her salad again, eyes on her plate. She didn't see the look that *passed between Briar and Linus, but I did. It was brief, a flicker, but enough to make me shift in my seat.*

Linus cleared his throat. "The Wishing Tree, eh?"

Fi nodded, still oblivious to the sudden ripple in the room's energy.

"I don't know why everyone makes such a big deal about it," she went on. "It's just a tree, right? They all dare each other to go and make a wish. What's so scary about that?"

Briar pushed her glasses higher on her nose and glanced sideways at Linus. This time, Fi caught it.

"What?" she asked, her mouth full.

Linus smiled, the kind of smile that didn't quite reach his eyes, and took a long sip from his glass.

"Tell you what, girls," he said, carefully. "Instead of a film tonight, I have a story for you. A story about The Wishing Tree."

Fi looked up sharply. "It has a story?"

"That it does," Linus replied. "And a lesson at the end. But let's finish up first, and see if Mum's made any pudding."

He winked, trying to return the mood to normal. And though the chocolate peppermint cheesecake that followed was divine, and we laughed and licked spoons and fought over the last bite, I noticed it: the occasional glance, the quiet, unspoken exchange between Briar and Linus. Something was definitely being left unsaid.

∞ ∞ ∞

Later, once we were fed and full and flopped out on the living room rug in a tangle of blankets and pyjamas, Linus returned with a mug of tea in one hand and a book in the other. He set the mug down carefully on a coiled grass mat that doubled as a coaster and lowered himself into the armchair with a sigh that sounded older than he was. The book was thick and bound in cracked leather, with a strange symbol pressed into the cover—one I didn't recognise, but it seemed to shimmer slightly when the lamp caught it.

Fi and I were wrapped in a shared patchwork quilt, its squares made from scraps of old dresses, pillowcases, and baby clothes, soft with years of use. Her foot nudged mine beneath it, cold toes curling against my skin like they always did when she was trying to warm them up.

Linus didn't open the book straight away. He looked at us for a moment, then reached for his tea, he gave it a short blow and the steam immediately vanished, he took a slow sip and winked at us.

"The story I'm going to tell you can vary depending on who tells it. This book has been passed down in my family for years and was handwritten by a distant relative. The version I have here might be biased but it is the version we believe to be true."

We both leaned forward instinctively. Outside, the night had gone still and strange. The earlier rain had passed, but the windows still glistened with a fine silver mist, and every now and then, the wind nudged the glass like it was trying to remind us of something forgotten.

"The Wishing Tree," Linus began, settling back, "is older than Wychbold Cove itself. Older than Evermore, older than the roadways and maps and the names people gave to the land. Back then, no one called it a wishing tree. It had a different name. One no one speaks now, not because it's a secret, but because the name has been forgotten... or maybe buried."

The fire crackled softly beside us. Fi's eyes were wide, her curls spilling across her shoulders, casting little shadows on her cheeks. I could hear her breathing, shallow, steady.

"It was many, many years ago," Linus continued, his voice low and rhythmic, like the opening of a spell. "And the world was a very different place. Back then, men and women lived as equals, working side by side in the fields, tending gardens, raising livestock, and caring for the children as one community. Land wasn't claimed or owned. It belonged to everyone and no one at once, shared, respected, loved. Villages had communal spaces where neighbours toiled together, and all reaped the gifts of the land with grateful hands."

We listened, curled beneath the quilt on the floor, the fire casting slow-moving shadows along the walls.

"But as with all good things," he continued, his gaze turning thoughtful, "change crept in. The power of the land, the richness in its soil, the strength in its yield, began to draw the attention of those far above the common folk. Lords. Landowners. Men who saw opportunity where others saw home. They wanted the land back. And so they took it. Piece by piece, they claimed it, fenced it, sold it off to wealthy farmers for pastures and ploughs."

He paused to take a sip from his drink, the steam curling gently past his cheek. His eyes met ours, bright, serious, and heavy with the weight of memory not his own.

"The great fields came next," he said softly. "Vast, privately owned stretches of green where once there had been laughter, shared bread, and handwoven baskets full of harvest. Communal plots dwindled to nothing. People *were forced to earn a living now, not through cooperation, but through wages paid by the very men who stole what once was theirs. And in this new order, the work of women, tending, nurturing, healing, was dismissed. Forgotten. No longer considered work at all."*

His voice deepened, the firelight flickering against his spectacles.

"The breadwinner became king. Not the breadmaker. And in households across the countryside, men were prized for their labour, while women were pushed aside. For those without husbands or children, it was worse. They were cast out, seen as burdens, broken pieces that no longer fit the new world."

Fi shifted beside me, silent, wide-eyed.

"These women," Linus said gently, "were abandoned. Forced to seek shelter in the woods, in crumbling cottages, makeshift shacks, any space they could call their own. They lived on scraps, depending on the fleeting kindness of those who still remembered them. But kindness is often short-lived when hardship takes root. Milk was refused. Bread withheld. And when they asked too often, too boldly... they were met with fear instead of mercy."

His voice lowered into a whisper.

"And so, when illness came to a family, or misfortune knocked at their door, it was not fate that was blamed. It was her. The woman

who had once been their neighbour. Their friend. She became a scapegoat. She became... a witch."

Fi gasped, indignant. "But they weren't! They weren't witches!"

Linus smiled faintly and nodded. "You're right, Seraphina. Most were not. They were ordinary women who had simply fallen on hard times. But fear has always been a louder voice than truth."

He leaned forward, folding his hands.

"At the centre of the old village, before it was carved apart, there stood a great tree. Vast, ancient, with a trunk so wide it would take five people linking arms to reach around it. No one quite remembered where it came from, but over time, it became a place of quiet hope. The Wishing Tree, they called it. Those women who had been shunned began gathering there. They whispered their pleas into its bark, wishes for food, for warmth, for mercy. No one knows exactly how it began. Perhaps desperation has its own rituals."

I felt a strange ache in my chest then, as if I could hear the whispers myself.

"And then," Linus went on, "something changed. Real witches, true witches, heard their cries. Moved by their suffering, they enchanted the tree. Magic wove itself through the roots and branches, and from then on, the tree could hear."

Fi and I looked at each other, wide-eyed and glowing with quiet joy. I saw a flicker of something fierce in her expression, something that looked like pride.

"Of the many women who came to the tree, there were two sisters," Linus continued, his tone shifting again. "One wished for goodness, that the tree would help the forgotten women of the woods. The other, bitter and hollowed by anger, wished for ruin. For vengeance upon the men who had turned their backs on them."

A shiver passed through me. I gripped the blanket tighter.

"The witches were divided. Some stood with the sister of light, others with the sister of darkness. A battle began, not with swords or fire, but with spells and secrets, curses whispered through leaves. From that day on, the Wishing Tree became more than a place of hope. It became a line in the earth, a boundary between the light and the dark. Between magic meant to mend, and magic meant to destroy."

He looked at us both, his voice slow and deliberate now.

"They say that if you visit the tree and speak your heart's deepest wish, you may hear the soft, guiding voices of light witches. They will lift you up, help your dreams take shape. But you may also hear something else. The darker voices. The ones that feed on bitterness. The ones that speak not of what you need,

but what you want most in your shadowed heart. The tree no longer knows who it serves. Its magic has been tampered with, tangled and twisted over centuries. And now... it's no longer safe. For no one, not even the purest, can know what side will answer their call."

I looked down. My arms were covered in goosebumps, the tiny hairs standing on end like a warning. Beside me, Fi rubbed her hands along her legs under the blanket, suddenly quiet.

"So it's dangerous?" she asked her dad, voice low.

Before Linus could respond, Briar entered the room, moving to stand beside his armchair. Her presence was like the scent of thyme and sun-warmed linen, strong, grounding, undeniably there.

"It is, my darlings," she said softly, her eyes resting on us. "There is dark magic beyond that tree. And it is no place for children. I was born in this land. I've lived through the stories, the superstitions, the truths too strange to ignore. Nothing good has ever come from stepping into that clearing."

Fi opened her mouth, as if to protest, but then shut it again. A rare silence settled on her tongue.

"There is no danger in the woods themselves," Linus added gently. "They are still as sacred as they've always been. But

promise me, don't go near the tree. Not that far. Not ever."

We nodded at once, solemn and small under the weight of what we'd heard.

Then Linus's face lit up again, like a curtain lifting at the end of a heavy play. "Anyway!" he said with a clap of his hands, his usual warmth returning. "Bedtime for you pair!"

He stood, and with a playful flick of his fingers, his empty mug floated from his hand and glided neatly into the kitchen with a clink.

Briar kissed us both on the forehead, soft, warm, and fleeting like a spell to keep us safe, and we scampered up the stairs to Fi's bedroom, hearts thudding, minds too full of stories to even pretend we'd be sleeping that night.

Fi's room smelled like lavender and the faint waxy scent of candle smoke. We climbed into her double bed and pulled the heavy duvet up to our chins, nestling into the softness like it might muffle the questions swirling between us. The fairy lights above the bed blinked softly, casting golden shapes across the ceiling.

"Do you believe it?" I asked, turning to face Fi in the dim light.

She gave a little shrug, her curls rustling against the pillow. "My dad wouldn't lie," she said. "But it was just a story. Folklore." She sat up suddenly, excitement tugging at her voice and the duvet with it, half of it falling away from me in the process.

"I've never heard of anything bad happening in those woods," she added, eyes wide. "And if boys from Jasper's school have gone in and come out just fine, then why wouldn't we? We know those woods better than anyone!"

I could see it happening, right there behind her eyes. The idea blooming like a wildflower. Trouble usually looked like this on Fi: spark-lit, unstoppable.

"Fi…" I said, my voice lined with warning.

"Let's go anyway!" she burst out, already halfway to standing. I groaned, propping myself up on my elbows.

"I knew you were going to say that."

She rose fully now, balancing on the mattress like it was a stage. Her shadow stretched up the wall behind her, tall and triumphant. "They've never mentioned it before," she whispered, urgent. "And they know I go into the woods all the time. If it were that serious, if it were real, why wouldn't they have told me?"

I shrugged, knowing full well that logic wouldn't stop her. I could already feel myself giving in.

"We'll go tomorrow," Fi said, plopping back down beside me with finality. "And we'll prove him wrong."

"But—"

"No buts, Sasha." She reached for my hand and squeezed it, eyes glittering. "No excuses. Let's get some sleep. Tomorrow we're going to find the Wishing Tree. And we'll make wishes of our own."

I sighed, lying back onto the bed, the quilt puffing up around me like a cloud. Once Fi had made up her mind, the universe itself would have a hard time changing it. She slipped on a silk eye mask, blue with little silver moons embroidered across it, and turned onto her side, already settling in.

I lay there staring at the ceiling, watching as her dreamcatchers swayed in the breeze from the slightly cracked window. The feathers drifted lazily, as if stirred by some unseen breath from the forest beyond.

It was just a tree. How bad could it be?

I rolled onto my side and closed my eyes, surrendering to whatever adventure Fi was dragging us into. Tomorrow, I'd be traipsing through the woods chasing legends, but if I'd known what else was going to be waiting out there, I would have begged, screamed, done anything to stop us leaving the safety of the cottage.

But hindsight, as they say, is a wonderful thing. And by the time dawn crept into the sky and warmed my face through the curtain's crack, it was already too late.

The worst day of my life had begun.

18

J asper

It's fucking typical, isn't it? The moment I finally get to kiss Sasha, the one thing I've thought about more times than I'll ever admit, and Mum interrupts, like the universe just couldn't even let me have that.

No... that's not fair. Mum's unwell. And I'd do anything for her. Even if it means putting what I want, what I need, on hold. Again. That's why I'm still here in Wychbold Cove at twenty, fixing the fences my dad walked away from and chasing down groundskeeping jobs while everyone else seems to be moving on. This place, it's stitched into my skin. I know every worn stone, every salt-cracked wall. I've always said I'd grow old here, build something real, something lasting. A home. A family.

But some nights I lie awake and feel this pull in my chest. That restless itch to see the world. To get lost in it. A few reckless years just to breathe, to be somewhere no one knows my name. Like Sasha's doing, off chasing sunrises in countries I've only seen on maps. I'd give anything for that. But I can't. Not with Mum the way she is. I swore I'd never turn my back on her. Not like he did. And I meant it. She deserves better than that.

Still, sometimes I wonder... if I'd even know who I was if I ever left this town.

She'd hate to know how much I've given up. How much of myself I've packed away just to keep things running. But I see her struggling at times, she can't keep up with Evermore for much longer, not with her health the way it is, so I stay. I always stay.

But then there's Sasha.

God, Sasha.

The other night, listening to her talk about her travels, all wide eyes and wild hands, it hit me like a punch to the ribs, an almost physical reminder that she would be doing these amazing things while I was stuck here.

Every place she described, I could see it. She made it real just by speaking it aloud. That's her gift. She belongs everywhere. There's nowhere on earth where she wouldn't fit in. She's magnetic like that.

And she doesn't even know. Doesn't see how she draws everyone in without trying. She's sunlight in a storm, she's a candle, and the rest of us, we're just moths to her flame. Just lucky to get a glimpse at her light.

When she fell into my arms a few weeks ago, flustered and rambling, I knew then. I wouldn't be able to hide it any longer. This had to be the summer I told her. All of it. It's been sitting under my skin like a slow burn for years. I told myself it was just friendship, back when we were kids. But then she would leave. And the silence she left behind didn't feel like missing a friend, it felt like more.

I dated other girls. Tried to distract myself. Chloe lasted the longest. Nine months. I really tried and she was a lovely girl but the second I saw Sasha again, barefoot in the garden, curls wild, laughing with Fi, I knew I'd been kidding myself. I could never love anyone like I love her.

So I drove to Chloe's house and ended it that night. It wasn't kind. It wasn't noble. It just was. I didn't want to waste any more of her time, and I couldn't keep pretending. Not when Sasha existed in the same world.

And now... the kiss.

It shattered something in me. That barrier I'd been holding up for years. She kissed me back. Not out of curiosity. Not because it was convenient. Because she felt it. I wonder if she has any idea how deep it runs in me. How her voice can calm the chaos in my head. How I ache to run my fingers through that wild mane of hers, even if she spends half her life trying to tame it.

But she's leaving. Again. Off to chase her dreams while I stay here. Maybe telling her how I feel will ruin everything. Maybe it'll make the goodbye harder. Maybe it'll make her stay and I'd hate myself for it. I don't want to be the reason she gives up the world. I couldn't live with that.

But still… if all I ever get is that one kiss, that one moment where time stood still and she was mine, I'll take it. I'll drag it with me through every dull day and sleepless night.

Because I love her. In ways I probably shouldn't. In ways that make it hard to breathe when she's not around. And maybe that love won't ever be simple, or easy, or even returned the way I want it to be.

But it's hers. Always has been.

19

The heat from the barbecue hit me full in the face, a sudden wave of warmth like that first step off a plane on holiday. I watched Jasper flip another burger, the shimmer of the grill distorting the view of the rose bushes in the distance. He looked so focused, brow furrowed slightly as he worked, and I couldn't stop watching him. My heart skipped—God, I'd fallen hard. This summer had cracked something open in me. I found myself replaying the memories in quick succession, little flashes of moments that now felt impossibly vivid. How had I missed this before? I'd been in relationships, sure, but nothing that made me feel like this. Nothing that had settled so quietly and surely under my skin.

Almost like he could hear my thoughts, Jasper turned, flashed me a grin, and winked before turning back to the sizzling grill.

I let out a breath, a quiet laugh escaping, and wandered barefoot across the patio. The tiles were cool beneath my feet, still damp from earlier splashes. The smell of cooking meat hung thick in the air, but there was something softer underneath too—the sweetness of jasmine from the flowerbeds nearby. Wooden troughs lined the patio, overflowing with bursts of pink, purple, and yellow petals that softened the clean, modern lines of the space. Vines curled up the white walls of the pool house, their dark green tendrils framing the half-glass door like nature reclaiming its place.

The pool stretched out in front of me, curved like a teardrop nestled into the patio's edge. Its surface gleamed in the sunlight, a deep, inviting blue. Ripples shimmered gently across the water, catching the light, and a few empty beer cans lay abandoned by the edge, their reflections wobbling on the surface like lazy echoes of earlier fun.

Around me, our friends lounged on pale green sunbeds, drinks in hand, laughter spilling into the warm afternoon air. The chairs were scattered at odd angles, evidence of weeks of use and no one bothering to put things back in order. Sloane, Joe, and Sebastian sat near the grill, legs dangling off their loungers, deep in conversation. Jasper, cheeks flushed from the heat, lifted a few sausages off the grill and laid them carefully on a plate. The hum of voices mingled with the upbeat pulse of "T-Shirt Weather" by Circa Waves, playing from someone's speaker. Every now and then, Jasper glanced my way, and each time felt like a secret passed between us.

I folded my arms around myself and smiled, content.

He'd arrived back at the house just before two, right as I was crumbling the last chunk of feta into the salad. He'd assured me Eva was fine, curled up in front of the TV watching reruns of her beloved WWE SmackDown. He'd made sure she had everything she needed: a giant bottle of water, snacks within reach, her phone plugged in, and strict instructions to call if anything came up. I'd laughed when he told me she rolled her eyes and told him to bugger off. Typical Eva, fiercely independent, always taking care of everyone else. The idea of anyone fussing over her probably made her itch.

I wandered toward the table, the scent of grilled food growing stronger with each step. As I passed the pool, I trailed my toes through the water, letting its coolness skim across my skin. It was a small relief from the heat, a ripple of calm against the sun's steady press. I reached the table and popped a wedge of sweet chili halloumi into my mouth just as Fi came bustling up behind me, a large stoneware platter balanced in her hands.

She wedged it neatly between the portobello mushrooms and the corn on the cobs.

"What the bloody hell are those?" Joe's voice rang out from across the pool, suspicion clear as he eyed the oily green bundles Fi had placed down with great ceremony.

"Stuffed vine leaves," she said pointedly, glancing around at the blank expressions that met her. She looked slightly offended, and I couldn't blame her. I leaned over the table, studying them curiously. They glistened in the sun, tight little parcels slick with oil. I'd never once questioned anything Fi handed me, her food, like her magic, usually held unexpected brilliance, so I plucked one up, careful not to let it slip through my fingers.

The taste hit immediately, sharp, salty, bright with lemon and herbs. The rice inside was soft and fragrant, spilling out slightly as I bit through the tough outer layer. I licked the oil from my fingers, catching Fi's proud grin with one of my own.

"Burgers are done!" Jasper's voice broke through the moment, and he set down a steaming plate of meat in the last open space on the table. He took a step back, surveying the spread with a satisfied smile. He'd barely been through the front door before declaring himself "The King of the Grill," and I'd been more than happy to let him take the reins.

"Hey, Sash," he said, leaning in until his breath tickled the edge of my ear. Goosebumps sprang up across my arms. He nodded toward the pool house, where Marcus sat hunched in a deck chair, nursing a beer and looking more like a man stranded than someone invited.

"I'm gonna ask Marcus to join. If that's alright. I feel sorry for the bloke."

I followed his gaze and sighed softly. Marcus did look a bit pitiful, sunk into himself, staring at nothing in particular as he drained the last dregs of the bottle in his hand.

"Yeah, okay," I said, though I doubted Marcus would be all that keen to join in. Still, I couldn't fault Jasper for trying.

I watched from my spot as Jasper walked over, clasping Marcus's hand in greeting, then giving him a firm slap on the back. Marcus looked mildly startled, but he took the offered beer as Jasper sank into the chair beside him. I glanced at Sloane, who was too focused on watching Joe stack his plate with an absurd mountain of meat to notice Marcus at all. She didn't even blink in his direction. Relief washed through me.

Across from us, Fi had settled into a wicker basket chair between Sebastian's legs. Her crocheted bralette barely covered anything, and her cheeks were flushed—whether from the heat or from Seb's fingers toying with the frayed hem of her shorts, it was hard to tell. She looked luminous, glowing with the kind of joy that radiates without effort. She held up a vine leaf to Sebastian's mouth, and he took it in one bite, eyes going wide with appreciation.

Jasper returned to my side, handing me a cold beer before dropping into the chair beside me. I curled my legs up, folding them onto the seat, my white linen dress bunching at my ankles.

"He's just changing out of his work clothes, then he'll head over," Jasper said, settling in close and draping an arm around my shoulders. "He's alright, you know. We got chatting about motorbikes."

His touch sent a little thrill across my skin, a warm ache that curled low in my chest. I didn't respond. I didn't have much to say about Marcus, but I loved that Jasper never wanted to leave anyone on the outside. He had this quiet confidence, this gentle steadiness I hadn't really seen before. These past few days, I was seeing him differently. And God, it was so incredibly attractive.

After the plates were cleared away and the girls had made a freshly mixed pitcher of margaritas, we settled back on the patio, the afternoon sun still clinging lazily to the sky. I nestled between Jasper's legs on the lounger, my head light and giggly from the margarita and my stomach pleasantly full. The low hum of voices floated around us, punctuated by the occasional clink of glass or burst of laughter.

Marcus had eventually wandered over, though he kept to the outskirts. I might not have noticed if it weren't for Fi's musical laugh cutting through the chatter, when I glanced over, I saw it was Marcus who'd made her laugh. He clapped a hand onto Sebastian's shoulder, the three of them doubled over about something.

"Ah, you aren't that tough!" Joe's voice rang out, pulling my attention to where he was teasing Sloane, playfully pinging the strap of her black bikini top.

"Hey!" she giggled, batting him away, her dark lashes fluttering. "I am too! Aren't I, Sash?" Her pale eyes met mine with a look that was both pleading and amused.

"Toughest old bird I know," I replied with a grin. "I'd never have survived school without you. Tanya Henrys would've turned me into a hermit if you hadn't stepped in."

"Tanya who?" Fi asked, her voice laced with curiosity. The conversation quieted, everyone now listening. Jasper sat up slightly behind me, snaking his arm around my waist and pulling me back against him. His warm skin pressed to my back, grounding me. Even Marcus pushed his sunglasses onto his head, squinting in my direction as he sipped his beer.

I sighed, placing my glass on the concrete beside the lounger.

"Tanya Henrys is a nasty bitch." An angry voice but out before I could speak.

"Sloane!" Fi gasped, covering her mouth as Joe let out a loud snort of laughter. I joined in, shaking my head as Sloane gave a little shrug, twisting the silver ring on her toe until the black gem faced upward.

"What? She is. Or was anyway. Fuck knows where she is now." She lay back with a sigh, dragging her oversized baroque sunglasses down over her eyes.

"Tanya was in our class when we were about twelve," I explained. "She used to constantly make fun of my hair. Made that whole year unbearable." My shoulders slumped slightly at the memory. It had been so long ago, but the sting still lingered. Without thinking, I reached up to smooth down my curls, but Jasper caught my hand and pressed a kiss to my fingers. I melted into him a little more.

"One day," I continued, "we were walking back to Sloane's after school, and Tanya and her band of morons started following us. She was spouting her usual shit at me, this time it was something about me needing to 'wash the bird's nest on my head.'" I added air quotes with a roll of my eyes.

"Silly cow," Sloane muttered under her breath, her jaw tensing.

"Anyway," I carried on, shooting my best friend a grin. "Sloane turned around with this sweet-as-honey voice, which was obviously shocking, and told Tanya that her mum, who was a 'natural blonde,' had gorgeous hair because she bathed it in rose petals."

Marcus straightened in his chair at that, one eyebrow raised in quiet amusement. His mum, Sloane's foster mum, had dark brown hair. Sloane caught his look and raised both eyebrows back, daring him to say something. He didn't.

"We were just passing Old Man Cleary's house," I went on, "and he had this insane garden, flowers everywhere, and a massive rose bush. Sloane pointed to it and told Tanya that Old Man Clearys car wasn't on the drive and he must be out so she should go pick some petals, and Tanya, the absolute air head, believed her of course."

Fi giggled. "Rose petals are completely useless for hair!" She collapsed into laughter, clearly thinking that was the end of the story.

I grinned, holding back a laugh of my own. "Oh, no. It gets better. Tanya had just started picking petals when Old Man Cleary's sprinkler system kicked in and absolutely drenched her. I mean, soaking. Her backpack was dripping when she scrambled back to the pavement. I don't think her books survived."

Sloane looked smug, sipping her drink behind her sunglasses.

"How did you know the sprinklers would go off?" Sebastian asked, rubbing his brow.

"I walked that way every day," she said simply. "You notice things when you're alone with your thoughts that often."

"You weren't alone," Marcus cut in. "I walked home too."

She shot him a look. "Basically alone, then, wasn't I?"

There was an edge to her tone, but she moved on quickly. "Anyway, I saw them come on like clockwork. Same time every day. I was done with Tanya's crap, she needed taking down a peg."

"And then," I jumped in, the memory now glowing with that strange warmth nostalgia brings, "Sloane yells, 'I know you wanted Sasha to wash her hair, Tanya, but I didn't know you were going to give her a demonstration!'"

The group erupted. Laughing harder than we had all afternoon, the margaritas only making everything funnier.

"Sash," Sloane said, still giggling, "I never told you what I said after. I told her if she ever talked about you like that again, she wouldn't have any hair left to get wet."

Joe erupted into a roar of laughter.

"That's my girl!" He boomed, pulling her face to his for a kiss. They pulled apart and Sloane blushed.

"I mean, I do feel a little bad now," she added, settling back, "but it worked. She avoided us for the rest of the year."

I raised my glass and finished the last of my drink, a grin still playing at the edges of my lips. Around us, the group slowly returned to their conversations, the lull of afternoon stretching on, as easy and warm as the sun on our skin.

∞ ∞ ∞

Later, I lay sprawled on the sun lounger, the last rays of daylight painting golden streaks across the garden. My limbs were heavy and content, basking in the warmth still clinging to the day. From where I was, I could see Sloane and Fi by the food table, heads thrown back laughing animatedly. It was a beautiful sight, two of the people I loved most, bonding so easily. Despite being complete opposites in almost every way, they'd grown closer these past few weeks, like gravity had slowly drawn them together.

Fi turned away from Sloane and took Sebastian's hand declaring they were going for a walk. The others hollered and whistled as they disappeared into the trees, laughter chasing after them. I smiled to myself, stretching my legs out and soaking in the fading heat, my ears tuning into the low murmur of Jasper and Marcus as they packed up the leftover food. Their conversation drifted over to me in broken fragments, nothing specific, just voices against the hush of approaching dusk.

Today had been perfect. I ran my hands up my bare arms, chasing the lingering warmth, and turned my head lazily to the side, one eye cracking open to watch Sloane and Joe in the pool. They were tangled up in each other, laughing as their wet bodies glistened in the evening light. Earlier, Sloane had challenged Joe to a swimming race, an overly confident wager that ended with her shrieking and flailing when she realised she was no match for him. Naturally, she tried to dunk him instead, but she'd failed miserably. It hadn't stopped them from ending up wrapped around each other, giggling like school kids.

My gaze shifted back toward the house just in time to catch Jasper and Marcus disappearing inside with the Tupperware. My eyes lingered, okay, stared, at Jasper's retreating figure. More specifically, at his ass. I wasn't proud of it, but I also wasn't sorry. He really was... unfairly hot. Every part of him. I could feel my skin prickling with heat that had nothing to do with the sun. I sat up straighter, trying to push the thoughts down, rein them in. We'd had one kiss. One incredible, mind-altering kiss. And now I couldn't stop thinking about him. Or about where this was heading.

But the thought brought with it a slow, creeping weight. If this was going to be real, if we were going to be real, I would have to tell him everything. Not just the good stuff. The truth about what I was. About the coven. About Silas. My stomach twisted. I could already feel the cold creeping in, despite the sunlight still clinging to the garden.

I reached for Jasper's jumper at the end of the lounger and pulled it on, the sleeves swallowing my hands. The familiar scent of him hit me, spice and pine and something warm, and I breathed it in like a tether. It calmed me, grounded me, even as my thoughts spiraled.

Something moved at the edge of the trees, and I looked up to see Fi returning alone.

"You okay?" I asked gently as she approached. Her usual glow was missing, replaced by a kind of quiet tension. Her eyes were glassy, worry tucked behind the flicker of a smile as she nibbled her brightly painted thumbnail.

"Yeah, um… Seb had to go. I think I'm gonna head up early, finish my book," she said. Her gaze flicked briefly to the pool, where Sloane and Joe were still tangled together. "I'm fine, Sash. Just tired. And a little drunk." Her voice was breezy, but I could hear the hollowness beneath it.

I saw the flicker of something behind her eyes, something unspoken, but I didn't press, she clearly wasn't ready to talk about whatever had changed her mood within the past half an hour.

"Okay, well… you know where I am if you need me," I said, squeezing her hand gently.

She nodded and gave me a small smile before turning away. I watched her disappear into the house, the screen door clicking shut behind her. A beat later, her silhouette was replaced by two taller shapes, Jasper and Marcus, stepping out with easy laughter. They looked relaxed, shoulders loose, Jasper nudging Marcus with a grin as they walked across the lawn. I blinked. They were actually... getting along? After thirteen years of hating Marcus, the sight felt almost surreal.

"...and then he crashed into that lamppost!" Jasper said, mid-story, as they reached me.

Marcus doubled over with laughter, a sharp bark that was startling in its sincerity. I'd never seen him like that, unguarded, unpolished.

They fist-bumped, and Marcus veered off toward the pool house, still chuckling. Jasper dropped down beside me and playfully knocked his knee against mine.

"That suits you," he murmured, his eyes trailing over me in his jumper. "Though I bet it'd look even better on your bedroom floor."

I rolled my eyes, even as my cheeks flared. "Good one," I muttered, trying not to grin.

Movement drew my gaze back toward the pool house, where Marcus reappeared and sank into a deck chair just outside the door. He cracked open a beer, took a long pull, and stared straight ahead. I followed his line of sight and found him watching Sloane and Joe. Still wrapped around each other in the water, their foreheads touching, moving with the lazy rhythm of the pool.

Their lips met like the soft collision of waves, slow and tender, and the water cradled them in a silence dance. They pulled apart and looked into each other's eyes, suspended in the cool depths as if time itself had surrendered to their embrace.

I felt like an intruder watching them.

Then, suddenly, Marcus stood. The beer can crumpled in his fist, liquid spilling through his fingers like spilled emotion. He turned sharply, his face unreadable, and disappeared into the pool house, slamming the door behind him.

I blinked, jolted from the spell, and looked up at Jasper.

He raised an eyebrow. "He does seem to have a problem with her."

I nodded, frowning. "He always has. I don't think it's his fault, though. His parents… they were awful to Sloane. I think they twisted something in him. Like he's been brainwashed."

Jasper shrugged. "Shame. He's a decent guy otherwise."

I looked back at the pool. The water had taken on a new texture, less calm, more insistent, like it mirrored the undercurrent of emotion rippling through it's inhabitants.

"Fancy heading inside before we get treated to PornHub's version of The Little Mermaid?" I quipped, raising an eyebrow.

Jasper barked a laugh. "What do you know about PornHub?"

I grinned, dragging my tongue slowly across my bottom lip. "Wouldn't you like to find out?"

"Oh, more than you know," he smirked.

I squealed as he jumped up, pulling me to standing. My legs wrapped instinctively around his waist as his hands gripped my hips, igniting sparks everywhere his skin met mine. His lips crashed against my own, hot and urgent, the kiss deepening as my fingers knotted in his hair. The world narrowed to just us, heat, breath, want. His grip tightened, and I melted into him, every cell alive with the need to be closer.

But then he pulled back, panting, a flicker of conflict crossing his face.

"However," he said breathlessly, lowering me to the ground, "I should go check on Mum."

I nodded, swallowing the disappointment blooming in my chest. I understood. I really did. But it still stung.

"Send her my love," I murmured, forcing a smile.

"Thanks, Sash." His hand found my chin, tilting my face to his. His eyes locked onto mine, warm and searching. "I'll text you later."

He kissed me again, slow this time, lingering, like he didn't want to leave. Then he turned and walked away, back toward the cottage.

I watched him go, the taste of him still on my lips, my fingertips brushing the spot where his kiss had been.

20

"Good morning, sleepyhead!"

Fi's voice lilted into my dream, soft and sweet like birdsong, tugging me up from the depths of sleep. I blinked against the morning light, disoriented for a moment, until a pair of enormous green eyes appeared inches from my face, startling me properly awake.

I groaned softly, but the delicious smell of coffee hit me before I could complain.

"Time to get up! I have a surprise for you," Fi said, practically bouncing with excitement.

Propping myself up on my elbows, I squinted at her. She was holding out a coffee, and not just any coffee, it was gorgeous. The foam shimmered in the sunlight like it had been dusted with something magical.

"What is it?" I asked, taking the cup from

her carefully and eyeing the sparkle with suspicion.

"A caramel macchiato, silly, what else?" She flashed me her most innocent grin, which only made me more suspicious. "I just… added a little twist."

I didn't bother asking. Fi's magic always had a way of making ordinary things extraordinary, and I wasn't about to question it before caffeine. I took a tentative sip.

"Oh, this is amazing," I breathed, taking another mouthful. Warm, sweet, smooth. Whatever she'd done, I wasn't complaining.

She looked smug. "Good. Now get up and make yourself pretty. It's gorgeous out, and we're going somewhere."

And just like that, she pirouetted out of the room.

I raised an eyebrow at her retreating form but didn't press for details. With Fi, it was always an adventure.

Once I'd finished my enchanted macchiato, I padded across the hall to the bathroom and turned on the shower. I hit shuffle on my playlist and grinned as Miley Cyrus's husky voice filled the room. I lathered up with cherry-scented shower gel, singing along to Malibu with an enthusiasm the whole house definitely heard.

Back in my room, I slipped into a

white off-the-shoulder summer dress with a scalloped hem that brushed the tops of my thighs. I left my curls natural, just tamed them with a little oil, and then headed downstairs barefoot, the wooden steps cool beneath my feet.

On the kitchen counter, a new postcard caught my eye. I drifted over to it instinctively. The photo showed sweeping golden dunes under a blue sky, with the endless shimmer of Lake Michigan beyond. Sleeping Bear Dunes, somewhere I'd only ever seen in pictures.

I turned it over, smiling at the familiar slant of my Dads handwriting. He'd written about hiking up to the overlook, saying the view of the lake had taken their breath away. One of the most beautiful places we've ever seen, he wrote.

I sighed, a warm ache blooming in my chest. I pinned it to the corkboard in the corner of the kitchen, where a handful others were already clustered, snapshots of faraway places, little reminders that they were thinking of me, even from the other side of the world.

∞∞∞∞

By late morning, Fi and I were making our way across the garden. We waved to Marcus as he emerged from the pool house, towel slung over his shoulder, and then veered around the edge of the woods. The path we took was worn into the earth, a trail of sun-dappled dirt and old memories. We hadn't been to the lake yet this summer, and as we walked, something in my chest loosened.

The lake had always been our haven growing up, a place tucked far enough away to keep secrets safe. As we got older, we stopped making flower crowns and started whispering about boys. We spent less time making potions and more time testing love charms, not real love, of course. That kind of magic doesn't work. But nudging affections? *That* I got the hang of.

Still, I couldn't shake the feeling something was... off. Fi was suspiciously empty-handed. No blankets. No baskets. Not even her bag. Which was weird. I was pretty sure Fi had never set foot outdoors at lunchtime without at least one baked good. My fingers toyed with the malachite bracelet on my wrist as I glanced sideways at her.

The breeze whispered through the trees, carrying the scent of the outdoors. As we reached the clearing, the lake revealed itself all at once, a glittering expanse of still water, fringed by tall reeds and wildflowers that looked like little cups. Eva used to say they were fairy beds, and the thought made me smile.

Then Fi gave a little giggle. "You go on ahead. I'm right behind you."

My eyes narrowed. Yep, definitely up to something.

But I let her have her secret and stepped forward, letting the beauty of the lake wash over me. The surface glittered like glass. The sky was a perfect blue dome, only a few clouds drifting slowly across it. I felt like I'd walked into a memory.

And then, a soft cough.

I turned to my left, and everything else vanished.

Jasper.

He was standing beneath the trees, the sun catching in his hair and on the pale cream of his linen shirt. The top buttons were undone, revealing a glimpse of tanned skin and the lightest dusting of chest hair. His shorts matched the shirt, showing off strong, sun-kissed legs. His hair was pulled back into a loose knot, a few pieces falling around his face. He looked relaxed, warm, and infuriatingly handsome.

Behind him, a red and white checked

picnic blanket was spread on the grass, strewn with cushions. A collapsible table stood nearby, a wicker basket beside it with an open bottle of chardonnay and two glasses already poured.

I gasped, my heart skipping. My gaze flicked to his, and the grin on his face told me everything I needed to know.

Sasha looked behind her and noticed Fi had disappeared.

Of course.

Jasper held out a hand. I walked toward him in a daze, my dress fluttering around my thighs, and slipped my fingers into his. He brought them to his lips and pressed a kiss to my knuckles, slow and deliberate.

"Jasper, this is... I don't even know what to say."

He smiled, brushing a strand of hair from my face. "I told you, I've always dreamed of going to the lake with you."

My breath caught in my throat. I stood on tiptoe and kissed him, wrapping my arms around his neck. He pulled me in, his mouth warm against mine as he pushed my lips open to let his tongue explore my mouth, and suddenly I wasn't thinking about anything else at all. I felt the fireworks in my chest and returned the kiss with the same fervour, the molten river of anticipation running through my body.

We pulled apart and he guided me down onto the blanket, settling beside me. One arm slipped around my waist as he leaned in again, pulling me into his firm body, his other hand gently tipping my chin toward him. Our lips met, soft at first, then deeper, like we were breathing each other in.

As his hands roamed my body his touch sent shivers through me, and I knew then, there was no way we were making it through this picnic with our hands to ourselves.

I broke the kiss, breathless, my chest rising and falling as I looked up at him. Something unspoken passed between us, a look, a question in his eyes that I didn't need words to understand. His gaze dipped over me, lingering just a little too long on the swell of my breasts which threatened to break free from my dress, before meeting mine again. I gave a small nod. I was sure.

Jasper's jaw tensed slightly, and then his hand found the back of my head, gently fisting the hair at the nape of my neck as he tilted it up so my lips met his. My hands found the buttons of his shirt and worked them open quickly, desperate to feel his skin, to expose the solid man beneath me. His touch trailed down my body, settling on my thigh before inching higher, until his fingers brushed the edge of my lacy underwear. I was suddenly very glad I'd worn that particular pair, not that I'd imagined any of this happening when I left the house this morning.

He pressed his other hand between my shoulder blades, guiding me into him as his mouth left mine and trailed kisses down the side of my neck, then my collarbone. I shivered. He moved with purpose, lifting the hem of my dress and pulling it over my head in one swift motion, leaving me bare in the warm summer air. I hadn't worn a bra, not wanting any straps to show and now the breeze moved across my chest, sharp and cool against my skin causing my nipples to peak.

Jasper took me in, his gaze slow and full of awe. And in that moment, under the weight of his eyes, I'd never felt more wanted. The man looked like he'd just been presented with sirloin steak, life he was starving, and she was his feast, ready to be devoured.

He shrugged out of his shirt and my breath caught. His body was sculpted and sun-kissed, and the sight of him made something stir low in my stomach and my mouth water.

When he leaned down, taking one of my nipples into his mouth, I let out a soft groan, my fingers threading into his hair, my spine arching instinctively toward him. The heat between us was dizzying. I reached for his waistband, then lower, feeling him, hard, solid, bigger than anyone I had been with before. He groaned against my skin as I held him through the fabric, it wasn't enough, I wanted to feel him.

I tugged gently at his shorts, and without hesitation, he freed himself, pulling them down and off with his boxers in one smooth motion. He sprung free and he was beautiful, I didn't waste any time resuming my movements from before.

"Sasha... fuck," he muttered, breathless, kissing a trail down my stomach. He moved up again, hovering over me, his skin warm against mine. He took both my wrists and pinned them softly above my head with one hand and slipped the other beneath my underwear, sliding them down slowly as he kissed every bit of skin he revealed. I felt like I was glowing, breathless, nervous, completely vulnerable, and somehow more alive than I'd ever been.

He looked down at me, and I looked up at him, the boy I'd grown up with, the one I used to follow around like a shadow. This wasn't really happening and I couldn't have been more ready for it.

My pulse quickened and I could hear my heartbeat in my ears as his hands found my thighs, gently parting them. I would've normally felt exposed, shy, even. But the way he looked at me made me feel like I was-

"Perfect," he whispered, more to himself than to me.

He took his time, sliding one finger along my entrance slowly, then adding a second. He sent tremors through me with just a glance, a breath. I whispered his name, begged, really, not out of desperation, but because I couldn't take the ache any longer.

He smiled, dipping his head, his mouth finding my clit, his tongue drawing circles. Every movement was precise, like he knew exactly how to unravel me.

My lips parted.

"G...God!" I croaked. My fingers reached for his hair, but he caught my wrists again, holding them gently at my sides as he continued, slow, steady, driving me wild, lightly nipping my tender bed as I writhed beneath him.

"I want you," I breathed, unable to keep the words inside. He looked up at me, his lips leaving a parting kiss then brushing softly against my skin before he let go of my arms and returned to my mouth, kissing me with such intensity that it stole the air from my lungs.

My freed hands reached for his cock again, smearing the drop of liquid around its large head with my thumb, the smoothness of his skin, the weight of him. He let out a low curse, and I watched as he reached for his shorts, his eyes never leaving mine as he pulled a condom from his wallet and rolled it down his large shaft with ease.

Then he was back over me, steadying himself. When he lined himself up against my opening, I gasped, the pressure was intense, but not unwelcome. He was careful, slow at first, then he filled me, all the way to the hilt. He palmed my thighs, stretching me open to him, filling me in a way I had never been filled before. My hands gripped his arms, needing something to hold on to.

He stilled for a moment letting me adjust to him as he let out a hiss of pleasure. His hand found the back of my neck as he pulled me towards him into a deep kiss. His tongue explored my mouth as he pulled back out slowly and I moaned into his mouth at the loss of pressure.

When he finally moved, the gentle movements from before were gone. It was like a spark ignited between us. His rhythm picked up, his breath rough against my ear as he whispered my name, and I felt myself unraveling all over again.

He hooked my leg over his arm, drawing himself in deeper with each thrust. I felt the pressure rising in my core, the eruption threatening to burst out of me. The world around us blurred into nothing. It was just him. Just us.

"Not yet," he murmured, his hand unhooking my leg and finding my throat, applying just enough pressure to make me catch my breath and come back from the edge. My eyes locked onto his, wide and wanting, marvelling at the way his body moved above me, the moment felt like an eternity suspended in heat and motion. This was the best kind of torture. Jaspers hard muscles tensed underneath my palms and my breath hitched in my throat. His eyes met mine as his fingers clenched around my windpipe as the speed of his hips picked back up, building the pressure inside me. I didn't think I'd be able to hold it off much longer.

And then—

"Come for me, Sasha."

That did it. His words were all it took.

My body clenched, a wave of pleasure crashing through me, sharp and deep and overwhelming. I cried out, holding onto him as tightly as I could. A second later, Jasper's body shuddered and he groaned my name into the curve of my neck, his own release shaking through him as we moved together, riding the waves of pleasure simultaneously.

Eventually, he slowed, brushing kisses

across my collarbone, his hands gentle again. I couldn't stop smiling. I felt weightless, like I was floating somewhere high above the world, and I never wanted to come down.

He rolled to the side and pulled me with him, our limbs still tangled as the sun warmed our skin. I bit my lip, glancing up at him, and his eyes softened as they searched my face. He reached out, gently tugging my bottom lip free with his thumb before leaning in to kiss me again, slow and sweet.

"You're incredible."

His voice was quiet but sure, and the way he looked at me, like he could see all the way in made something shift inside me. Not just butterflies, but something deeper, steadier. Like a knowing. I felt his words settle into my chest, warm and steady, and I couldn't help but smile.

"Honestly?" I said, grinning back. "You're not so bad yourself."

Our eyes met again, and for a moment, neither of us said anything. We just lay there, tangled up in the warmth of each other and the lazy hum of the lake around us. His fingers traced slow, reverent circles across my bare skin, feather-light and unhurried, like he was still committing every inch of me to memory.

Then, with a playful flick of his gaze down

my body, Jasper said, "Hungry?"

His tone was casual, but the glint in his eyes gave him away. I laughed.

"Starving," I replied, my voice still breathless with the afterglow. "Though maybe not just for food."

He sat up and reached for my dress, handing it back with a smirk. As he tugged on his shorts, I noticed him subtly pocketing something.

"Jasper."

He turned, all mock innocence, as I spotted the delicate white thong balled up in his fist.

"I'm keeping these," he said with a wicked grin, shoving them into his pocket like a trophy.

"You are not!" I gasped, half-scandalized, half-delighted. "I'm literally only wearing a dress. What if it gets windy?"

"I'm hoping it does," he said smoothly, handing me my wine glass and clinking it with his. "Maybe I'll get lucky twice today."

I rolled my eyes at him, but couldn't stop the laugh that escaped. Same Jasper. Same cocky smile and offhand charm. But now it hit differently, now it was edged with heat and history, and it was mine.

He downed his wine in one go, then refilled both glasses before turning his attention to the picnic basket. As he unpacked it, I watched him, the way his hands moved, the curve of his shoulders, the sunlight catching in his hair. I'd known Jasper for years, but something about today, the way he touched me, looked at me, wanted me, made it feel like seeing him properly for the first time.

We spent the rest of the afternoon wrapped in that golden haze, drinking wine and picking at strawberries and soft cheese while the lake glittered beside us. Later, when the sun climbed high and the heat pressed close, we stripped off again and slipped into the cool water. The moment his arms found me under the surface, our bodies pulled together like magnets, and just like that, the world melted away again.

I couldn't remember the last time I'd felt so blissfully, thoroughly happy. The wine, the sun, the water, the sex, it all soaked into my skin, until I felt like I was glowing from the inside out. And this time? This wasn't some fleeting summer fling. This was Jasper. My Jasper. I knew him, had always known him, but this was something new, something deeper. Something I didn't need to be afraid of.

When we finally started to pack up, I caught myself smiling like an idiot. I glanced at him, and the look on his face, the way his eyes softened when he looked at me, told me he felt it too.

We walked back slowly, the path winding through dappled shade and warm light. On the narrower strips, Jasper trailed behind me, claiming he was just being polite. But I felt his gaze on me, lingering on the curve of my back, the bare skin beneath my dress. I smirked to myself. So predictable.

At the edge of the woods, we paused. He had to check in on Eva, and I was starting to wonder what the girls had been up to without me. He pulled me in for one last kiss, and this one was slower, longer, like he didn't really want to leave. His hand lingered at my waist, and his eyes stayed on mine even after he pulled away.

"Incredible," he murmured again, before heading across the lawn toward the cottage.

I watched him go, heart still fluttering, and when I turned back toward the house, I spotted them, Fi and Sloane, both sprawled by the pool, wearing matching knowing grins.

I made my way up the hill, trying and failing to stop the flush rising in my cheeks.

"Well…" Sloane said, raising an eyebrow. "You definitely look like you've had a good day."

"Care to tell us all about it over girls' night?" Fi added, biting back a smirk.

I laughed, tossing my hair over one

shoulder like I could somehow play it cool. "That sounds amazing. I need to keep this buzz going."

I leaned in, lowering my voice playfully. "Trust me, I've got so much to tell you both."

Sloane let out a dramatic gasp as Fi squealed, and I winked at them both before adding, "But first... I need to go find some underwear."

I've decided something. That man in the
program was going to kill that girl but the police got his. Im
going to actually do it. They wont get me. Those girls dont even
know that I've been watching them and even mum keeps asking
me where I've been going and she believed me when I said I
was doing a school project. I am going to kill them though, I
am going to kill them though. I've found such a gold place to
do it. It's all ready and Im so excited. I've thought it
through perfectly and tomorrow is the day. Im going to

21

*T*en years old

The sun streamed through the sheer curtain in Fi's bedroom, casting soft, dappled patterns across the duvet as I blinked myself awake. I lay still for a long moment, letting my eyes wander the familiar walls, lined with shelves of curious oddities, glass bottles holding dried herbs, and a string of feathers and bones that twisted lazily in the breeze from the open window. My gaze settled on the painting above Fi's desk, the butterfly Briar had made for her when she turned seven. I'd always adored it. The shimmering blue wings, dusted with gold leaf, glowed like stained glass in the morning light. It was beautiful, delicate.

I breathed in deeply, letting the soft, herbal scent of chamomile from Fi's duvet calm me. But the calm didn't last long.

"Wake up, Sash!" Fi burst through the door, sunlight trailing behind her like she'd brought the whole morning in with her. She was already *dressed, her pale yellow top tucked into her favourite frayed denim shorts, and in her hands were two steaming glass mugs, each filled with a translucent pinkish brew, petals and leaves swirling slowly within.*

"I've been up for ages," she said with that signature Fi grin. "Made us adventure tea. Keeps our heads clear."

I pushed myself up on my elbows as she placed my cup down on the nightstand. The warmth of it curled up into the air between us, sweet and a little earthy. Fi disappeared out the door and returned almost instantly with her ever-overflowing satchel, plonking herself beside me on the bed.

"I packed lunch," she said proudly, flipping open the flap. "Sandwiches, fruit salad, some of Mum's cakes..." Her eyes sparkled as she revealed the bag's chaotic contents: food nestled amongst spell jars, bundles of wild herbs, a crystal net bag, and a feather quill poking out the side like it had taken root there.

I couldn't help but smile. This was so Fi. But even as I laughed and reached for the tea, a nervous knot twisted itself into my stomach.

"Looks good," I said, "but... are you sure we should go to the Wishing Tree today?"

She paused only for a moment. "Yeah. I woke up feeling weird, you know how my gut is. For a second I thought maybe it was a sign, but then I had a cinnamon bun and felt fine. I think I was just hungry."

I nodded slowly, trying to ignore the unease that hadn't left me since Linus told us that story.

Half an hour later I was dressed and standing in the cottage's kitchen chewing on the last remnants of a cinnamon bun, I shifted my weight nervously from one foot to another as I waited for Fi to come back downstairs from whatever she was doing now. My eyes wandered over the quirky decor, the space was a charming jumble of mismatched patterns and bright colours with an assortment of knick knacks scattered about. I tried to keep my distance from Briar who was seated at the kitchen table, absorbed in her breakfast and the newspaper. I felt the awkwardness of the moment, my gaze drifting around the room to avoid any unnecessary conversation. My attention was drawn to a painting on the wall, its vibrant blue frame standing out amongst the otherwise busy decor. The painting depicted a man in a long purple cloak, proudly standing next to a tree he had clearly just planted in a field. The man's expression was almost whimsical and there was something oddly captivating about the scene. The artist had clearly poured a lot of personal style into the piece and the man's stance was both proud and peculiar. I noticed a signature at the bottom, but it was too small and intricate for me to decipher from where I stood. As I continued to study the painting I heard the soft shuffle of footsteps coming down the stairs. Fi emerged from the hallway, running her hands through her hair, her expression brightened as her eyes landed on me.

"Ready to go?" She asked, her voice cheerful and eager. I nodded, giving one last glance at the painting before turning to follow Fi and waving goodbye to Briar who was still sat at the kitchen table.

"Where did you tell your parents we were going?" I whispered as we crossed through the raised flower beds at the back of the cottage and underneath the sweet pea arch that led into the woods.

"To the lake." Fi said simply, "Had to pack my swimming costume and everything." She laughed and I snorted in response.

"What are you going to ask The Wishing Tree for?" I mused as I stared at the back of Fi's braided head as we traversed the narrow pathway around the edge of the woods. Fi's head tilted in front of me and I could picture her scrunched up nose as she thought of her response.

"Hmm... I'm not really sure. I was thinking about it last night, about how all those poor women had nothing and how important their wishes were. I'd hate to sound ungrateful for my life."

My brow furrowed as I thought about what Fi had said and a small wave of guilt washed over me when I remembered how I was thinking of asking the tree to make Ryan in my form class pay more attention to me. I thought hard, delving deep down inside and trying to access that part of me that Fi always told me about. Where my intuition was. I reached into my pocket and rubbed the sodalite that Fi had given me a few weeks ago.

"I think I'm going to make a wish for Sloane." I said finally. "For her to eventually be free from her foster parents and for her to be able to come to Evermore with me one day. She would love this you know..." I trailed off sadly, "she loves going on adventures. She always says anywhere outside of her house is an adventure." Fi dropped back slightly as the pathway widened up and took my hand squeezing it lightly, a melancholy look on her face.

"I know." She said softly, as we walked on a bit further in silence.

The ground beneath us was damp and the smell of petrichor hung in the air like a blanket on a washing line. It had rained heavily overnight and the leaves on the trees glistened in the rays of the morning sun. Light droplets fell around us every time the wind blew but none ever landed on us, I assumed Fi had something to do with that. The forest always bent to her will.

We had just got about five minutes past the clearing that we had made our den in, the surroundings suddenly not looking familiar, when the hair on the back of my neck began to prickle. I suddenly felt vulnerable, like I was exposed. I stopped still, my eyes scanning the surroundings.

"What's wrong?" Fi had stopped abruptly behind me, nearly crashing into my back whilst not paying attention. Her eyes followed mine around the treeline.

"I... I don't know." I responded honestly. "Something feels off."

"Look over there!" Fi's finger pointed over to my left towards a large sequoia tree that had a black jacket hanging over one of the lower branches.

We both made our way towards the discarded garment slowly, it looked weathered and dirty, like it had been forgotten about a long time ago.

"Creepy." Fi murmured. "A weird place to forget your coat, we're pretty far out now." Her statement was met with silence and she looked over at me. I was tracing my fingers over the dark trunk of the tree. The forest was much more dense where we were now and once the sun dipped behind a cloud it was much darker than when we had set off this morning.

"They look like knife marks." I said, my eyes not moving from where my fingers moved over deep and erratic slashes.

"Oh poor thing." Fi stroked one of the branches in front of us sympathetically. "Why do people have to ruin what we're so blessed to have."

My breathing was still shallow, something about our day had changed and I could feel it. "Come on." Fi tugged my hand away. "Jasper said it was only a bit further up this way."

I followed my friend further into the woods, her bare feet tinkling with the sounds of anklets as she walked. She was babbling on about some spell her dad had messed up the other day which resulted in his temporary baldness. She was giggling to herself, her hands moving animatedly, but I couldn't focus on the story properly. I pulled my lilac cardigan further over my shoulders as I shuddered slightly, I knew it wasn't cold but I couldn't warm up. My eyes darted around as we walked, looking for a reason I felt this way. I noticed the remnants of an old campfire through the trees to my right and although the sight itself wasn't sinister it still bothered me. Fi stepped on a pile of wet leaves and the light squelch made me grimace, everything felt off balance.

"Look!" Fi gasped and my head snapped upright ahead of us. "That must be it."

A gigantic tree stood in front of us, its

branches gnarled and knotted out in every direction. It was huge, I had never seen anything like it, it looked straight from a storybook. It reminded me of the front cover of The Faraway Tree, Eva used to read it to me when I was younger and I'd loved it so much. I'd once even asked Fi about it, I thought maybe like so many other stories by non magic folk it had derived from something real and I had been so excited at the idea of going up into the clouds and visiting other lands. Especially the land of birthdays, that was my favourite. Fi had looked thoroughly bewildered when I'd first asked and after I'd shown her the book I was completely devastated to find out it wasn't real. I made a mental note to ask Eva if she still had the book once we got home.

The sun's rays beamed out from behind the tree highlighting the dust motes dancing in the air, lifting my mood immediately, it really was beautiful. The huge trunk had deep crevices etched into it, some of them shelved items such as fallen acorns and leaves, others looked like they had been made into homes for various critters. The tree itself stood in its own clearing, like the forest had made room specifically to showcase it, the surrounding trees bent in towards it like they were bowing down to its presence and its giant roots jutted out of the ground, anchoring it in place. I noticed that around the base of the tree various items were placed neatly; an old bunch of flowers gently wilting, returning back to the earth and a small wooden box that looked like it had been there for so long one of the large roots was slowly swallowing it. Fi looked over, noticing me inspecting the items.

"They look like offerings." She said, as she leant over to caress a herb swag that had been tied from one of the lower branches. "I didn't even think about that.." She trailed off, kneeling down and lifting her bag onto her lap. She started rummaging inside, muttering to herself. "Aha!" She exclaimed, pulling a medium sized peridot out followed by a bunch of foliage, she gently removed one sprig of rosemary and then carefully tied the herb onto the crystal with a long blade of grass she plucked from the ground. She inspected her work happily, and then pressing the bundle to her heart she said a few words to herself under her breath then placed it carefully at the base of the tree trunk.

"For Sloane." She said matter of factly, smiling over at me. I returned her smile. I wasn't entirely sure of the magickal properties of the stone and herb but I was grateful to Fi anyway. She knew what she was doing.

We straightened up and admired the large tree in front of us, Fi walked closer to the main trunk, gently tapping her fingers on the bark as she went. I could hear her speaking words *of thanks to it, for all its wisdom and for the care it had shown people. I was pretty sure the tree wasn't replying but Fi seemed not to notice, either that or she could hear something I couldn't. She carried on her conversation as I explored the area I was in. I could hear Fi asking the tree something about the goddess Gaia when out of the corner of my eye I noticed something smooth hidden amongst some of the underbrush surrounding the roots. I made my way over and parted the grass, it was dirty and worn, years of being touched by the seasons by the look of it. I dug my fingernails in the ground around it, I didn't know what had drawn me into this item. It didn't look like anything special, it was a dull white with weird indents in it and it was much bigger than I'd first thought. I finally managed to wiggle it loose as I heard Fi approach from behind me.*

"What have you found?" Fi was now peering over my shoulder as I freed the item from the ground. Turning it over in my hand we both let out loud screams as I let the skull roll from my palm.

"Fi, is that human?!" I was on my feet, my chest heaving as I kept my eyes on the hollow bone in front of me.

"It looks like it. The eye sockets and nose and everything. It even has a few teeth left in it and they aren't sharp enough to belong to an animal."

315

The sun disappeared once again behind a cloud in an almost sudden motion, plunging the clearing into an eerily dim light. I felt cold again and my heart seemed to be beating out of my chest so loudly it was the only sound travelling into my ears.

"I don't like this anymore Fi, can we go?" I knew I sounded like a baby but the feeling I'd been having all day had returned tenfold and I had to get out of there. A rustle came from next to us and we both startled. Fi grabbed my hand as we stared into the bushes, her chest rising and falling rapidly. My gaze flicked back to the skull lying in front of me. Whose was it? Was it an offering? And if so, who left it here? Were they murdered? Questions flew around my mind. I wanted the answers but I knew I wouldn't get them. We could never tell Briar and Linus that we'd come here, I knew we'd be in too much trouble. And telling my parents or Eva was even further out of the question, they'd never understand.

"Yeah, let me grab my bag, let's get out of here." Fi made to move, releasing my hand as she bent down to grab her belongings. A coldness set into my bones. I took one last look up at the tree, what had seemed so beautiful and magical only a few moments ago now seemed to tower above us in judgement, ancient and knowing and I on longer felt welcome in its presence. I exhaled, trying to

steady myself as a loud crack of a tree branch sounded out directly behind us and then... everything went black.

22

I was really trying to pay attention to what Fi was saying about the protective properties of the rowan tree, honestly, I was. But every time my mind slipped, just for a second, it was like I could feel him again. Strong arms around me. Fingers grazing the tips of my nipples. His hand around my throat.

My face burned.

"Sasha?" Fi's voice cut through my haze. I looked up and met her gaze, mildly annoyed, lips pursed, one brow lifted.

A choked sound escaped my throat before I could form anything resembling a sentence. Sloane glanced up from the book she was practically inhaling, squinting behind it, and snorted.

"Leave the girl alone," she said with a grin. "Poor thing's got a serious sex hangover."

"Sasha, I was just talking about the rowan tree in the cottage garden," Fi went on, ignoring Sloane completely. "Remember when we were underneath it that time and —"

The doorbell rang, slicing through the air like a lifeline. I bolted upright, flashing Fi an apologetic smile before rushing out of the room and into the hallway.

"Saved by the bell!" Sloane called after me.

I pulled open the front door. "Pizza?"

A girl about my age stood on the doorstep, drenched from the sudden downpour. Her dark hair was tucked beneath a bright blue cap, wisps of it clinging to her cheeks. Water dripped off her coat, the rain still dancing on the rooftop above us, echoing under the overhang in that hypnotic, endless rhythm.

"Thank you!" I smiled as I took the warm boxes from her.

She nodded and darted back toward her little red Fiat 500, desperate to escape the wet.

I shut the door behind me, already enveloped in the rich, buttery scent of melted cheese and garlic. My stomach growled, loud and unashamed, as I made my way back into the living room, balancing the boxes like they were treasure.

Sloane had sprawled out belly-down on the chesterfield, legs crossed and kicking lazily in the air. She wore a short pleated black skirt and one of her favourite chunky knit jumpers, black and slouchy with a white collar peeking out beneath the neckline. Her legs were mostly covered by thick black socks, her chunky Mary Janes kicked off in a heap beside the sofa. Her face was buried in a heavy, hardcover book, one Fi had fetched from her house earlier. More books lay scattered around, colonising the floor and overtaking every available surface.

Hozier's voice melted through the room like honey as Work Song played softly from the TV. I turned toward Fi. She was leaning over the console table, another book laid open before her. As I watched, a page turned by itself. She fidgeted with the tie on her long emerald cardigan, the fabric brushing the tops of her thighs as she shifted her weight. Her dark brown skirt brushed the floor, and the silver jewellery stacked on her wrists and fingers sang softly every time she moved.

"Food's here," I called, dropping the boxes onto the coffee table and flipping one open in search of my usual.

"Mmm, I'm starving," Fi said, abandoning her book and snagging a slice immediately. The cheese stretched in long, gooey strings before snapping.

"Beer?" I offered, watching the trail of cheese land unceremoniously on the table.

Fi gave me a thumbs-up mid-chew. Sloane just grunted.

The air smelled of rain on hot concrete —thick and sweet, almost steamy. I padded into the kitchen, cracked open the fridge, and grabbed a few cold bottles. Outside, through the open doors to the garden, Evermore's lawn shimmered under the storm. It was still warm, the air thick with late summer heat, but the rain brought a hush, a kind of peace. It matched our evening perfectly.

I curled back up in the armchair I'd been in earlier, folding my bare legs beneath me. I was still in the white dress I'd worn that morning, though I'd pulled on a pale blue cardigan when I'd gone upstairs earlier, for underwear. My cheeks warmed again at the thought of the thong still tucked into Jasper's shorts pocket.

Nope. Not thinking about that again.

I grabbed a slice of pizza and delicately picked off the gherkin perched on top, popping it into my mouth. Heaven. Sloane had mocked my "weird" pizza order for years, but I knew it was just because she was a certified pickle-hater. People were either passionately for or aggressively against pickles, there was no in between. Luckily, it worked in my favour. Sloane always gave me the gherkins off her burgers, and I always gave her the small, extra-crispy fries at the bottom of the bag. We balanced each other out. I smiled to myself as I took a bite, she was the yang to my yin.

I let my eyes wander around the living room as I chewed. We hadn't spent much time in here this summer, but it had always been one of my favourite rooms. Most of the house had been designed by the interior designer Mum hired before that first summer here, but this room, this one was all Gabrielle.

Floor-to-ceiling windows made up most of the walls, and right now the rain outside painted them in streaks of gold, each droplet catching the light like a tiny jewel. Soft curtains in pale greys and whites framed them. The sofas were solid and heavy but covered in plush grey fabric that gave them a sleek, modern feel. All the furniture was pale wood, maybe pine, or bamboo?

But it was the fireplace I loved most. A tall brick column that reached all the way up to the high ceiling, its hearth framed in black metal. On our occasional winter visits, we lit roaring fires there and drank hot chocolate wrapped in duvets. It made the whole place feel like magic. Tonight, though, the room looked like chaos. Books, pizza boxes, random clothing, it was a glorious mess. Eva would lose her mind if she walked in right now. I promised myself I'd tidy before going to bed.

"You not eating, Sloane?" Fi's voice pulled me out of my thoughts.

Sloane blinked up, stretching with a groan and cracking her neck. Fi winced.

"I am," she said. "I'm starving." She pulled a box into her lap and started digging in with the enthusiasm of someone who hadn't eaten in hours.

"What were you so into?" I asked, nodding toward the book still open beside her.

"Dark magic…" Her voice was quiet, almost embarrassed. "I'm just curious about it, that's all."

Fi groaned and raised a finger, still chewing.

After swallowing, she rolled her eyes. "Sloane, how many times? It's not a bad thing. I'd be more worried if you were reading the Malleus Maleficarum!"

She laughed, a loud, abrupt bark, and looked at us expectantly. I glanced at Sloane. She shrugged.

"Honestly," Fi muttered. "I'm wasted on you two. Where's my dad when I need him? He would've howled at that one. I'll have to remember to tell him."

She giggled to herself and finished her pizza. I had no clue what she was talking about and didn't dare ask, not if it meant sitting through another of Fi's history lectures. I made a mental note to look up Malleus Maleficarum later.

Fi wiped her hands on a napkin and went on. "Anyway. Sure, there are bad witches. But that goes for everything. Humans. Animals. You wouldn't assume every dog was dangerous just because of its breed, right?"

Sloane raised an eyebrow. "That's exactly what people think, Fi."

Fi faltered, then regrouped. "Well, those aren't the people you want to listen to, are they? Normal, sane people know there's good and bad in every race, religion, breed, or belief. Same goes for witches. Same goes for dark magic."

"I get you," Sloane said, nodding. "Just... why does it have to be called dark magic? It sounds evil."

"It's not," Fi said with a satisfied smile. "And anyone in the know knows that."

"Fair enough." Sloane shrugged and bit into her slice again.

For a while, we ate in companionable silence, flipping through books, occasionally reading aloud spells or strange facts about herbs or crystals. It was the kind of quiet that felt alive.

"This is cool..." Sloane's voice cut through the lull. She didn't look up.

Fi and I glanced at her.

"Hexes," she went on. "Apparently, they're abilities you're born with. Rare, and powerful. Can't be taught."

"I thought a hex was just a curse," I said, frowning.

"That's how humans twisted it," Fi replied, stretching out on the sofa, hands over her stomach. "They turned it into some Disney villain nonsense. But a real hex is different."

Sloane flipped a page. "Says here a hex can be good or bad for the witch who wields it, and even more so for the people around them. Control is everything."

"What kind of hexes are there?" she asked, eyes flicking up to Fi.

Fi shrugged and started scanning the spines of nearby books. "My mum once told me her great-aunt could heal bones just by touching the affected area. That's the only one I've really heard about... but there must be some more information in one of these books somewhere... aha... "

She pulled out a thick, brown volume and flipped through it quickly before handing it to Sloane. "Try this."

Sloane propped it over her current book and read, brow furrowing. "Mind reading... healing..." She barked out a burst of laughter. "Manipulating bread!"

I laughed along with her. "Finally, a power

I could use."

Sloane grinned. "Ooh, listen to this one. 'The ability to stop a beating heart. This hex enables the witch to stop a heart dead inside someone's chest. Side effects include a temporary loss of magical ability... and a strong smell of burning from the body.'" She wrinkled her nose. "Imagine dying and smelling like a blown-out candle."

The room spun.

My blood went cold, a memory coming back to me. My eyes glanced up, finding Fi who was listening to Sloane with interest, her face a mask of calm. I swallowed, my saliva sticking in my dry throat. My senses suddenly felt flooded and I was transported back to another time. The air around me cold and a tightness around my wrists, plastic cutting into my skin causing blood to surface, screaming, struggling, tears.

And the sharp, unmistakable smell of burning...

...as a body crumpled to the ground.

∞ ∞ ∞

I lay in bed hours later, the soft rustle of sheets the only sound in the room aside from the steady pulse of rain. Each drop whispered against the world, gentle but insistent, like it was trying to speak a language only I could hear. Normally, rain soothed me, wrapped me in a kind of sleepy comfort. But tonight it felt different. Heavier. Like it was carrying something it wasn't saying.

I'd made it through the rest of the evening by faking it, smiling when I was meant to, laughing at the right beats. The girls had noticed something. I could tell. They'd both shot me little looks here and there, but thankfully, neither of them said anything. I wasn't sure I could've handled being asked what was wrong.

The rain changed, its uneven cadence coming in surges now. One moment soft and tentative, the next loud and urgent, slamming against the roof like it had a score to settle. It reminded me of my mind, how it pinged between short stretches of calm and sudden flares of anxiety. Even the pauses between drops felt too short, the silence unable to hold for long before the storm pushed through again. My heart matched its rhythm: erratic, unpredictable, a wild flutter against my ribs every time the windows shuddered beneath a gust. It was as though the storm outside was echoing the one inside me. The night felt too full, too thick, like even the sky couldn't settle.

I'd called Jasper before bed, hoping his voice might anchor me. It didn't. Not really. I couldn't tell him the truth, couldn't even come close to it, and the distance between what I felt and what I said made the call feel hollow. I'd told him I was tired, said I needed to sleep. I wished I could've curled into him, let his arms close around me like a shield. But at least I'd remembered to ask about Eva. He told me the bruise was now a vibrant purple, but she wasn't in too much pain. She'd gone up to her room with a lemon-shaped ice pack. I'd told him about our night, about the pizza, the girl talk and the laughter. I left out the spell books, the hexes, the unspoken thing clawing at the edge of my chest.

I rolled over with a sigh, yanking my pillow over my head like I could smother the thoughts out. My eyes squeezed shut, but the moment I did, his face appeared. Not Jasper's, the one I'd tried for years to forget. Groaning, I sat up, rubbing my face with both hands. Why couldn't my mind go back to the delicious daydream of Jasper's hands on my skin? That was supposed to be my comfort. My distraction. I closed my eyes again, willing myself to see Jasper, imagining his fingers tangled in my hair. Nothing. Just static.

I gave up, swung my legs over the side of the bed, and padded downstairs barefoot. The cold kitchen tiles grounded me a little. I filled a glass of water, leaned against the counter, and took small sips. The house was quiet but the rain was relentless, still thudding against the windows. I glanced out at the dark lawn beyond the glass doors of Evermore and shivered.

Could Fi really not remember the smell?

It had been so strong. Acrid and sharp, like burnt wires or scorched fabric, an unnatural kind of burning. I swallowed the rest of the water, rinsed the glass, and marched back upstairs, heart pounding with something closer to certainty than fear.

"Fi," I hissed as I pushed open her bedroom door.

Darkness met me like a wall, and for a moment I stood still, waiting for my eyes to adjust. Fi was curled under the covers, her hair a golden halo fanned out across the pillow. She looked so peaceful I hesitated.

Then I crossed the room, knees sinking into the rug beside her bed. "Fi," I said again, gently placing my fingers on her shoulder.

"Ah!" she gasped, jerking upright. "Sasha? What the—?"

She rubbed her eyes and blinked at me through the low light, confusion written all over her face.

"Fi," I said, leaning in, my voice barely above a whisper. "Do you remember the smell? The burning smell? That day…"

She flinched. Just the memory seemed to knock the sleep from her bones.

"Sasha, what are you talking about?" she asked, voice groggy but clearing quickly.

"That day. With Silas. When he… when he fell. There was a smell. Like burning. Do you remember?"

She blinked again, slower this time. "Yes, Sasha. I do. But…"

"The hex," I cut in. "The one in the book Sloane was reading earlier. It said that when the heart stops, there's a smell. Burning."

Her hand came to rest on my shoulder. "No, Sasha. No. He went missing. He was one of the missing kids. There were posters, television appeals—"

"Yes, exactly!" I stood up, shrugging off her hand. "He went missing after that day. No one saw him again."

I grabbed her hand and pulled. "Come on. I want to read that book."

I was already halfway down the stairs before I heard her footsteps behind me. We slipped back into the living room like ghosts. I hauled the big brown book onto my lap, flipping it open to the page.

"Right," I muttered, my finger tracing the

words. "…strong smell of burning from the now deceased body." I picked up where Sloane had left off. "Signs that a witch possesses this power can only really be confirmed after a post mortem has taken place. The heart affected will be rock hard inside the body. Calcified from the inside out and turned to stone."

I looked up at Fi. "I need to know, Fi."

She was pacing, her hands twisting together like they did when she was thinking too fast.

"Sasha… what are the odds?" she said softly.

I shrugged. "Same as the odds of me and Sloane both being witches. Same as my parents choosing this exact house in this exact sleepy village. Same as me meeting you, and everything we went through."

She exhaled, long and slow, and sat down beside me, taking my hand in hers.

"A hex is rare, Sasha. Like, really rare. They usually only show up in old bloodlines, families that have been practising for generations."

"But not impossible," I said, running a hand through my hair. "There was this one time… years ago. Sloane and I were about thirteen. She was telling me about something Mallory and Rory had done, I don't even remember what now, but it was awful, as usual. I was fuming, Fi. We were just sitting on the grass outside my house. Doing nothing. And then, out of nowhere, a bird dropped out of the sky."

I stood, arms flying up in the air as the memory surged back, vivid and terrifying.

"It just fell. Dead. Wings outstretched mid-flight. It was horrible, we both screamed and ran inside. My dad had to come out with a spade and a bag to pick it up. We even buried it. Had a little funeral under the apple tree."

I turned to her, heart pounding in my throat.

"But Fi..." My voice cracked. "The bird. It smelled like burning."

Fi stared at me. I could see her mind ticking through everything I'd said, every flicker of memory, every possibility.

Finally, she sighed. "Okay, Sash. What do you want to do?"

Relief washed over me like a wave. "I want to go back there. I have to. I need to see if there's anything... if there's something I missed. I need to know."

She nodded slowly, her voice trembling. "I'll come with you. But not now. Not in the dark. Let's wait for morning."

I nodded, accepting the logic, even though the urgency inside me felt like it was burning a hole straight through my ribs.

"Okay." I squeezed her hands. "Thank you. Come on. Let's go back to bed."

23

Ten years old

I forced my eyes open as we spun around, freezing in place. The angry boy from Chaihu was standing right behind us. His eyes glowed with the same rage from before, but this time there was a terrifying smile stretched across his pale face. I never realised such icy blue eyes could hold such burning hot fury.

Fi screamed beside me, the initial shock of someone being there, coupled with the clear, malicious intent plastered across his features, sent her into a panic. I grabbed her hand in comfort. We needed to leave. Now.

My brain screamed at my legs to run, but before my body could react, he lunged.

He towered over us by at least a foot, his lean frame showing the first signs of wiry strength.

"Don't fucking move." His voice cracked in the middle, the gravelly rasp of puberty

straining to assert dominance.

Fi broke into a sob beside me. That was when I noticed it, the glint of a large kitchen knife in his hand.

I darted my eyes back up to his face. That smug look of satisfaction. He knew he had us. He tossed a cable tie onto the ground at my feet and gestured with the knife in my direction.

"Tie her hands together. Tight."

My eyes flicked to Fi's. Her usually sparkling green eyes were bloodshot and brimming with fear. I hitched in a breath as she held out her trembling wrists. My eyes darted desperately around the deserted woodland, but I recognised nothing. We'd wandered too far. We should've listened to Linus.

"DO IT!" The shout shattered through my thoughts like glass. I flinched. Fi sobbed louder.

I wrapped the clear plastic around her wrists, threading one end through the small hole and pulling it closed.

"Tighter!" he barked.

I obeyed, wincing as the plastic cut into her skin, pressing against the fine bones in her wrists. He stepped closer, causing Fi to cower, her blonde hair spilling over her tear-streaked face. With the knife in one hand, he reached for her wrists with the other, testing the bind.

Satisfied, he turned his attention to me.

Shoving a hand into the pocket of his stained, oversized jeans, he pulled out another cable tie. He nodded to my hands, the rage still blazing in his eyes. It was my turn.

I sniffed, lifting my chin in defiance, an instinct I regretted immediately as the stench of sweat from his body hit my nose like a slap.

He scowled. Then, without warning, he grabbed Fi by her hair. She let out a panicked scream, followed by another sob.

He brought the knife up to her face, dangerously close to her eyes, his own gaze locked on mine.

"Fine! Stop! I'll do it!" I snatched the tie from the dirt and held it out. "Just leave her alone."

He smirked, clearly pleased with himself. Slipping the knife between his teeth, he wrapped the plastic around my wrists and yanked with all his force.

I hissed as pain shot up my arms, the plastic biting deep into my skin. Welts rose immediately.

"You're both going to walk in front of me," he said. "I'll tell you where to go. If either of you tries anything, I'll fucking kill you both. Then I'll go to your houses and kill everyone there too. Don't think I fucking won't."

He nodded to the left. Fi turned to comply, and I followed.

I felt useless. I could hear the blood rushing in my ears, every sense heightened to a painful degree, but none of it helpful. Fi was catatonic, the threat against her family seeming to *paralyse her entirely.*

We walked in silence, the boy mumbling directions. The forest grew unfamiliar. Every tree looked the same. I glanced at Fi, hoping she might know the way. But she stared ahead blankly, her red-rimmed eyes vacant.

There was no use. If I ran, he'd hurt Fi. Even if I tried to grab her and flee, we'd never make it, he clearly knew these woods.

The trees thickened, cutting off most of the light, until a derelict cabin appeared through the brush.

It looked like it had been swallowed by the forest, peeling dark wood, a crumbling brick base, vines crawling through gaping cracks. But there was no magic here like there was at Evermore. Just decay.

A once-functional hunting cabin, now gutted by nature and time. The broken windows, the heaps of debris, everything about it screamed danger.

He pushed us through the doorway into a ransacked room.

A filthy, frayed rug lay in the middle, its faded red pattern stained beyond recognition. Shattered glass littered the floor, and the threadbare sofa looked like it had been used for knife practice, its guts spilling from torn seams.

A pile of wilted red petals sat abandoned on a side table, the sight of them making my stomach churn.

The door slammed shut behind us, jolting both Fi and me.

She wasn't crying anymore, but her fear was plain. Her eyes darted around the room before landing on mine. She twisted her wrists and winced. Blood had begun to smear her pale skin, she'd been trying to wriggle free.

Suddenly, Fi was yanked backward again, her scream muffled by the thud of her body being dragged.

"STOP IT!" I shouted, the words ripped from my throat.

He smirked again, revelling in our fear.

Fi's sobs returned, raw and broken, echoing through the rotting walls as he threw her across the room.

She hit the ground hard, winded, her body convulsing with sobs.

Tears pricked my eyes, but I clenched my jaw. I wouldn't give him that satisfaction.

Desperate, I brought my wrists to my mouth and began gnawing at the plastic, praying, begging for it to snap.

"OI!"

He'd seen me.

He flung himself across the room and yanked me upright, dragging me toward a rusted radiator in the corner. Another tie appeared in his hand.

"No! Please, no!"

My voice cracked, desperate and raw, but he didn't care. He tied my wrists to the pipe, securing me in place.

He snorted, pleased, and walked back to Fi.

He picked up the knife again and began pacing beside her as she trembled on the floor.

His expression had shifted, no longer angry, just... disconnected.

He mumbled under his breath. I caught pieces. Something about a man on TV. About doing what that man couldn't.

I pulled at my restraints, pain lancing up my arms, but the plastic wouldn't give.

I gasped in frustration. The sound must've broken his trance. His head snapped toward me, eyes dark and hollow.

He scratched at his scalp with the knife, sweat patches blooming under his filthy t-shirt.

Then he turned back to Fi.

A maniacal laugh burst from his chest as he lowered himself on top of her.

"STOP!" I screamed, but he didn't even flinch.

Fi began to fight back, kicking, thrashing, her sobs morphing into screams.

"Stop fucking moving!" he snarled, trying to wrestle her still. "Shut the fuck up, you stupid bitch!"

My panic consumed me.

He reached for the knife, fingers brushing the handle.

God, no. No.

Warm blood trickled down my arms as I fought against the ties.

"Ha!" he barked triumphantly, one hand on the knife, the other popping open the button of her shorts.

Fi screamed again as he pressed the blade to her chin.

Her breath came in ragged gasps, her body frozen in fear beneath his weight.

He laughed again, tugging hard at the denim.

My eyes slammed shut.

"NO!!"

The scream erupted from me, primal and gut-deep.

Then,

Silence.

A silence so thick it rang in my ears.

I opened my eyes.

The boy's expression was blank. His body crumpled forward with a dull thud.

Fi screamed again, shoving him off with all her strength, scrambling back to the wall.

We stared at him.

Silent.

Still.

Only the faint smell of burning in my nose

reminded me to breathe.

I looked up.

Fi's sunken eyes met mine.

She stood, her steps shaking. Kicked the knife away. Then grabbed it.

With trembling hands, she sliced through my ties.

I freed her in return.

"Come on! Now!" she hissed over at me as if not to wake the unconscious body in front of us.

She grabbed my wrist and dragged me out, the door slamming behind us with a final, echoing bang.

We ran.

And ran.

And ran.

Pain seared my lungs, my throat scorched raw.

We didn't know where we were going. We just needed to go.

Only when we passed The Wishing Tree did the woods begin to look familiar.

Fi veered right, leading us back toward Evermore.

The red petals came into view and bile rose in my throat.

We burst out of the trees and onto the lawn, collapsing in sobs and gasps.

Loud sobs burst from Fi's mouth as I grabbed her towards me, cradling her head against my chest.

"Shh, shh Fi it's okay. We're safe now. We're home." I stroked the dust covered hair off of her sweaty forehead. I felt anything but safe at that moment, but I knew for now we had gotten away from the monster in the woods.

24

5:47 a.m.

That's what the screen said when I finally caved and looked. I'd been pretending not to check it all night, clinging to the vague hope that I might've dozed off at some point without realising. But no. My body felt like it had been wrung out and left to dry, tight with anxiety, loose with exhaustion.

I unfolded myself from the twisted sheets and crept toward the pale green armchair in the corner, the one that had unofficially become a second wardrobe. My jeans were still there, slouched and half-crumpled. I tugged them on, followed by a soft white jumper that hung low at the sleeves. My hair went up next, messily twisted into a knot on top of my head. The motion exposed the sigil at the back of my neck, cool air kissed it, and a small shiver crawled down my spine.

I grabbed a pair of socks from my top drawer and padded down the stairs as quietly as I could, the old floorboards creaking despite my best efforts.

The kitchen was dim, pale morning light just beginning to stretch its fingers across the countertops.

"Jesus fuck!"

I jumped, nearly dropping my socks.

Marcus sat at the breakfast bar, silent as a ghost, a steaming mug of coffee clasped between his hands. The smell hit me, bitter, strong, slightly burnt.

"Sorry, Sash," he muttered, rubbing the back of his neck like it might undo the startle. His voice was husky with sleep or silence, I wasn't sure which. He looked... tired. More than usual.

He stood, stretching the thick muscles in his arms as he drained the rest of his coffee in a few slow gulps. "Just heading out for work."

He rinsed the mug, popped it into the dishwasher, and gave me a small, apologetic smile.

"See you later."

I didn't say anything back. Just nodded. Watched him walk out of the room like the weight of the world had grown heavier overnight. His shoulders hung lower than usual, his broad chest seeming to cave in on itself. He looked... hollow.

Through the window, I watched him slide on his helmet, tug his leather jacket over his navy polo shirt, and straddle the motorbike with practiced ease. The engine snarled to life, loud and jarring against the stillness of Evermore's morning.

But I couldn't worry about Marcus today.

I had my own demons to face.

I made a coffee of my own, trying to ignore how my hands shook just enough to spill a few drops on the counter. I sat where Marcus had been, the warmth of his seat already fading.

I fired off a quick message to Jasper.

Hope it goes okay today.

He was spending the day with his dad, some pre-arranged visit he couldn't get out of. I hadn't decided if I was relieved or disappointed. It would've been impossible to explain where I was going today.

I set my phone down, face first, and stared into the steam rising from my mug. I twisted the rings on my fingers, one by one, until my coffee went cold. By the time I glanced back at the clock, it was just after six-thirty.

That's when Fi walked in.

She was already dressed, carrying a

bundle of things in her arms. Her wide-leg trousers, pale blue linen, looked like they'd been plucked off the floor without much thought. Her jumper was cream and slouched off one shoulder, exposing the butterflies inked in delicate lines up her arm and curling along her collarbone.

She looked… different.

No jewellery. No layers. No floaty shawl or jangling bangles. Just Fi, stripped back and bare-faced, her hair pulled into a plain ponytail. Her eyes were rimmed in pink, and her hands kept twitching at the sleeves of her jumper like she didn't know what to do with them.

"Morning," she said softly, the word more breath than sound.

I offered her a weak smile, not trusting myself to speak yet.

"Before we go," she said, shifting the bundle in her arms, "I want to do a quick spell."

I nodded. Of course. It made sense, she was doing something to ease our fears. The last time we'd walked this walk, we hadn't come back the same.

I could feel it in my stomach even now, a tight knot of unease twisting itself tighter with every minute.

Fi knelt by the bifold doors, crossing her legs and laying out her tools in quiet, methodical movements. I watched her for a moment, then drifted to the door and stood there, chewing the inside of my cheek, eyes scanning the creeping dawn outside.

The air in the house felt thick. Safe, somehow. Contained. But it wouldn't last.

"Come on," she said gently, not looking up. "We need to get this done."

I joined her on the cold tile floor, legs folded beneath me. Her little collection of supplies was already arranged, candles, the glint of glass, and the soft sound of cork being pulled from a vial.

She handed me the salt.

"Close your eyes," she said. Her voice was steady now, focused. But I could see the tension in her fingers, the way she kept clenching and releasing her jaw.

"We're going to weave the protection around us first, from the inside out."

I obeyed, shutting my eyes tight.

The air around us shifted.

Fi's chant began low, melodic, like something ancient. The rhythm of it washed over me, grounding and strange. I could feel the hum of it, deep in my bones. The space around us seemed to pulse, warm and familiar, like the magic recognised us, like it remembered we'd been hurt.

She whispered again, more urgent now.

"The salt."

I opened my eyes just in time to see her hold out the tiny glass vial. My fingers trembled as I uncorked it. The grains inside caught the light like powdered stars.

Slowly, I began to pour them, careful and deliberate, watching them fall like snowfall into a circle around us.

"This is our line," Fi said, her eyes locked on mine. "It'll protect us once we leave the house. As long as we remember our intent, the magic will hold. Nothing gets through unless we let it."

I swallowed, nodded.

A flicker of warmth sparked in my chest, hope, maybe. Or maybe just the memory of it.

With the last sweep of salt, the circle closed.

A soft click in the air, like a door sealing shut.

We sat in the silence for a moment longer, letting the spell settle. Then Fi stood, brushing off her palms.

"Let's go," she said. Her voice didn't shake this time. "We'll be okay. Just trust the magic."

I stood too, my hand already on the doorknob.

And for a moment, just one, I let myself believe her.

∞∞∞

We hadn't walked this path since that day.

Every snapped twig and gust of wind still felt like a warning. My feet moved on their own, one step after the other, but my thoughts were spiraling, impossible to settle. The silence between us felt heavy, like we were both afraid to speak it into existence, to name the thing we were really here to find.

Fi didn't say anything, and I couldn't either. My brain was too busy panicking. Terrified that the thoughts I'd been thinking all night were about to stand up and confirm themselves in front of me. That I'd find whatever was in that cabin and know, without a doubt, that I was a murderer.

We passed the Wishing Tree, tall, gnarled, and unmoved by time, and I heard Fi suck in a sharp breath beside me. Her fingers brushed mine, and I instinctively reached out and took her hand, squeezing tightly. I didn't want to look at it either. Not after what happened. Not with the memories flaring up behind my eyes like an old film reel set on loop.

We trudged on. The air grew cooler as

we moved deeper into the trees, and then...
there it was.

The cabin.

Or what was left of it.

I stopped in my tracks, my breath caught somewhere in my chest. It had been ruined back then, half-rotted and unfit for anything but nightmares. But now? Now it was barely even a structure. The back room had completely collapsed, revealing the twisted skeleton of an old camping cot, its metal frame poking through shredded canvas like broken bones. Rotting wood was scattered in a heap around it, half-swallowed by dirt and weeds. The front door hung sideways on a single hinge, and wild brambles twisted around the foundation like claws, desperate to drag the place back into the earth.

I stomped through the tangled undergrowth, my trainers doing a better job of protection than the sandals Fi had on. I was halfway to the entrance when I felt the shift, Fi wasn't beside me anymore.

I turned and found her standing still, frozen in place like something had reached inside and turned her to stone. Her eyes were glassy, brimming with tears, and she was staring at the cabin like it was speaking directly to her. Her whole body trembled, the same panic I felt mirrored in the set of her jaw, in the way her arms hung uselessly at her sides.

She was back there, in her head. Reliving it.

I knew that look. I saw it in my own reflection more often than I cared to admit.

"You don't have to come inside, Fi," I said softly, careful not to startle her. "I can go on my own... I just... I have to know."

Her eyes snapped to mine, like I'd broken the trance. She blinked fast and shook her head, her voice hoarse.

"No, Sash. I'm coming with you."

I reached for her hand again. Her grip was firmer this time.

Together, we nudged the broken door off to the side and stepped into the shadows.

It took a moment for my eyes to adjust. The room smelled like damp earth and old ash. Ivy crept in through the cracks in the wall, draping across broken beams like a veil. The place was even darker than before, more overgrown, more decayed, but somehow... unchanged.

The sofa was still there, its cushions flattened and torn. The rusty radiator I'd been tied to still clung to the wall by a single bolt, sagging under its own weight. My gaze dropped to the floor, to the plastic zip tie still looped around the pipe. Another lay discarded nearby, brittle and yellowed with time.

I shivered.

The rug, what was left of it, was mouldering into the floorboards, its floral pattern eaten away by dirt and weather. And there, in the centre of it all, was the thing I'd been dreading most.

A skeleton.

Fi gasped, her breath catching sharp in her throat.

We didn't speak. We didn't need to. The torn blue fabric tangled in the ribcage, the way the bones lay collapsed like a puppet without strings, there was no question.

"Silas." His name slipped out before I could stop it.

It was definitely him, the remnants of his raggedy blue t-shirt lay in strips around his torso, clearly a by-product of whatever animals had left those nicks and grazes on the few remaining ribs left sticking up and the denim of his jeans still clung to what was left of his lower limbs.

I didn't realise I'd moved until I was nearly standing over him.

My legs didn't want to carry me forward, but I forced them to. I stopped just short of the skeleton, heart hammering behind my ribs. My knees wobbled. My fingers trembled at my sides.

"Well…?" Fi's voice came from behind me, barely above a whisper.

I opened my eyes.

Inside the hollow of his ribcage, nestled among splintered bone, was something smooth and dark. A stone. Rounded, polished by some invisible force, but unmistakably heart-shaped.

His heart.

My stomach dropped. A sob burst from me so suddenly I didn't even try to swallow it. I crumpled to the ground with a broken sound, the old rug scratching at my palms, dust catching in my throat.

"I did this," I gasped. The words tore out of me. "I did this…"

Fi was already there, pulling me into her arms, cradling me the way I'd once done for her when we escaped this place. Her warmth against me was the only thing keeping me upright.

But then—

The door finally gave way behind us, slamming to the ground with a deafening thud.

We both screamed, clutching each other like children. My breath vanished from my lungs as I turned, expecting—

"It's me! It's just me!"

Sebastian's voice cut through the panic, and then he was there, framed in sunlight.

His eyes swept across us, wide with confusion and concern, then landed on what lay behind us on the floor.

"Girls..." he breathed. "What the fuck...?"

Fi sagged against me, her tension breaking all at once. Relief. Her shoulders dropped, and I felt the shift in her body as she reached down to take my hand again.

She helped me to my feet, our fingers tangled like lifelines.

"We can explain..." Fi started, her voice cracking. She looked at me, a silent request to give them a moment.

I nodded. Wordless, numb. I turned toward the shattered doorway and stepped outside, brushing past Sebastian with a ghost of a smile. His brows furrowed, but he let me go.

The clearing welcomed me with quiet birdsong and dappled sunlight, so at odds with everything inside that house. I sank down onto a log, folding my hands in my lap, twisting the rings on my fingers one by one.

The tears came again, silent and slow.

I had killed someone.

Even if he'd deserved it, even if he'd meant to do worse to us, it didn't matter. He was gone. Because of me.

His face drifted behind my eyes again. The missing posters. Curls matted across his forehead, eyes like ice. I could never forget those eyes.

He was someone's son.

And they'd never known what happened to him.

Never would.

His body had been left to rot, to be picked apart by time and animals, hidden in this cursed place while the world moved on.

I felt hollow.

I didn't even hear the cabin door creak open again until Fi and Sebastian stepped out into the clearing. Fi's face was streaked with tears. Her eyes were raw, swollen. But she was holding his hand tightly, and leaning against him like she could finally breathe again.

She looked at me and gave me a small nod. No words, just that. But it was enough.

They crossed the clearing, and Fi reached down for me, her fingers outstretched and waiting.

"Come on," she said, her voice gentler now. "Let's go home."

25

I didn't want to get out of bed. Not now, not ever. If the universe would let me stay buried here, tangled in these sheets and swallowed by guilt, I'd stay until the end of time. Who would even care? Who would want to be friends with someone who'd killed a fourteen-year-old boy?

Sure, he was a horrible, vile little shit who would've raped and murdered me and Fi if he'd gotten the chance, but still, he was dead now. And it was because of me.

I burrowed deeper under the duvet. I hadn't moved since yesterday, not really. When Fi, Sebastian, and I got back to Evermore, I came straight upstairs, stripped off my clothes, and collapsed into bed. That was twenty-one hours ago. I'd drifted in and out of sleep ever since.

A knock on the door pulled me out of my spiral.

I grunted in response.

Fi poked her head in, her face full of soft sympathy. "Sash," she said gently, "can I get you anything?"

I shook my head.

She sighed. "Okay. Seb and I are basically having a bed day. I just got up to make drinks, but I'm just across the hall. If you need anything, just shout, or ring me."

I nodded, barely lifting my head.

"Oh, and Sash," she added hesitantly, "Seb knows everything. I told him. About the magic, the cabin, us."

Her voice was shaky, but she smiled. I guess that meant it had gone okay.

I nodded again. I couldn't even process that right now. "Where's Sloane?" I croaked.

"She's in the shower. She's spending the day with Joe, they're going to some party tonight. She invited us, but I told her we were giving it a miss. She knows something's wrong, Sash. We're going to have to tell her soon."

I groaned, already overwhelmed by the thought. Telling her about the hex was eating me alive.

"She'll understand," Fi said firmly. "You know she will. I need to talk to you too…"

Her voice trailed off, and I peered at her over the top of the duvet.

"Not now," she said, catching my gaze.

"Just when you're ready. Oh, and Jasper called. About twenty minutes ago. He said he couldn't reach you, texts, calls, nothing."

I looked toward my discarded jeans. My phone was still in the pocket from yesterday, a forgotten bulge.

Fi noticed. She walked in, pulled the phone out, and plugged it into the charger on my bedside table.

The screen lit up: six texts and four missed calls from Jasper.

Guilt slammed into me.

"Don't ignore him," Fi said firmly as she crossed back to the door.

"On, and Sasha..." She paused, her head appearing back around the doorframe. "Have a shower, you stink!"

She winked and was gone. I threw the covers back over my head and lay these for a moment, my chest rising and falling with my breath.

She was right, I did stink.

I sat up slowly. The duvet slipped to my waist. My eyes flicked to the door. I stretched, stiff and sore, and figured that a shower was the least I could do before facing the mountain ahead.

Jasper deserved the truth, every raw, terrifying piece of it. If I wanted any kind of future with him, he had to know what I was. What I'd done. He didn't even know I was a witch, let alone that I had a hex buried so deep inside me it could stop someone's heart.

After the shower, I pulled on black cycling shorts and an oversized T-shirt. I left my hair wet and down, towel-dried and curling at the ends. As I stood at my dressing table, smoothing SPF onto my cheeks, I heard the sound of a car pulling up outside.

My heart jolted.

Jasper.

It lifted, really lifted, for the first time since we left that cabin. I shoved my feet into my red Crocs and flew out of the room, bolting down the stairs. I threw open the front door and sprinted across the gravel driveway, heading for the little cottage just as he climbed out of his old Jeep.

I launched myself into his arms. He caught me, holding me tight, burying his face into my neck.

"Sash," he murmured, inhaling deeply. "Where have you been?"

He pulled back a little. His smile faded into something more serious.

"I've been trying to call you. Fi said you were sleeping?"

"I'm sorry," I whispered, my chest aching. "I can explain."

His shoulders eased. He nodded, gently brushing a damp curl from my forehead and tucking it behind my ear.

Our eyes locked. Then he kissed me.

His tongue moved with mine, slow and deep, and the world around us disappeared. It was just him, just this, just the soft press of his hands on my back and neck. I melted into him. I was about to kiss him again when someone cleared their throat.

"So," said a voice. "This is what you two have been up to?"

Eva stood in the doorway of her house, arms crossed, grinning.

"Mum—" Jasper stammered, face flushing.

Eva laughed. "Don't think I haven't noticed, you lovesick fools."

She walked toward us and took both our hands in hers, holding them tight. "I'm overjoyed. My two favourite people."

I smiled, unexpectedly breathless with relief. I hadn't realised how much I needed her approval until I got it.

"I always knew there was a spark between you two," she said. Jasper rolled his eyes, but he was grinning too.

Eva winked and headed back toward her door. "Ah, the beautiful babies you'll make."

Jasper groaned and buried his face in his hands. I laughed.

When she disappeared inside, I turned to him. "Do you need to unpack?"

He shook his head. "Not yet. I've missed

you. Let's go inside."

His gaze traced over me, slow and wanting. My stomach fluttered, but then the familiar dread returned, coiling in my gut.

I pulled away.

"I need to talk to you."

He frowned. "Did I come on too strong?"

"No," I said quickly. "You're perfect. It's not you. It's me."

I walked to the bench by the flower beds and sat down. He followed and sat beside me, worry etched into his face.

And then I told him everything.

I didn't stop. Words spilled out of me, a torrent of secrets and pain. I told him I was a witch, explained the truth behind what that meant. I told him about the hex, how when I'm under extreme duress, I can stop hearts. I told him about Silas. Why I left his house so suddenly that night. What happened in that cabin. What that boy did to Fi and me.

I cried. I couldn't stop.

Jasper didn't say a word the whole time. He just sat there, his fists clenched, jaw tight, expression unreadable.

When I finished, I wiped my face and whispered, "So that's everything. I understand if you never want to see me again."

He reached out, cupping my face. Gently,

he tilted it up so I had to meet his eyes.

"Sasha," he said. "I've lived in this town my whole life. I've spent eleven summers growing up with you, watching from the sidelines. You think I don't know the stories about the magical folk around here? You think I haven't noticed you and Fi are a past of that community?"

His voice was soft, steady. "*You* are the most beautiful and enchanting girl I've ever met. You might feel like you fade into the background, but I've spent every summer noticing every little thing about you."

Tears blurred my vision again.

"But Silas," I whispered. "I killed him. I'm a murderer."

"You are not and never will be a murderer, Sasha," he said fiercely. "What you are is a protector. You were given no choice in your actions and because of your powers you and Fi are still alive today. You have no idea what he planned to do with you and I will never think badly of you for protecting yourself and your friend."

I broke. I fell into him, sobbing uncontrollably. He held me, cradling me, stroking my hair as I shook in his arms.

When the tears finally ebbed and the shuddering gasps subsided I felt Jasper looking down at me.

"Sasha..."

I looked up to met his gaze, self conscious of my puffy eyes and red face.

He smiled.

"I love you."

A laugh burst out of me. "If you love me like this, after hearing all of that, I think I'm safe."

He laughed too. "You look beautiful."

"I love you too," I whispered. I wrapped my arms around his neck and kissed him. Ours eyes met and the connection felt electric, a silence understanding passed between us.

He cupped my face again and kissed me deeply, then whispered, "Let's go inside."

We barely made it through the bedroom door, Jasper only just managing to push it closed behind us with his fingertips before we were tangled together on the bed.

My fingers curled into his shirt, tugging him closer, feeling the steady beat of his heart against mine. Our kisses grew hungry, tongues dancing, mouths tasting, until we had to pause just to breathe.

His eyes searched mine, no longer requiring my silent permission to take things further. I gave a soft smile, my heart filled with trust and anticipation.

We stood, undressing slowly. Every piece of clothing dropped to the floor, barriers falling with them. I stepped out of my thong just as he kicked off his boxers, his cock springing free, and for a second we just stood there, drinking each other in.

Then we crashed together again, collapsing onto the bed.

His hands moved over my skin, urgent but tender. He kissed down my neck, across my collarbone, then lower, his tongue swirling around my nipple before pulling it into his mouth. I gasped, threading my fingers into his hair.

When his hand slipped between my thighs, I moaned. His fingers found me, moving expertly, teasing and pressing until I was shaking. I reached for him, wrapping my hand around his thick cock, stroking him slowly in time with his movements.

His breath hitched.

I pushed him gently onto his back, moved down, and took him into my mouth. I licked up the length of him, hollowing my cheeks and flicking my tongue, working him deeper with every movement. I looked up at him through my eyelashes, his head was thrown back, his eyes were closed and lips were parted. I smiled.

Just before he lost control, he stopped me. His hands gripped my shoulders and he pulled me up to face him.

"I want to see you," he said, voice rough.

He kissed me again, pulling my lower lip into his mouth, sucking and nibbling softly.

He pulled away momentarily, his hand reaching down to his jeans and fumbling urgently in the pocket. I placed my hand on his arm, stilling it.

"Jasper, I'm on the pill," I breathed. "I want to feel you."

He straightened back up and stared at me, heat blazing in his eyes as the unspoken agreement passed between us. He nodded, taking a breath and eased into me, slow and steady, until I was full.

We moved together, bodies perfectly attuned, our moans filling the room as everything else slipped away.

When I opened my eyes, his were on mine. The connection between us was electric. The pleasure built in my stomach, growing and growing until it was almost unbearable. And when we came, it was together, everything shattering and building and spilling over like light flooding into darkness.

Later, wrapped in each other, I traced the lines of his body, heart finally steady. I rested my head on his chest and listened to the rhythm of his breath, feeling myself slide into the deepest, safest sleep I'd ever known.

26

Ten years old

A week had passed since the attack, and we hadn't left the house once. Luckily, the weather had turned early this year, rain had poured nearly every day, so no one thought much of our change in routine or questioned the long sleeves we wore, even indoors.

We were curled up on my bed, the curtains half-drawn to keep the gloom at bay, though the windows were still open. The air was thick with moisture, the scent of damp earth seeping in, as if the storm outside mirrored something brewing between us. Raindrops clung to the glass like scattered jewels, and I watched them absently, tracing their slow descent with my eyes. Though it was only 4pm, the sky was heavy and dark, smothered by leaden clouds. A cold wind surged through the open window, tossing my sheer curtains in slow, ghostlike *waves, an eerie sort of dance.*

'Rocks and Water' by Deb Talan murmured from the radio in the corner of my room, the melancholy melody settling over us like fog. I lay on my back, staring up at the ceiling. A copy of Cosmopolitan rested open on my lap, abandoned halfway through the agony aunt column. One girl had written in complaining that her sister kept stealing her clothes. I'd tried to care, read the same line four times ,but my eyes rolled so far back in my head, they practically stayed there, fixed on the crystal light fixture above.

Fi lay on her stomach beside me, wearing the pink, fluffy onesie she'd shown up in that morning. Her hair was a tangled nest on top of her head, legs bent at the knees, feet swaying lazily in the air. She was half-scribbling in a notebook, half-staring into space, drifting somewhere far away.

Two days earlier, Eva had dragged me into town with Jasper, chirping about a farewell lunch before I left for the end of summer. Fi hadn't come. She said she couldn't, but I knew better. She was scared. And I didn't blame her.

We'd just turned onto the high street when I saw them, his eyes. Pale, icy blue, locked with mine. My stomach dropped. I felt sick. A freshly laminated missing poster was taped to the bakery window. His face stared out at me. Silas Burns, the text underneath read. He was only fourteen. I'd thought he was older.

Missing. He hadn't gone home.

Had he been on his way back when it happened?

I couldn't make myself feel sad for him, not really. But I let my mind wander to his parents. Did they know who he really was? Or was he someone else entirely at home, kind, even funny? I tried to picture it, but all I could see was the fury that had burned in his eyes. I couldn't imagine him any other way. I stared until Eva noticed and gently tugged me away, steering me down the street toward the café.

That evening, I told Fi what I'd seen. She frowned, staring at her feet for a long beat before giving a half-hearted shrug. She didn't have the words, but when she looked up at me, I could see the relief in her eyes. He was gone. That was enough for her. And maybe, for me too.

There were still so many things I wanted to say to Fi, but time was slipping through my fingers. My packed suitcase sat in the corner, a silent reminder: we were leaving in the morning. Apart from a few scattered phone calls or letters, I wouldn't see her again for nearly a year.

I glanced at her hands. She gripped her pen tightly, each fingernail painted a different colour, though most of the polish had chipped, leaving patchy smudges behind.

"Fi…?" I swallowed. My voice came out softer than I intended. "The other day… didn't you feel like something was off? Your intuition's usually so good. I swear I felt weird as soon as we left your house."

Fi looked up slowly through her lashes, exhaling before she spoke.

"Yeah, I know." She paused. "I felt weird in the morning, too. But I thought it was just because… you know, we weren't supposed to go. And you know me, I just wanted to focus on the fun parts."

She sat up cross-legged at the edge of the bed, tugging her sleeves down to cover the faded bruises on her wrists. That gesture had become second nature this past week.

"Sash… we can't ever tell anyone. You know that, right? We'd be in so much trouble. Dad would kill me for going. He told me not to. He'd never forgive me for putting us in danger." Her shoulders slumped, and a single tear slipped down her cheek.

"Hey… hey, Fi, don't cry." I reached over and gave her knee a gentle squeeze. "You didn't do anything wrong. None of this was your fault. I went because I wanted to, okay? You didn't make me."

And it was true. Fi had always been fiercely protective of her friends, loyal to a fault. She'd never put anyone in harm's way if she could help it. She cared about everything, down to the smallest bug on the windowsill.

She wiped her face on her sleeve and gave me a small, grateful smile.

"What actually happened, though, Fi?" I asked, voice lower now. "I remember him on top of you... then I screamed, shut my eyes, and when I opened them, he was just... gone. Did you hit him? Or something?"

Fi's expression tightened. She wrung her hands, nervous.

"No... I didn't do anything," she said finally. "Honestly, Sash. One second he was on top of me... and then he just fell. No noise, nothing. He just fell."

I sat up, watching her carefully. But in the end, it didn't matter. He was gone. We were safe. Whether he ran or something else took him, he wasn't here anymore. That was enough.

"Let's stop talking about it," I said gently. "Mum and Dad said we could order pizza tonight. It's our last sleepover, so let's make it count. I asked Mum earlier if we could watch that witchy film we saw advertised, she said it was rated 12, but we could watch it with her!"

Fi's face lit up. We'd spotted Practical Magic on the movie service earlier that summer, but Eva had said no. There were two witches on the cover, sisters. Fi had said they reminded her of us.

I jumped off the bed and zipped my purple

onesie up to my chin. I had a vest top underneath, but the temperature had dropped sharply, and distant thunder rumbled through the open window. I scraped my hair into a messy bun, clicked the radio off, and with Fi by my side, we headed downstairs on a mission for food, or more accurately, my dad, who could order it.

We spent our last evening stuffing our faces and watching the best film we'd ever seen. Even when Gilly got possessed and Mum reached for the remote, we begged her not to turn it off. We watched, spellbound. Later, tucked under the covers, we whispered about it for hours. Fi said it was pretty accurate. We decided to look up the screenwriter, just in case she was a real witch.

Morning came too soon. A knock at the door and my mum's soft voice nudged us awake. She peeked in, offering a sad smile.

We dressed quietly. I knew that if we started talking about goodbyes, I'd cry.

Downstairs, the smell of fresh coffee greeted us. Rounding the corner, I saw Eva, Briar, and Linus already in the kitchen with my parents. Eva had laid out one last breakfast spread. They were all there to see us off.

We joined them at the oak table as conversation bubbled around us. Linus told my dad about a leak at The Alchemy, Eva recommended a plumber, and our mums were cackling about something unintelligible at the far end.

Jasper wandered in through the back door and dropped into the seat beside me. He smelled faintly of vanilla, and I inhaled instinctively stopping when Fi shot me a look across the table.

"So... you're leaving, huh?" he murmured, grabbing a waffle and the syrup. I nodded.

"Sucks," he said under his breath, eyes fixed on his plate until my dad pulled him into a conversation about school.

I looked around the table, and a quiet smile crept across my face. I'd be back next summer. Maybe that'd be the year we finally convinced Mallory and Rory to let Sloane come too. I couldn't wait to show her around, to introduce her to everyone here. Well... minus my parents of course.

After breakfast, the adults loaded the car while Jasper, Fi, and I sat on the front steps in a peaceful, reflective silence.

When it was time, I hugged Briar and Linus tightly, followed by an emotional Eva, who made me promise I'd write. Jasper gave me a quick one-armed hug before turning abruptly and walking back toward the cottage without looking back.

But it was saying goodbye to Fi that broke me. We clung to each other and cried, unable to speak, until our parents gently pulled us apart.

I was bundled into the car and buckled in.

I waved through the window, watching Fi until she was out of sight. The tears slowed as we reached the motorway. I fished my iPod out of the seat pocket, slipped in my headphones, and pressed shuffle.

Leaning my head against the cool glass, as Evermore faded away behind us.

27

I lay on my side, nose just an inch from Jasper's. His eyes were closed, his breathing steady and deep, warm against my cheek as he exhaled. I didn't move. I just watched him, taking in every detail, how his jaw curved so perfectly, the way the early stubble shadowed his cheeks, the mess of dark hair falling across his forehead. I felt this quiet pull in my chest, a need to reach out, to trace the edge of his face with my fingertips. But I didn't want to wake him, not yet. Instead, I edged a little closer, letting my body gently align with his, our legs brushing together beneath the covers.

As if he could sense my closeness without even opening his eyes, Jasper stirred and wrapped an arm around my waist, pulling me into him. I exhaled softly, a quiet little sigh escaping as he buried his face in my neck. His lips brushed my skin, sleepy and tender, in a series of featherlight kisses that made me shiver.

"Good morning," he murmured, his voice thick and husky with sleep.

"Good morning," I whispered back, turning toward him, our mouths meeting in a slow, lingering kiss. The morning light filtered softly through the curtains, golden and warm, casting everything in a kind of hush. It was as if time had paused just for us. Our kisses deepened, urgent now, like a spark catching fire. My fingers slid up into his hair; his hands found my waist. Our bodies shifted closer, tangled completely beneath the sheets, every inch of us pulled into the gravity between us.

Eventually, the kisses gave way to something more, something breathless and sacred, a shared rhythm that stole the air from our lungs and left us wrapped up in each other as the day quietly began.

My hair clung damply to the back of my neck, sticky with sweat, and as I slid my hand down Jasper's chest, I felt the same warm sheen on his skin.

"Shower?" I murmured.

He didn't answer, just grinned and launched out of bed, scooping me up in his arms without warning. I yelped, laughing in protest as he shouldered the bedroom door open.

"Jasper!" I squeaked, eyes darting

anxiously down the hallway. "We are literally stark bollock naked. What if someone comes out of their room?"

"Lucky them," he said with a wicked grin, carrying me like some victorious caveman toward the bathroom. "People usually have to pay good money for this."

I rolled my eyes, but the laugh slipped out anyway. I couldn't help it. He was impossible and ridiculous and... completely mine.

He set me down and turned on the shower. Jets of water thundered from the ceiling, and then more from the walls as he adjusted the settings. I watched his back flex as he moved, all those muscles carved from endless days in the gardens. His ass looked particularly smug with itself.

"Like what you see?" he teased without turning around.

I blinked, cheeks flushing, I'd totally zoned out. Before I could respond, he pressed his bare ass to the shower glass, squashing it in the most absurd way.

"Oh my God," I burst out laughing, startled and breathless.

He reached out, caught my hand, and tugged me in with him.

Steam curled around us, warm and thick, wrapping us in a cocoon. We kissed again, hungry and unfiltered, and made love under the pounding water, our bodies slick and clinging together, our laughter and gasps lost beneath the rush of heat and movement. When we finally decided to wash our hair and soap up properly, the bathroom was a fogged-up jungle, dripping with condensation.

I cracked the window open, gulping in some fresh air, still flushed from everything. Jasper was smiling as he rummaged in the cupboard for towels. He brought one over and began to squeeze the water from my hair, gentle and careful like I was something precious.

I closed my eyes. Let him take care of me.

He brushed the towel along my shoulders, then down my back, his lips following in a trail of soft, damp kisses that sent shivers racing through me. My skin prickled with goosebumps, and when I turned around to face him, I reached up and brushed a wet curl from his forehead, my fingers lingering against his skin.

"I love you so much, Jasper," I whispered, eyes locking with his.

His lips found mine in the kind of kiss that made the whole world feel quiet.

"I love you too, Sasha."

And in that moment, I believed nothing else could ever matter more.

∞∞∞

The scent of coffee hit me before I even made it into the kitchen. I padded down the stairs with Jasper close behind me, his warm hand brushing against the small of my back as we rounded the corner and before I could even register the room, I was engulfed in a mass of frizzy curls and excited limbs.

"I've missed you so much!" Fi squeaked, right in my ear. I winced, half-laughing, half-choking as I tried to peel her off me and spit out one of her hairs that had somehow made its way into my mouth.

"Fi, what are you even on about?" I spluttered, squirming in her grip.

She pulled back, gripping my shoulders, her eyes wide and earnest. "I just feel like I haven't really seen you in ages. Even when you've been here, it's like… you haven't been here. But this morning? You're back. You feel like you again. And I'm so happy."

Behind me, Jasper let out a low chuckle and made his way over to the breakfast bar, clapping Sebastian on the back like they were old mates. Sebastian just nodded, his mouth full of bagel.

I rolled my eyes at Fi's dramatics but couldn't help the smile that tugged at my lips. She wasn't wrong. I did feel more like myself this morning. Probably something to do with the multiple divine encounters I'd had in Jasper's arms; bed, shower, take your pick. I glanced over at him and felt my cheeks flush as heat bloomed beneath my skin.

God, get a grip, Sasha.

"I need coffee," I muttered, turning toward the machine. "Jasper?"

"Please," he replied, settling in.

I paused as I reached the machine. "It's not on?" I muttered, frowning as I felt the cold surface beneath my palm. "But... I can smell it?"

Fi's face bloomed pink. "I may have been sending the smell upstairs with magic. I was trying to lure you down."

I blinked at her, then looked at Sebastian, who just shrugged with a mouthful of bagel and a look that said, Witches, right?

"You sneaky little..." I grinned as I popped Jasper's favourite pod into the machine and pressed it on. I leaned back against the counter and closed my eyes, picturing the exact mugs I wanted. Something cute. Familiar. Cosy. I concentrated and heard the gentle creak of the cupboard door swinging open, followed by a soft gasp and a clatter as

Sebastian dropped half his bagel.

When I opened my eyes, two mugs floated serenely through the air and landed on the counter beside me.

"Sorry, boys," I said sweetly, casting them a smug little grin. "You're going to have to get used to that."

Sebastian recovered his bagel and took another bite, shaking his head, while Jasper just beamed at me like I'd just summoned the moon itself.

Fi, meanwhile, looked like she might actually burst.

"This is so nice!" she gushed. "Although… where's Sloane?"

"In her room?" I guessed, pouring Jasper's coffee into his mug before popping my own pod into the machine.

Fi shrugged. "Haven't seen her."

The kitchen settled into a quiet rhythm, Jasper got up to make breakfast for us both, Fi drifted toward Sebastian, picking absentmindedly at the crumbs on the table. I focused on the sound of the machine, the comforting clink of mugs, and the steam curling in the air.

"Do you want this toasted?" Jasper asked, holding up a slice of bread.

"Yes please," I replied, taking my coffee. "What shall we do today?"

He looked out the window, his brow

furrowing slightly as he took in the scene beyond the glass. The sun was strong, heat hanging thick in the air, but the leaves were already curling at the edges, tinged with the first signs of fire-orange.

"It's hot," he said, "but I don't think it's going to last much longer."

"Mabon is coming," I nodded, wrapping my hands around the warmth of the mug.

Jasper tilted his head. "Mabon?"

"The autumn equinox," Fi explained softly. "The tipping point. When light and dark balance for just a moment before everything shifts again."

He hummed like he understood, and I smiled to myself. There was so much he didn't know but I'd teach him.

His toast popped up, saving him from any further confusion, and he reached for the Marmite.

"Have you been up to the peak yet this summer?" he asked as he dipped his knife into the jar.

Sanderson's Peak. My heart gave a little jolt at the thought of it. The views. The wind. The way the air felt different up there, thin and wild and almost magical.

"That's a great point," I said, sipping my coffee. "We haven't! That would be the first summer in years we've missed it. We have to go."

I turned to tell Fi, but something stopped me. She and Sebastian were leaned in close, heads nearly touching, voices hushed. I couldn't hear what they were saying, but I could feel it, Sebastian's face was tense, drawn. Fi's brow was furrowed. She shook her head and he rubbed his hands down his face.

His eyes flicked to mine and he straightened abruptly. Fi noticed and turned toward me, her expression morphing into something bright and brittle.

"Did you say something?" she asked, too cheerfully.

"No..." I said slowly, eyes narrowing. "Is everything okay?"

"Yes! Yes!" Fi sprang to her feet, smoothing the fabric of her long skirt, adjusting her lilac headband like she hadn't just been in the middle of a secretive, heavy conversation.

"We were thinking of heading up the peak today," Jasper interjected, his voice light, purposeful. "Coming?"

"Ooh yes!" Fi clapped her hands. "We have to go! We haven't been at all this year!"

"That's what we thought," Jasper said, nudging my arm. "Didn't we, Sash?"

I blinked, pulling myself back into the moment. "Yeah," I smiled. "Probably one of the last good days before the weather changes."

Fi was already raiding the cupboards, ingredients flying to the counter in a flurry of magical excitement.

"I'll make the picnic!" she announced, catching a tin of tuna that zoomed through the air. Jasper stared, wide-eyed, peering behind her like he expected to see someone chucking things.

I glanced at Sebastian, his expression was amused, but his hands were wringing in his lap. Nervous. Tense. He smiled at me when our eyes met, and I returned it, but something about the whole exchange sat wrong with me.

I finished the last of my coffee and set my mug in the dishwasher. I wasn't going to let it ruin today. I'd talk to Fi later. I just wished Sloane was around, I missed her. She'd found someone good, someone who really saw her, and I was happy for her. Really. But I missed her.

"I'm going to check on Sloane, see if she wants to come," I said, slipping out of the kitchen.

Upstairs, I paused outside her door, pressing my ear gently to the wood. Silence. I knocked once.

"Sloane?" Nothing.

I turned the handle and pushed the door

open.

Empty.

Clothes were scattered across the floor in her usual chaos, but the bed hadn't been slept in. I stepped back, pulling the door shut with a small frown. She hadn't come back from the party last night.

I crossed to my room and picked up my phone, calling her. One ring. Voicemail.

I sighed, dropping it onto my bed and grabbing a notepad from my desk. I scribbled a quick note:

Sloane—if you and Joe see this in time, meet us at Sanderson's Peak. We're heading out soon. Miss you x

I placed it gently on her pillow and stood for a moment, just looking at it, willing her to find it. I hated the heaviness in my chest. It wasn't like her to vanish without a word.

Trudging downstairs, I rounded the Yule post and crashed straight into Jasper.

"There you are!" he grinned, lacing our fingers together. "We're all set. Fi's packed enough food for a week. You okay?"

I considered telling him about my reservations about Sebastian but quickly decided against it. Jasper and Sebastian were getting along, and Fi and I had always dreamt about a time our boyfriends were friends too. I didn't want to ruin the day.

"Yeah," I said breezily. "Just left a note for

Sloane. Looks like she didn't come home last night. I'm guessing she's with Joe."

"Are you worried?"

"No, no," I said, running a hand down his arm. "Just wish she was coming with us."

"Yeah, shame we're not all going. Try calling her?"

"I did. Straight to voicemail They're probably still asleep."

"Or…" He grinned, stepping closer, his hand sliding down to cup my ass. "Maybe they're spending the morning like we did. Fancy round three?"

I laughed, swatting at him. "You're incorrigible."

He narrowed his eyes. "That's it."

I squealed and backed away, hands raised in mock surrender, but he lunged and scooped me up over his shoulder, laughing as I shrieked.

"Ready!" he called as he marched into the kitchen. "I've got everything I need!"

He spun me so I was facing Fi and Sebastian, who looked bewildered and slightly concerned. I raised my hand and waved at them, my other was still clinging on to Jasper's t-shirt for dear life.

"Perfect," Sebastian said with mock seriousness. "I'll bring mine too."

Then he stood and promptly lifted Fi over his shoulder. She shrieked, laughing uncontrollably.

"Don't forget the picnic!" she called out between giggles.

Jasper hooked the basket on his free arm and nodded to Sebastian, the two of them heading out the door, their giggling girlfriends bouncing on their backs.

I looked over at Fi, her face flushed with laughter as she reached her hand out to me. I took it without hesitation, our fingers lacing together as we bobbed along like two ridiculous, delighted children.

God, we must've looked like absolute lunatics making our way down towards the town. But I didn't care.

I beamed.

We were going to have the perfect day.

28

By the time we finally reached the summit of Sanderson's Peak, nearly three hours had slipped past us like water through my fingers. The boys had carried us for only a few playful minutes before setting us down, and the rest of the climb had been steady, sun-drenched, and beautiful, just the four of us, weaving through wild countryside and overgrown trails like explorers in a forgotten world.

Now, standing at the top, the whole world opened up beneath our feet. Sunlight gleamed on the brook that cut a silver ribbon across the ridge, its waters bright and alive, like something out of a dream. I peeled off my shoes with a small groan of relief and dipped my feet into the stream. The coolness was a revelation. My toes tingled, the icy current easing the heat that had built in my soles from the climb.

I stood slowly, letting the water rush

around my ankles. From here, the land fell away on all sides, endless, wild, and impossibly wide. It felt like standing on the edge of everything. The wind tossed my hair back from my face, and I breathed in deeply, the mountain air crisp and sweet in my lungs. My heart beat in time with the breeze, fast, alive, untamed.

Behind me, the soft crunch of shifting rocks announced Jasper's approach.

"Fi's making the picnic blanket fly around again," he muttered, stepping up beside me. "I'm the most open-minded guy I know, but it's gonna take me a while to stop freaking out about that stuff."

I laughed, the sound carried off by the wind as I stepped out of the stream. I wrapped my arms around his neck and kissed the tip of his nose.

"You're cute," I said, smiling into his skin.

Jasper frowned, puffing out his chest. "I am not. I'm a manly man, I am."

I grinned and took his hand, leading him back toward the others, my heart light, buoyant and full.

Fi had picked the perfect picnic spot on a grassy knoll tucked beneath the limbs of a sprawling oak. Half in the sun, half in the shade, the heat was tempered by the tree's dappled canopy. The food looked like it had arranged itself: sandwiches stacked haphazardly, bowls of fresh fruit, and tall bottles of lemonade beading with condensation.

It was simple. But perfect. Full of Fi's little touches, crusty baguettes layered with her homemade jam, cucumber slices with mint, and fresh juice squeezed that morning. I bit into my sandwich and closed my eyes, the sweet tang of jam bursting on my tongue. Everything about this moment felt like a soft embrace, the sun, the breeze, the laughter.

I lay back on the blanket, my head resting against Jasper's thigh as Fi passed around berries. Gratitude hummed quietly through my chest, not just for the view or the food, but for Fi. For always knowing exactly what I needed often before I knew it myself.

Laughter bubbled around us as we drifted into old stories, reminiscing about long, golden summers, poolside games, marshmallows charred over bonfires, and that one wild hike where we'd gotten lost and stumbled upon a secret waterfall.

"Remember when you thought you saw a bear, Fi?" Jasper cackled, tossing a crust in her direction. "You nearly scrambled up my back like a squirrel."

Fi rolled her eyes, but her smile gave her away. She chucked the crust back. "Hey! It was dark. I was trying to protect us. All of us. It looked exactly like a bear."

"A very scary bush," Jasper laughed. "I thought Sasha was going to cry."

"Me?" I gasped, scandalized. "I was the calmest person there. It was you who bolted down that hill with Fi screaming on your back!"

Jasper grinned through a mouthful of sandwich, too proud to argue. Sebastian's eyes darted between us, amused, as we bickered like old sitcom characters.

After we ate, we wandered back to the brook. The water sparkled like shattered glass in the sun, and soon we were splashing around, our laughter echoing off the rocks. Jasper and Sebastian started a stone-skipping contest, their pebbles slicing the surface with impressive skips and dramatic flair.

"You're going down, Seb!" Jasper called, his stone skipping five times before vanishing beneath the surface.

Sebastian narrowed his eyes, tossed his, and watched it skip six times. Jasper groaned theatrically and flopped onto the bank like he'd been mortally wounded.

Fi and I waded knee-deep into the water, squealing at the icy shock before we settled onto a wide, sun-warmed rock in the middle of the stream. I watched the boys for a while, but my mind drifted.

"Is everything okay with Sebastian?" I asked, keeping my voice low.

Fi looked up, her fingers tugging absently at the hem of her skirt. "Yeah, why?"

I picked up a stone, mimicking the boys' skipping motion. It dropped into the water with a pitiful splash.

"I dunno. He just seems kind of on edge. And this morning... the conversation you two were having at breakfast, it seemed a bit intense, that's all."

Fi was already shaking her head. "No, Sash, it's not like that." She reached over, her hand warm against my bare thigh. "Everything's okay. I promise. I know you don't know him super well yet, but he's wonderful. He loves me. And I love him."

Fi's face was let up and I let out a breath. The tightness in my shoulders started to ease.

"You promise?"

She nodded. "Honestly. But..." She hesitated. "I do need to talk to you about something. It's important. Just... not today. I don't want to cloud this."

I raised an eyebrow. "That sounds ominous."

"It's not," she said quickly, giving my hand a squeeze. "I promise. Me and you, we've been through hell together, haven't we?"

I met her gaze, and I saw it, that flicker in

her eyes. Emotion glimmering just beneath the surface like light under water.

"Fi," I said gently, "what's wrong?"

She wiped at her cheek, surprised by a tear. "Absolutely nothing," she laughed, a little shakily. "I don't even know why I'm crying. I think... I think it's just relief. We're okay, Sash. After everything. It's done. We know what happened, and we're safe now. We can finally draw a line under that whole horrible time."

I nodded, my heart aching with the weight of understanding. We'd carried this for years, a terrible secret tucked into the corners of our lives like dust. We had been just kids, trying to make the best choice we could. Maybe it hadn't been the right one, it seemed crazy now that we had dealt with this all alone and never told anyone, but it had brought us here. To this.

I breathed in the scent of grass and sun-warmed earth. "Yeah," I murmured, and smiled.

Later, we dragged the blanket out into the sunshine. Sebastian and Fi disappeared down toward the brook again, her laughter floating back to us on the breeze.

I stretched out next to Jasper, still damp, still glowing. We shared a pair of earphones, the soft sounds of The Calling's Wherever You Will Go filling one ear as Jasper's foot tapped lazily with the beat.

"You know," he said, "I could stay here forever."

I smiled, wrapping my legs into his, and he shivered slightly at my cold skin. "We're going to remember this summer for the rest of our lives."

He kissed my forehead, slow and soft. "Yeah. It's been the best. My life genuinely feels changed. But what happens when it ends?"

I looked up at the sky, that endless stretch of blue. "I've been thinking about that too," I said. "You know I want to go in to journalism. I want to write like my parents but about real things not fiction. I want to write about real people. Real stories. I think life's incredible enough without having to invent it."

Jasper traced lazy circles on my arm.

"But first," I added, "I'm going to travel. Take a year off. I want to learn more, about the world, about myself."

He smiled. "Where?"

"Everywhere," I said, laughing. "I want to explore places connected to my heritage. Like Salem in America and Pendle Hill in Lancashire. I'm fascinated by the history of witchcraft, and I want to see those places, feel the history in them. And then I want to go to Jamaica, where my mum's family is from. I want to learn more about Obeah, that's what my grandmother practised. There's a whole side of my family's history I don't know much about, I feel like it's time I connected with it."

Jasper's eyes crinkled with excitement. "It sounds incredible Sash, I can already see you with a notebook, writing down stories from all those places. I wish I could come with you. I mean, imagine the things we'd see together."

I smiled, wistfully. "You could, you know. Come with me. I know your mum needs you, but she'd want you to live your life, wouldn't she? To have adventures of your own?"

Jasper sighed, looking away for a moment. "I know she would, but it's complicated. She's been doing better lately but she still relies on me. I don't know how I would feel about being so far away if anything happened."

I reached over and squeezed his hand gently. "I get it Jasper, I really do. But don't let that be the thing that holds you back okay? If you want to come there's always a place for you with me. Think about it. You don't have to decide right now."

Jasper looked at me, a small smile tugging at his lips. "Thanks babe. It does sound like an adventure I wouldn't want to miss."

We sat in silence, a soft quiet that only comfort can bring. The brook babbled nearby. Fi's laughter echoed faintly. She and Sebastian reappeared, cheeks flushed, hair tousled.

I smirked as Fi gave me a look that said everything and nothing all at once.

I closed my eyes. The sun soaked into my skin, my heart full, and my future, finally, wide open.

∞ ∞ ∞

Traipsing back into the house, I shivered as the cool air kissed my skin. The descent from Sanderson's Peak had felt twice as long as the climb, each step heavier than the last. Now, with the last remnants of daylight spilling through the windows, the house felt like a sanctuary, a quiet exhale after the adrenaline of the day.

The four of us collapsed in the living room like fallen leaves, limbs tangled and loose with exhaustion. Dim evening light draped itself over the furniture, and the soft hum of the ceiling fan whispered above our heads like a lullaby. I curled into Jasper on the sofa, my cheek pressed to the steady rhythm of his heartbeat. Across from us, Fi leaned into Sebastian, his arm draped protectively around her shoulders, their bodies tucked together like puzzle pieces that had always belonged.

"I swear," I murmured, my voice lazy with sleep and mischief, "you two always look like you're decoding some ancient manuscript whenever we do any witchcraft."

Sebastian chuckled, the sound low and warm. "That's because you two have all these herbs and crystals, talking about energies and moon phases. Wouldn't be shocked if Latin chanting started next. And that thing you did to me with the feathers and salt last week?" He gave Fi a sideways glance. "What even was that?"

Fi giggled, her eyes catching the last bit of light and glinting like river stones. "That was to ward off bad energy, obviously. I explained that to you."

"You explained," Sebastian said, "but that doesn't mean I get it."

"You girls have a whole secret world," Jasper added, lifting one arm lazily. "It's cool. Kind of freaky. But cool."

Before I could respond, the air shifted. Sloane burst into the room like a gust of wind that had lost its way, her face tight with worry, her eyes wide and electric with urgency. Behind her came Marcus, tense and quiet, his jaw locked like he was bracing for impact.

"Sloane?" I sat up fast, my pulse jumping as I clocked Marcus's rigid stance. "I thought you were with Joe today. Where is he?"

But Sloane didn't answer. Her eyes swept across the group, her mouth tightening. "I need to tell you something," she said, voice sharp and direct.

I raised an eyebrow, already bracing. "If you're about to tell me you're shagging your brother, I swear to God—"

Fi gasped, then dissolved into giggles. I followed, our laughter bright and loud, spilling into the room like sunshine through a window. Jasper and Sebastian blinked at us, baffled.

But Sloane didn't laugh. Her expression didn't even twitch.

"I'm serious," she snapped, her voice cutting clean through the laughter like a blade. "Can you just shut up for one second and listen?"

The laughter died instantly.

The tension coiled, tight and immediate. Sebastian sat up, his body alert. Fi stilled, her face pale. I felt my chest tighten as if something invisible had crept into the room.

"What is it?" I asked softly, my voice steady but my insides beginning to churn.

"What's going on, Sloane?"

Sloane's hands trembled slightly as she took a breath. She glanced at Marcus, who gave her the smallest nod, an unspoken You can do this.

"Something's happened," she said, her voice trembling now, heavy with something I couldn't yet name. "I need you all to listen."

The air turned cold. I felt the hairs on my arms stand up, like the room itself had started to hold its breath.

"I know what's happened to the missing kids," Sloane whispered.

Silence. Pure and absolute.

Then, just as she began to speak again—

"And also, Fi, we're—"

The lights flickered violently. Shadows danced across the walls in strange, unnatural shapes. A sharp crash echoed from the hallway, loud enough to make Fi squeal and grab Sebastian's arm.

My heart kicked against my ribs. I twisted toward Jasper, who was already looking at me, his brow furrowed. The room felt charged, like the seconds before a lightning strike.

"What the hell was that?" Jasper muttered, scanning the shadows.

And then, without warning, something stepped into the doorway.

A figure, tall, hooded and faceless loomed

in the threshold. The moment shattered. There was a sudden burst of blinding white light, flashes so intense they burned the outlines of furniture into my vision. Smoke poured in thick and choking, curling like fingers around our ankles. The air pulsed with static, thick with power, and then,

everything went black.

CLEO SWEETLAND

Salt Playlist

Find us on Spotify and Youtube

1. Death By A Thousand Cuts - Taylor Swift
2. Season Of The Witch - Lana Del Ray
3. Billie Bossa Nova - Billie Eilish
4. I Put A Spell On You - Nina Simone
5. Everywhere - Fleetwood Mac
6. This Is What Falling In Love Feels Like - Jvke
7. Harbinger - Kiki Rockwell
8. This Kiss - Faith Hill
9. T-Shirt Weather - Circa Waves
10. Malibu - Miley Cyrus
11. Work Song - Hozier
12. Rocks And Water - Deb Talan
13. Wherever You Will Go - The Calling
14. Evermore - Taylor Swift (Ft. Bon Iver)

Sasha's Banana Fritters

Ingredients

For the fritters:
4 overripe bananas
60g all purpose flour
3 tbsp brown sugar
½ tsp vanilla extract
½ tsp ground cinnamon
¼ tsp ground nutmeg
A pinch of salt

To dust:
2 tbsp icing sugar
1 tbsp ground cinnamon

Peel the bananas and mash them
in a bowl with a fork

Add all other ingredients into the bowl and
mix until you get a soft paste, a slightly
denser consistency than pancake batter
Add your preferred cooking oil to a large
pan and bring to a medium heat
Spoon palm sized portions of the
batter into the pan and fry for approx.
1 minute or until golden brown.

Flip fritter with a spatula and repeat
Once removed from the heat pat both
sides of the fritters with dry kitchen
roll to remove any excess oil
Dust the cinnamon and icing sugar mix
over the top and serve whilst still hot.

Afterword

And that, dear reader, brings Sasha's whirlwind summer to a gentle pause, note we didnt say "end". Close the cover for now, but listen, another narrator is already clearing her throat. Serephina is eager to guide you back to Evermore and Wychbold Cove, where her magic runs as sure and deep as the midnight tide. The choices she's about to make will send ripples through every sandy street and shadowed grove. When we revisit this summer again, she'll step into the spotlight, ready to illuminate some of the secrets Sasha only brushed against.

Join us in 2026 to watch Serephina prove just how a single summer can transform her world, and we hope, yours too.

- Helen & Claire aka Cleo Sweetland

The Evermore Trilogy: Sage
                 COMING 2026

Printed in Dunstable, United Kingdom

63721881R10238